Powers
of Arrest

Books by Jon Talton

The David Mapstone Mysteries
Concrete Desert
Cactus Heart
Camelback Falls
Dry Heat
Arizona Dreams
South Phoenix Rules

The Cincinnati Casebooks
The Pain Nurse
Powers of Arrest

Other Novels
Deadline Man

Powers
of Arrest

A Cincinnati Casebook

Jon Talton

Poisoned Pen Press

Poisoned Pen Press
6962 E. First Ave., Ste. 103
Scottsdale, AZ 85251
www.poisonedpenpress.com
info@poisonedpenpress.com

Printed in the United States of America

For Susan

Saturday

Chapter One

The Licking River crooks slightly to the northeast before it empties quietly into the broad, swift-running curve of the Ohio at the foot of downtown Cincinnati. That faint turn allows it to work unnoticed, like a stranger hiding in the underbrush. Across the big river that warm May afternoon, the young man walked alone beneath the trees at the park above the Serpentine Wall, the undulating concrete public space that stepped down to the Ohio River. It was part flood control, part amphitheater and work of art. The landing was filling up with couples and families watching boats ply the blue-green water and shedding memories of the winter's ice storms. The skyline, voluptuous with a century of towers, shimmered from the scrubbing of April rains. Sculptures of flying pigs gazed down benevolently from their perches atop blue pillars. A Reds game was being played a quarter-mile west at Great American Ballpark, and when the cheers echoed out of the stadium he thought for a moment they might be for him.

This day would be different.

John walked with all the inner awkwardness of twenty. His mother told him he was handsome but he didn't believe her. He was tall, with a high forehead, intense eyes, and a long nose. He might grow into handsome in his thirties. But his features hadn't broken out of teenage chubbiness, and he was all too aware of it. He also had hair so pale it lacked any of the appeal of the surfer's blond mane; as a baby, he was told, it had been the color of cotton. He was so sensitive that he kept it cut very short. On bad days, he thought he looked like a freak. On those days, he hated to pass mirrors, hated to look at himself. No mirrors here, thank god. He checked his cell phone: four o'clock.

He saw Heather in the distance and waved. She smiled and walked toward him. Her long, wavy chestnut hair caught the wind and she looked like the most beautiful woman he had ever seen. She wore khaki shorts and a lightweight, teal-colored top that accented small, enticing breasts. He didn't stare at her body but looked her in the eyes, his mother had taught him that much. When they came close, he impulsively kissed her and held her close. He was very conscious of the feelings emanating from his groin. She gently broke the kiss and patted his arm.

"What am I going to do with you?"

John's answer involved them both naked somewhere, as he had fantasized a hundred times since he had found her again. He wanted to make his answer another kiss. But he stayed silent, his voice stuck in his mind. Her comment was cryptic. What should he say? He had asked her here and now didn't have the first idea of what to do. He didn't know how to take the lead. The thoughts of meeting her today and where it might take them had kept him up all night. Now he couldn't manage the first word. He looked away at the boats speeding up and down, dodging a long barge pushing upriver, the engine of the tug straining against the current.

"I brought a picnic!"

For the first time, he saw the basket in her hand. It was expensive-looking woven dark wicker with leather trim and brass hardware. They settled on a spot to sit as he struggled to find the voice that had come so easily that first night they had talked. He knew that if he spoke at that moment he could barely get out her name. He loved her name. Heather. So feminine, such poetry in it. Heather was his favorite name. He knew that much.

"Ants!" She emptied two-dozen small, black creatures out of a Ziploc bag. He almost recoiled before realizing they were made of plastic. She set them out across the concrete surface between them, playfully putting one on his shirt. He pretended he was going to eat it and she made a face, her eyes lovely saucers of mock surprise. That was progress, no?

"I saw your dad on TV," she said. "Does he ever talk to you about his work?"

"He's my step-dad," John managed.

His step-dad was still convinced he was a druggie, all from a single night two years before when John had stayed out until three a.m. and had come home smelling like pot. *Running with the wrong crowd*, his mother put it. She sent him to a high-priced counselor in Montgomery. It was the only time he had smoked pot. But his step-dad was a hard ass and John felt forever branded. Druggie. Pothead. Addict. Two years and nothing had changed in his step-dad's mind. Later, his first and only lover had told him how impressed she was that he had good judgment for someone his age, but what did that mean?

"So, Mr. Portland, how did you like the Northwest?"

"It was amped. I really liked it. They say it rains a lot but it doesn't rain that much. It's not like here, where you don't see the sun for a month at a time. There's so much to do, like all these indie movie theaters and a real local music scene. They have light rail and trains…" He felt as if he was running on.

"So you're going back to Portland State? What does your mom think about that?"

"She hates it."

"She's thinking, 'Why did we spend all that money sending him to Summit Country Day and he's not already finishing Harvard?' "

Her laugh was a magical sound, making him laugh, too. She was right, of course. His mother was impatient with him and didn't understand the Portland adventure at all. He had only spent a semester in college and didn't do well. But looking at Heather, and beyond to the limitless blue Midwestern sky and electric green of the trees along the river, it was easy to put those worries away.

"I was accepted at Yale and Princeton and Stanford and, oh, Northwestern," Heather said, ticking them off on slender fingers. By this time they were relaxing on the top steps, watching the people and the river. The sun gave her hair a rich, dark copper glow.

She said, "So it's Yale for me and I start in the fall."

"Very good."

But something sank inside him. He was building a life around her in his fantasy world. She was two years younger but he had a crush on her that went back to the elite prep school they had both attended. They both sang in the choir. He never even thought she noticed him until he got back to Cincinnati and she called out to him one day when he was at the Kenwood Towne Center mall. Since then, they had been to a movie and a concert. He had sent her roses from Jones florist. And she had let him kiss her. Something about him was traditional and romantic.

She was smart, creative, and interesting. She read books as he did, and somehow she seemed different: maybe she was an outcast like him. Her looks did not carry the perfection of many of their classmates. Her mouth was wide and her features were beautifully off-center. That imperfection drew him. Now his brain calculated: perhaps he could go to Yale, too, or she would stay in Cincinnati, even though he hated Cincinnati and hated living off his mom.

He had the kind of rich fantasy life peculiar to young men. He watched the curve of her cheeks, but it could not save him from the growing angst. He already knew she wanted to become a doctor. Her announcement should not be a surprise. Now… well, maybe they could have a summer together. He bargained in his own mind, trying to find the words.

"Heather!"

The shout was a girl's voice, calling from a boat as it made a dramatic curve, cutting a frothy wake, and came to a stop at the foot of the Serpentine Wall. One young man and two teenage girls were aboard.

Heather stood and ran gracefully down the wide concrete slabs, almost as if they didn't exist. John enjoyed the view of her svelte legs and hips as she moved down to the embankment. Her bottom nicely filled out the shorts. He saw other men watch her, too.

"It's Zack Miller!"

Her voice sounded different. He looked longingly at the picnic basket, stared at the little plastic ants, counting them until she returned.

"Come on, John. Bring the basket."

He didn't even think of keeping the disappointment out of his face as he saw her beckoning him. He packed up, taking time to replace each plastic ant into the Ziploc bag, hooked the hasps of the picnic basket, and rose. He went over to the steps, moving carefully and down, with none of Heather's easy agility. He had never been well coordinated.

The trio was laughing and making easy small talk with Heather from the sleek new boat. It was towing what at first glance looked like a blue-and-gray lifeboat with an outboard attached. On closer inspection, it was sturdy and, of course, expensive. On the side was an emblem: "Zoom." John was familiar with that kind of boat.

"You remember John," she said and the two girls nodded distractedly. They both wore bikinis even though the weather was a little cool for that, their bodies young and flawless, both with long manes of golden hair. They looked so alike that it was difficult to tell where one ended and the other began. But they were ordinary princesses, with none of the special attractiveness of Heather. Zack Miller was at the wheel, skillfully using the engines to hold the boats in place, and he barely acknowledged John.

"We're going up the Licking," one of the blondes said. "It's party time! Hop in, Heather."

Heather looked over her shoulder and smiled at John. "Come on, it'll be fun."

He was barely aboard when Zack gunned the engines and swung around, knocking John into a seat. "Sea Ray 260," Zack called to no one in particular.

"Isn't this the most epic boat?" Blonde No. 2 said. They were all younger, all classmates. To John, they were rich, stuck-up, and shallow despite their star-quality SAT scores. Exactly the kind of people John hated. Even though his mother had become well-off working at the bank, John identified with the working-class roots of his stepdad. He knew, too, that most of his classmates came from old Cincinnati money and held it against him that his mother had started out as a mere teller at Fifth Third Bank.

The boat accelerated effortlessly, the empty Zoom skimming playfully along behind, as they shot under the big arched bridge that carried Interstate 471. Painted a yellow gold, it was not surprisingly nicknamed the Big Mac Bridge, even though it officially honored Daniel Carter Beard, one of the founders of the Boy Scouts. They moved east, upriver on the wide Ohio, with the condominium towers on the Cincinnati side sprouting out of the lush slope that led up to East Walnut Hills. The headwind destroyed the hair he had so carefully combed. Heather's lush shoulder-length mane caught the breeze like an auburn sail. Spray from the river made the air wet and warm.

The girls all looked great, of course. And Zack. Zack Miller was Mister Perfect, with preternaturally bright blue eyes set into a classically good-looking face. Chiseled chin, a bit of stubble, an arrogant tilt to his head. The last time John had seen Zack, he boasted thick, dark-brown hair. But he was a champion swimmer and now his head was completely shaved. Of course, he made the look cool. It helped that his skin was tanned and flawless. Zack's father was a high-ranking executive at Procter and Gamble.

The two blondes laughed, talked, and texted, all at the same time. John tried not to be too obvious about hanging on against the rough ride. He hated being on the river, especially at this speed. Looking at the extravagant white wake behind them only made his foreboding grow. Other boats flashed by, boats they could collide with. It happened all the time. The inner gyroscope of his mind was calibrated to disaster. The river could be as much as forty feet deep and so soupy thick you couldn't see two feet in front of you if you tried to swim underwater, a river filled with two centuries of effluent from the Industrial Revolution, and god knew how many dead bodies. Dead bodies from the gangster glory days of Newport, Kentucky, the carp and catfish having long since picked them to skeletons, the remains from yesterday's mishap upriver. When the river ran at flood stage in the early spring, all manner of mayhem ensued. Once he had been sitting at one of the floating restaurants when the river was running high and fast and had glanced over to see a dead pig slip by. It was not a flying pig. Every now and then, one of the restaurants was lost to flood season.

"You okay?" Heather patted his arm.

"The river makes me superstitious."

"Oh…"

John's biological father had a sailboat in Boston, and took him out on it when he visited in the summers. A few years ago, the man had decided he wanted to be part of John's life again. The sailboat and the open sea really frightened John. And the company of his stepbrother and stepsister, such as it was, and his father's chirpy young girlfriend of the moment—they all looked alike, attractive, and slender—made him feel even more alienated from the world. His father looked like the kind of man Zack would become at fifty, right down to the flawless blue eyes. He despised such men.

By this time, Zack had come about and brought them back downtown, then they turned south into the mouth of the Licking River. As the boat slowed, the dread in John's middle eased.

"Brought along the Zodiac in case we picked up more to party," Zack said to Heather, indicating the small craft he was towing. John's real father owned the exact same boat and had taught him how to pilot it in Boston Harbor. The man had done it, John knew, to help him overcome his fear of the water. Part of John wondered if he had also done it out of a streak of cruelty. But John had mastered the Zodiac out of spite, even if it didn't fully cure his sure knowledge of the sorcery of the river. He even grew to like the little craft. It was similar to ones used by Navy SEALS.

Zack said, "Should we cruise for company or go up the Licking. We don't have an even number of guys and girls…"

"Let's go," Heather said. "Maybe we'll find more people we know."

"Or make new friends. Lot of licking goes on in the Licking River," Zack said over his shoulder, and the blondes laughed as if it was the funniest thing they had ever heard. Indeed, the tributary had a reputation for summer socializing: men in fast boats picking up young women at the Serpentine Wall and bringing them up here for sex. John looked at Heather and could only dream. He didn't own a fast boat or have the inclination to be such a man or even know how to become one. It came so easily to guys like Zack Miller. It was in their DNA. Could it even be learned? Heather detached herself from the other two girls and sat next to him as they moved slower up the narrowing river.

"Better?"

"I'm fine." He was feeling anything but.

"We'll have fun. I made plenty of food to go around. It's good to make new friends."

The levees that protected Covington and Newport rose up. The boat crossed under bridges, passing several boats and fishermen. The northern Kentucky towns lay on either side, downtown Cincinnati to the north, but down on the river itself, dense trees growing right down to the bank blotted out any other views. It was like being in the country. A canoe and two kayaks passed, going the other way. He noticed another boat, a trim cabin cruiser, tied up under a railroad bridge. The portholes to the cabin were opaque and the boat barely registered the passing of Zack's Sea Ray.

They cruised deeper into Kentucky as the sun went down and the other boaters found their places closer to the city. They passed under the bridge that carried the Cincinnati beltway before Zack cut the engines and tied up at an old, abandoned dock beneath a thick canopy of branches.

"So John Borders." Zack spoke to him for the first time. And that was all he said, as if rendering a judgment.

Zack turned to Heather and soon they all were talking schools. They could switch from the latest slang to jokes to perfect adult conversation. Zack was starting at Harvard in the fall, pre-med, but after a month in Paris on his own. One of the blondes was doing an internship in John Boehner's office this summer. She was going for an MBA after finishing her undergrad at Brown. Everyone but John was impressed.

Zack hooked up an iPod to some speakers and they belted out a play list from the 1980s. It was so Cincinnati, frozen in time. Then he opened up a cabinet and pulled out liquor bottles and glasses.

"Red Hook cocktails, anyone?"

"Me, me," Heather purred, and the other girls laughed.

"That is so legit," Chelsea, one of the blondes, said. "I had my first last week. Wow." The prospect even made her stop texting and put away her cell phone.

As Men at Work sang, Zack expertly mixed the drinks, which looked like brown martinis and tasted of whiskey. Heather broke open the picnic basket and passed around food, but John didn't feel hungry. Soon, they were on the second drink, talking about friends he didn't know, and college plans he didn't care about. They had all recently graduated and yet appeared so focused. They were younger, but he felt out of his league, felt, depressingly, like he was back at prep school.

He had never fit in. He wasn't Catholic, wasn't an athlete, geek, academic star, or secret goth. Since graduating, he had drifted. John didn't know what the hell he wanted to do. He only knew he didn't want to be back in Cincinnati. Heather might have changed that, but she was barely with him now. It was a dynamic he had felt so many times before. He fell into a dark silence, feeling the knife he carried in his pocket, imagining what it might do to Zack's handsome face. It was only a passing thought. His imaginings of how well this night might go were quickly fading.

"And a chaser." Zack passed around a bag of pills. Everybody took one but John.

"A little ecstasy won't hurt you, Borders, unless you're narc'ing for your old man."

"Look, I don't like ecstasy. That's it." John didn't even especially like hard liquor, and he was feeling the Red Hooks.

Heather popped one of the pills and drained her glass, letting out a war whoop.

John had never done ecstasy, never done the hookups that were popular in school, especially among the rich Catholic kids at school. He had never been invited. He didn't even want that. He wanted Heather. But his mind shifted into momentary optimism. Maybe the night would turn into something after all. He retrieved the bag and took two of the pills. Chelsea and Jennifer giggled.

Zack smiled. "Now if anybody wants to use the little boat back there for some privacy…"

The river rocked the boat rhythmically and a sweet smell came from the foliage on the bank. Maybe the boat would sink and he could rescue Heather, be a hero, and she would fall in love with him. The other blonde, Jennifer, was telling a story, the ghost ship of the Licking River…a paddle wheeler in the nineteenth century that suffered a boiler explosion killing everyone on board, but for years people would see that ship at night, passing noiselessly down the river.

John couldn't feel any effect from the pills. But he started talking.

"See over there, to the west beyond the trees? It's the old Decoursey Yard of the L&N Railroad. It was huge. Now it's mostly abandoned and deserted, but the CSX main line between Cincinnati and Corbin runs through it." He was like that. He knew odd things, but somehow they didn't add up to much that anyone was interested in.

"We should hike up there and see it," Jennifer said. She was only wearing flip-flops.

He kept his eyes on Heather. "You might not want to. There's a story, where sometimes people see a man standing on the tracks, waving a red lantern. Like a warning. They say he's dressed in railroad clothes from the nineteen-thirties. Nobody knows who he is. But he waves that red lantern across the tracks at the old Decoursey Yard, and when he does, the railroad shuts down for a while. The old timers say the red lantern means there's going to be a wreck. So they stop the trains." He paused, and saw they were paying attention to him. "So listen…No trains. That means the man must have been seen tonight. He's right up that riverbank, over the trees."

"That's a great story," Heather said.

"Trains are yesterday," Zack said.

John's stomach was feeling the drinks. He should have eaten something. He set the glass aside and wondered how to keep Heather's attention. He thought about talking her into the Zodiac and they could go off together, get away from these bores. The play list from the Reagan years ran on. Huey Lewis and the News gave way to Journey. *I Want to Know What Love Is.* John had always thought the song was a maudlin oldie. Now it filled his heart and he thought, *yes, Heather, I do want to know.* He tried to catch her eye.

Sunday

Chapter Two

The moan awoke him, and for a second he thought about the mysterious man with the lantern, about the ghost ship. But it wasn't that kind of moan.

John didn't know how much time had passed. The sky beyond the overhang of trees was inky, filled with stars. Jennifer and Chelsea had disappeared. A few feet away, he saw Heather embracing Zack. He was sitting in his captain's chair and she was in his lap. The chair was turned to face the stern, where John was sprawled on the bench.

"You were so busy up front with the Jennifer and Chelsea that I didn't think you were interested in me," Heather said.

"Saving the best for last," Zack said.

The two were kissing deeply and he had his hand in her shorts. She moaned again.

John felt sick but not from the liquor. Yet he sat there and pretended to be asleep, watching the thing unfold. Zack slipped off her light top and expertly unhooked her bra. Her skin glowed in the starlight as she sat on his lap, facing away from John. After a few minutes, she dropped to her knees and unzipped him.

"My, my, what's this?"

It was a woman's voice, husky, alien.

"You like, babe?" Zack said.

She laughed. "What do I do with it?"

As she moved her head, John stared at Zack's penis, transfixed.

"Let me help." Zack reached down to undo it. Heather leaned forward and her hair covered what came next. But it was clear what was happening. Her head bobbed up and down. The boat rocked gently and John wanted to kill them both. He wanted to kill himself. It was a feeling that only grew as he saw, through the slits of his eyes, Heather kick off her shorts and black panties, climb astride the captain's chair, and reach down to put Mister Perfect's penis inside her.

"Fuck me!" she whispered.

John felt his face grow a hot blush.

They rocked against each other. Heather laughed and arched her back.

It seemed to last for years. He watched the whole thing, the drill of betrayal boring into his middle, but also…arousal. Maybe he was a peeping Tom. A freak.

They moved with ever-greater urgency until both were groaning loudly.

Heather's voice split the night. "Oh! You're making me come."

John closed his eyes and tried to think of nothing. After awhile the powerful engines of the boat started and idled.

"Hey, Borders, good nap?"

Zack was grinning at him, his stubble no longer so perfect, his clothes half-on and half off. Heather hung on Zack, looking like a new Burberry scarf around the neck of a homeless man. She didn't look at John.

"It was what it was." John sat upright on the bench.

The two other girls appeared from the front of the boat, ahead of the open cabin, which held two seats where you could stretch out.

"Did you girls have more fun?" Zack asked. He walked aft, leaned past John, and made fast the rope holding the Zodiac. "I love that boat," he said.

"Me, too." John glared at him.

They retraced their route back to the city, going slower this time, the little skiff barely noticeable behind them. The river was deserted now, the water nearly flat except for their unwelcome wake. He looked at his cell phone: almost four a.m.

"Check it out," Zack said. "We're not the last ones at closing time."

The two other girls were exchanging embarrassed looks while giving John dirty glances. They dug into their bags and pulled on more substantial tops and jeans.

Zack pointed to the cabin cruiser, still tied up by the railroad bridge. On closer inspection, it was an older boat.

"Rinker Fiesta 330," Zack said. "Let's have a little fun. Bet you somebody's fucking in there. Probably one of our dads cheating…"

"Don't," John said.

"We wouldn't want sex happening on a public waterway," Zack said augustly.

Heather laughed. She said, "Do it."

He aimed the spotlight and shot its powerful beam into the cabin. All John could think of was the memory of Heather's back and pelvis moving against Zack, how her head went up and down on his lap as if she couldn't get enough, stopping only long enough to pull her hair over one shoulder. And the sight of Zack's cock out of his pants…

Jennifer let out a gasp.

John saw it. Bright slices of red were painted against the glass of the oval-shaped portholes. He could swear it wasn't there when they went upriver.

"That looks like blood," Jennifer whispered.

"We should get out of here." Heather pulled herself away from Zack and slumped in the seat beside him.

Zack played the light all across the boat. The decks were empty.

"I mean it, we should go." Heather put on her bra under her blouse.

Zack stayed, holding the craft with the engines. They idled loudly, echoing off the trees and levees. Anyone inside couldn't help but hear them.

He yelled across. "Hey! Ahoy! Need help?"

The cabin cruiser rocked gently at its mooring.

"Why don't you check it out, Borders? You should know this kind of shit, being a cop's son and all."

John stared at the dark boat, now no more than ten feet away.

"Stay here, John." Heather looked at him, a blurry expression in her eyes.

"Come alongside," John said, standing.

"John!"

He ignored her and as the two craft gently bumped together he stepped across onto the stern of the other boat. "Got a flashlight?"

Zack tossed him one, a heavy two-cell with a metal case, and he miraculously caught it.

The boats were now side-by-side, but somehow Zack's glistening Sea Ray seemed impossibly distant. The other boat was shrouded. John could not see the faces of his companions onboard the Sea Ray. The deck beneath his feet felt slick and breakable.

"Anybody here?" he called, trying to keep the fear out of his voice.

He ran the flashlight beam forward, past a bench, sink, and the driver's seat. The helm. He didn't know many nautical terms, despite his sailing trips from Boston. Here nothing looked amiss. The seats were pearl colored and clean, and there was no evidence of any partying, no beer cans, nothing.

Ahead was the rectangular entrance to the cabin. It was totally black. The flashlight didn't cut through the gloom at all. John felt his stomach tighten. It was only a few steps but they looked dangerous and the cabin far off. His interior voice was telling him not to go in there, to return to the Sea Ray and leave.

He thought again of Heather, willed his feet forward, and ducked inside the cabin, taking the single step down.

"Anybody…"

The blood lay everywhere in the confined space, an area as tight as a funeral vault. A large amount pooled on the floor, soaking into the carpet, nearly reaching his shoes. More was flung in great spurts against the walls and portholes. He thought of photos he had seen in school, of Jackson Pollack painting.

The flashlight exaggerated the color of the blood and its freshness, sluiced along cushions and dripping from a bench. Everywhere, that is, except on the face of the woman who lay on the bench staring at him with empty eyes. She had short wheat-colored hair and a face that maintained its attractiveness despite what had happened here. Her legs were parted wide. A stab of recognition hit him and he had a moment's desire to venture deeper into the cabin, but no, he stopped.

He wanted out with sudden panic. He ran a hand nervously through his hair and backed out quickly, the skin on the rear of his neck prickly. Then, again with unaccustomed grace, he hopped back across to Zack's boat. Zack was in the rear, again working on the knots that secured the Zodiac. He was teasing the girls. "You take the little boat out for a love cruise…?

"No," a pouty response came.

"She's dead in there…" John tried to speak calmly, still supremely aware of Heather's presence. "We've got to call the police."

Zack walked back to the helm, speaking over the exclamations of the girls.

"What do you mean, dead?"

"Dead, asshole," John shouted. "Murdered. It's a fucking Freddy Kruger house in that cabin."

Zack opened his mouth and nothing came out.

He gunned the engine and they leapt out of the water. John fell painfully to the deck, but scrambled up again. He pushed his way forward, the images he had seen burned in his brain, grabbing Zack's shoulder. The other man pulled away roughly and steered to the middle of the channel.

"We have to go back!"

"Back off, dawg, it's my boat."

"She's dead back there."

"Then there's nothing we can do."

John fought for the wheel, unsuccessfully.

"Go back!"

"Are you crazy?" Zack shouted. "I've got a boat of ecstasy and drunk underage girls. No fucking way."

It was no use. The bright lights of downtown Cincinnati were in their faces and reflecting off Zack's sleek, shaved head, as if they had suddenly emerged from the past into the present.

Zack steered over to the Serpentine Wall and cut the engines, jumping out to tie up. He leaped back in and took the cell phone from John, rage in his bright blue eyes.

"Don't you get it, cop's son? We'll be the first goddamned suspects."

Monday

Chapter Three

With an hour to spare before her meeting started, Cheryl Beth locked her car and began her walk across campus. It was the loveliest day she had seen this year, as mother nature felt the intoxicating sense of her power to give rebirth. A rainstorm had come through in the early morning and now the day was sunny and warm. She gloried in the bright green of the Ohio buckeyes, the sweetgums with their star-shaped leaves, the dense beech trees. A woodpecker was working on an oak, a scarlet crown on his head. Her mother had taught her to identify trees when she was a little girl. She had given her that, at least.

The morning fast-walks were important, Cheryl Beth knew. After she had turned forty, she could no longer keep weight off effortlessly. She was still an attractive woman, with light brown hair worn in a long shag cut and large brown eyes in a face that still held the too-young look that had often caused her to be underestimated. She smiled easily and men still noticed her. But she was trying to be healthier. Too many years as a nurse had taught her the senseless, incomprehensible ways our bodies could go wrong; no need to help the process along.

Her surroundings made such worries seem impossible. The surreal beauty of Miami University never failed to move her. It was like a college setting out of a novel, with stately brick buildings, a lush, precisely maintained campus, and the quaint town of Oxford. The sense of safety was overwhelming. What a change from the grittiness of the old hospital in Cincinnati. She started through the dogwood grove that would take her to the Formal Gardens. It was one of her favorite spots.

This was the first time in her career when she wasn't practicing as an RN on a hospital staff. It felt strange to go to work as a teacher of nursing, not to be in scrubs but dressed up. She had worn scrubs for more than twenty years, working in the hardest jobs at the hospital that handled the toughest cases. She was known as the best pain management nurse in three states and wouldn't dispute it. But she needed this break. She was a natural teacher, and the clinical part of the job still gave her hospital time.

She liked her students, even though their reputation at "J. Crew U." was supposedly that of clueless privilege. Many were older, starting new careers. A few were her age, and quite a number were men. The clinical work in the hospital came naturally. She cared less for the nursing classes that were held in Middletown and Hamilton, the onetime industrial towns being so forlorn. So she appreciated the few times she actually got to teach on the main campus. Some days she thought about moving to Oxford and saving the drive from Cincinnati, but it was still early in this new work and she couldn't shake her love of the city. Her black Audi A4, her one serious indulgence, made the trip easier.

Much of the time she missed the old hospital for all its flaws. She missed the patients, and especially her old coworkers and their mostly endearing eccentricities. The university had plenty of smart, pleasant people, but it was very politically correct. The old Redskins mascot had been changed to the Red Birds. The nursing faculty was highly capable, but she knew she could never make the dark jokes or have the irreverent fun with them that she so enjoyed with the staff at the hospital, things that had kept her sane.

As she came closer to the Formal Gardens, she saw the police cars. She had only seen so many in a single place one other time. The cars were from the campus police, Oxford Police and

Butler County Sheriff, all crowded together, many with their lights flashing.

"I can't let you go closer, Professor Wilson."

A young man with close-cropped hair, wrap-around sunglasses, and uniform stood on the sidewalk. He was a campus officer she had become acquainted with when he helped her get a jump-start on her car back in the winter. He had all manner of things on his uniform belt besides his gun and handcuffs, and she couldn't say what half of them did. "Professor Wilson" was still new to her, and she urged her students to call her Cheryl Beth. But this young man was one of those who couldn't break the habit. Maybe saying "professor" made them feel as if they were getting their money's worth.

"And you're probably not going to tell me why." She smiled and he reluctantly smiled back, shaking his head.

"You know how it is." He slipped off his sunglasses. Over his shoulder, she saw some officers erecting a blue tarp beyond the circle of benches that stood at the heart of the Formal Gardens.

"Kind of ruining my walk," she said, and instantly regretted it, not even knowing what tragedy was unfolding at the head of the long string of police cars. As if she herself hadn't had enough dealings with the police to last a lifetime.

Then she saw his eyes.

"Are you all right, Jared?"

He stared at her and then looked at the ground. Even with the activity, it was quiet enough to hear birds singing. His eyes were red and his complexion had that greenish-gray tint of the nauseated, reminding her of when nursing students attended their first autopsy.

"It's really bad," he said. "Things like this don't happen here." He paused and kicked absently at the asphalt. "I was the first officer on the scene. Oh, my god…"

"You might want to get on your haunches and try to lower your head," she said. "It might make you feel better."

He remained standing. He whispered quickly. "I've never seen so much blood."

"Dead?" she inquired, but her middle was already cold.

"Two girls." He hesitated. "Somebody used a knife. I've never seen anything like it."

"Oh, no."

She saw another man walking toward them from the direction of the tarped-off area. He had sergeant's stripes on his uniform and an unhappy expression.

"Be good to you, Jared." She turned to leave.

Then she saw the movement out of her left peripheral vision.

It was a man, running and stumbling through the bushes at the foot of a stand of thick trees.

He was completely naked, and seemed to be wearing war paint. But Cheryl Beth had spent enough time in emergency rooms to know that it was dried blood caked on his hands, arms, and face.

"Stop! You, halt!" This command came from the uniformed group near the tarp. Now the sergeant and Jared focused on the man, who was running parallel to them twenty yards away. He was young and his face held a confused madness.

Both officers drew their weapons and ran toward him.

The naked man screamed, "Hostiles! Hostiles! I have wounded!"

Cheryl Beth watched the spectacle with a momentary, anes-thetized detachment, unaware of the messenger bag over her shoulder.

Another cop in a different style uniform dashed straight toward the naked man and tackled him, driving him into the grass. He screamed and thrashed but was quickly surrounded as eight men and women in uniform converged on him. He struggled and moaned.

"Quit fighting!"

"Quit resisting!"

The commands came quickly and atop each other. But the naked man dragged himself on the wet grass underneath the cop who had initially tackled him, regained his footing, and ran. The cop tried to grab his ankle but missed and fell face-first onto the grass, taking two other officers down with him.

She knew this man.

It was Noah Smith, one of her nursing students. Grass and mud now mingled with the caked blood on his naked body. Across the grassy distance, their eyes connected, his were full of terror.

"Cheryl Beth! What are you doing here? Help me!"

A female officer used a black baton to strike him in the side of the ribs, the knees. Pain centers. He moaned but ducked past her. She reached for him but lost her balance, spun around, and fell backwards, her equipment belt rattling loudly.

He ran directly toward Cheryl Beth.

Part of her was alarmed, but another was clinical, amused as the Keystone Kops scene unfolded before her. The campus police, city cops and deputies, a dozen now, caught up and surrounded him.

"No, no! Help me!" He dashed toward one cop, then another. They closed the ring, leaving him no escape. Cheryl Beth was now terrified they would shoot him.

"Tase him," the sergeant said and it was done. The naked young man snapped backwards and arched his back as surely as if he had been defibrillated. Then he lay still on the spring grass, face up.

They turned him over, handcuffed him, and dragged him toward a squad car, opened the back door, and shoved him inside horizontally, hands on his shoulders, legs, and feet. The door shut loudly.

Shock wobbled through her own body. What was Noah doing here, naked and covered in blood? He was a good student, quiet, friendly. Wasn't that what people always said about serial killers after they were exposed?

"What happened?"

A co-ed asked Cheryl Beth the question, and she realized a crowd had gathered.

"I don't know," she said quietly.

"Do you know this man?"

It was the sergeant. He was a deputy sheriff, not one of the campus police officers. He had red hair and a wide, muscular body.

"He's one of my students."

"Here?"

Cheryl Beth nodded, and the sergeant wrote down the information, including her name and phone number in a small notebook.

"When was the last time you saw him?"

"Last week. He's doing his clinical work."

She stared at the squad car that held Noah.

"Someone should at least check his pulse."

"We'll take care of all that. Now you need to leave." The sergeant then raised his voice. "You all need to move on. This is a crime scene."

Cheryl Beth walked back the way she had come, her legs feeling weak and stringy, her mind wondering what had happened. She would read about it in the newspaper, but that would never tell the whole story. She actually knew a cop. But it had been a long time since she had seen him.

Chapter Four

"Pee-eye-pee-eye-oh!"

"What do you want, Dodds?"

Will Borders swung his body out of the bed with difficulty. The clock said 6:45. He thought about reaching for his cane and standing, then thought better of it. He already had the cell phone in one hand and his legs were feeling both tight and uncertain. He sat and listened to his old partner sing off-key.

"It's a homicide, buddy." His voice dropped into its normal roomy baritone.

"I kind of figured, since you're a homicide detective."

"Here in Over-the-Rhine, waiting on your white ass."

"So? A homicide in Over-the-Rhine? I can record something later on the info line for the reporters, post it on the blog."

"Not this time," Dodds said. "A white man in a new Lexus with a blade sticking out of his chest. Two television news crews are already here, and we need our PIO on scene."

Will muttered a profanity.

"Can't be hard," Dodds went on. "You're living in the ghetto already."

"All right, fifteen minutes."

"Make it ten." The line went dead.

Will took his seven a.m. Baclofen early, reached for his black steel cane, and stood. He knew the drill: Tight abdomen, stand with the interior muscles of his legs, and pull his shoulders back and down using his lats. It worked. The days when he could roll out of bed, shower, dress, and be at a crime scene in fifteen minutes were gone. But so were the days, after being discharged from the hospital, when dressing left him exhausted and in tears. Today he used the electric shaver, brushed his teeth, and combed his hair almost like a normal person. In the closet, he sat on a bench and dressed in a suit and tie with only moderate pain and discomfort. At least he could feel something below his waist. At least he was off the pain meds.

He had been dreaming before the phone woke him. He dreamed all the time now. The reason was easy to understand: his legs were twitching, keeping him from falling into a deep sleep. In this dream, he was interviewing for a job in Homicide again, or maybe it was for the first time. It wasn't the real office, but a sleek, two-level workspace with Danish furniture and nobody he recognized. He was waiting to see Lieutenant Fassbinder. And waiting, and waiting, and then he had missed his interview. He always walked normally in his dreams and awoke filled with anxiety.

Now fully alert, he clipped his badge, holster, and extra cartridge magazines in his belt. In the holster was a Smith & Wesson M&P 40-caliber semiautomatic pistol. He was sweating from the effort by this time. The quads muscles in his right leg were already feeling the strain from the work. He stood again in front of the mirror and straightened his tie. Take away the cane and he almost looked normal: Six-feet-two inches, broad shoulders, and a full head of wavy hair. In better days, Cindy had nicknamed him "TDH" for tall, dark, and handsome. He certainly didn't feel that way now. Working his way carefully down the stairs, he headed out. The upright Baldwin piano in the living room stood unused, silently judging him.

The dark blue unmarked Ford Crown Victoria with five antennas on the roof and emergency lights under the grille sat unmolested outside his townhouse on Liberty Hill. It was a stub of a street that marked the beginning of the rise of Prospect Hill, which was sometimes called Liberty Hill. Cincinnati could be confusing that way. The little street was a collection of nineteenth century homes, two and three stories, closely spaced and right up on the sidewalk, in various states of repair. Many, like Will's, had been restored. Now he was glad that his was the only one that required only one step up to enter. A few doors up sat the three-story Pendleton House, with its light-blue mansard roof. It was a National Historic Landmark, having been owned by a senator who led reform of the federal civil service.

Being in only the municipal civil service and yet carrying a badge, Will had an informal deal with the neighborhood homeboys: they kept the car safe and he didn't bother them. So far it had worked. Downtown glistened to the south. He made himself walk the way he would at the scene: an easy, if slow gait, the cane barely visible, the weakness in his left leg concealed. But he was conscious of every step. Every step was hard as hell. Don't show it, he told himself for the thousandth time. Don't show it.

The city of Cincinnati comprised fifty-two neighborhoods in a geography that began with the basin at the river landing and rose onto three-hundred-foot high hills into which were tucked dozens of valleys, hillsides, and ravines. Each neighborhood had its own history, culture, and feel. But none was like Over-the-Rhine. With its narrow, snaky streets immediately north of downtown and dense rows of four- and five-story tenements and commercial buildings, it had once been the old German enclave. Its five square miles held America's largest urban historic district, its jewel box of architectural styles mostly unscathed by massive teardowns or urban renewal. It also was the home to Music Hall, Washington Park, and the Findlay Market.

It was half time capsule to the nineteenth century and half slum. Most cops had no sentimental attachment to it. Yet Will liked the place.

A hundred years before, Over-the-Rhine held nearly fifty thousand people. Now, despite the rough-at-the-edges splendor of its buildings, the neighborhood was home to little more than ten percent of that population, and almost all were poor, uneducated, and black. The gentrification of the nineties had

paused with the riots, but the place was so magnetic that yet
another attempt at a Renaissance was under way on Main Street
and elsewhere. The old Stenger's Café, where he bought coffee
for years, was being reborn as a wine shop. There was talk of
connecting O.T.R. to downtown with a streetcar, but change
came slowly to Cincinnati. Parts of it were amazing in their
beauty, others scary even to the cops.

He turned onto Race Street and briefly flashed the vehicle's
emergency lights so a uniform would let him pass. The street
was blocked and half a dozen marked and unmarked units were
parked in front of a dingy little market that still had a faded
Hudepohl beer sign hanging from a rusty overhead rod. It was
one of the few places to shop here. Kroger kept threatening to
close its small, run-down store over on Vine. It's not as if this
were a place with the demographics or incomes to attract retail-
ers. It attracted plenty of yellow crime-scene tape, which was
now being wrapped.

The buildings stood between the street and the low-hanging
sun, shrouding the landscape in the half-dark of the hour before
real morning. Dodds was standing on the curb with his hands on
his hips. He was hard to miss: big as a door, shaved head, with a
complexion like strong coffee, and always dressed to the nines.
A hundred feet down the block were two television news vans.

Will stepped up on the curb, made his left leg crook up to
catch the sidewalk, cheating by using his left hand to push off
a car fender, and walked toward him, conscious of every bump
and disfigurement of the sidewalk that might trip him.

"What have you got?"

"Thirty-one-year-old male, name Jeremy Snowden, address
in Mount Lookout, sitting peacefully behind the wheel of his
automobile enjoying this historic neighborhood."

He followed Dodds, moving as fast as he could but still
trailing behind. A silver four-door Lexus was parked directly
in front of the little store. Race was a one-way street running
toward downtown and the river, so the car was parked on the east
side of the street with the driver's door by the curb. A lithesome

young man with dirty blond hair to his shoulders sat exactly as
Dodds said. His eyes were open as if he were surprised by the
commotion. His shirt was light blue sporting a Ralph Lauren
Polo logo over the breast and a silver-handled knife was protrud-
ing from his chest at a ninety-degree angle. Will took it all in as
the experienced homicide investigator he had once been, before
the tumor and the hospital.

"Was the door open?" he asked.

"Closed but unlocked. Anonymous 911 call at 5:52 a.m. No
witnesses, of course."

Will looked around at the blank black faces watching them
from windows and gritty doorways.

"How do you know his name?"

"Wallet."

"So not a robbery?"

"Probably a robbery," Dodds said. "The vic was making a
purchase from Nubian pharmaceutical salesmen late last night
and something went wrong, then they were scared off by something else and didn't get the wallet."

"Maybe."

"You're not on homicide anymore, Mister PIO." Dodds
gently stuck a cigar-sized finger in his chest at exactly the place
where Jeremy Snowden had met his fate.

Will knew this too well. He was the public information
officer. The PIO. His job was to walk over to the reporters and
give them a statement that told them the basics of the crime,
but not too much. Not the victim's name, for next-of-kin would
have to be notified. Not specific information about the crime,
especially details the detectives wanted to hold back. Nothing
that a clever defense lawyer could later use to undermine the case
once they had a suspect. He'd be on the newscast with "Detective
Will Borders" under his image as he relayed as little as possible.

At that moment, he saw a young woman ambling up the
other side of the street. She saw him.

"Hello, Detective Will."

"Can't talk now, Tori," he called. "You'll have to go back and wait."

Tori was Victoria Missett, a reporter for WCPO.

"Get that girl outta here," Dodds commanded and a uni-formed officer walked toward her, even though she was already retreating.

"Not that I wouldn't do her," he said. "Young enough. I'd teach her how to fuck. Speaking of which, have you called that nurse? Cheryl."

"Cheryl Beth. And no."

"Why not? You're a free man. Divorced. God, wish I were free of my ball-and-chain. Twenty-two years of ball-and-chain."

Will badly wanted to change the subject. He said, "I'll tell Karla that and let her kick your black ass up and down the street."

"Cheryl Beth's a cutie. I'd do her.

"You want to do everyone."

"Why don't you call her?"

"Because I'm a cripple."

"You have a serious confidence problem, partner. Nobody's going to notice that cane. I bet you could use it as a kick-ass police baton."

Will didn't answer. Instead, he leaned in the open car door, shifting his body to rely even more on the cane. "Went right into his heart, right between the intercostal spaces." The shirt showed little more than a trickle of blood. He had bled out inside his body. If the assailant had twisted and pulled out the blade, it would have released a torrent. Will went on, "That's either major luck, or a lot more care than a random robber would take."

"So here's the statement you're going to give the media. Quit doing my job."

Will stood and faced Dodds. "That's not a knife," he said. "That's a letter opener. Looks expensive. Maybe sterling silver. I think it's Tiffany."

Dodds almost pushed him aside to peer inside the car again. "God damn," he said.

"Obviously a drug dealer of letters."

"Whatever. He stole it. Makes a nice weapon, as you can see."

"What's that in the back seat."

"You don't give up." Dodds shot him an annoyed glance, then bent into the car again. "Guitar case. So what? He looks like a hippie.

"There haven't been any hippies for thirty years, Dodds."

"This is Cincinnati, Borders."

"Whatever. It's not a guitar case. Too big. Cello."

Dodds faced him. "Now how the hell… Oh, yeah, you were a music-fucking-minor in college, weren't you? That was helpful in the career choice you made."

"It helps me now." Will wanted to sit down. His legs were aching and tired. All the muscles he was using to make the walking and standing look normal were stabbing at him. He pushed this aside. "It doesn't take college to know a cello case."

"You." Dodds pointed to a uniform. "What's your name?"

The young man gave it.

"Tim, I want you to go to the other side. Use these." He handed the uni some latex gloves. "Open that back passenger door and pull out that case. And do it carefully."

"Yes, sir," the young cop squeaked. It was probably his first homicide.

When the cello case was out, Dodds had the uni place it on the trunk of the Lexus.

"You know what they call the color of this car? 'Starfire Pearl.' I want one."

"Not on an honest cop's salary," Will said.

"There's always overtime." Dodds carefully undid the latches. The case was fiberglass, purple, and well worn. What was inside wasn't.

"So Mister Music, it's a cello. You're right. Now, go get those fucking reporters out of here."

Will stared at the instrument and didn't speak for several seconds. "That's a Domenico Montagnana."

"So? Sounds like a baseball player from the Dominican Republic."

"It's one of the finest cellos in existence," Will said, a tingle running across his chest. "Yo-Yo Ma plays one. I think he calls it Petunia."

He stared at the fine wood, the intricate workmanship on the scroll at the top, the neck, and fingerboard. Dodds exhaled heavily. He knew what Will was going to say next.

"Maybe it was dumb luck this didn't get stolen, like with his wallet. But this is no freshman at CCM." The College-Conservatory of Music at the University of Cincinnati.

Dodds stared at the ground.

"Music Hall is two blocks away," Will added.

Dodds waved a finger in his face. "Now don't try to make this some hoity-toity symphony thing, Mister President. You know as well as I do that most homicides are simple."

Will smiled mischievously and walked back to his car.

Yes, most were simple. That's why cops didn't read murder mysteries or watch police television dramas: they made the business sound too interesting. In real life, the homicide beat was tedious, repetitive, and unexciting. Most victims knew their killers. Drugs were a big motive: A deal gone wrong, a mule stealing from a dealer, a small-time dealer ripping off a bigger supplier. Domestic violence was another common denominator. Husbands killed wives and their new boyfriends, and often finished the job with a bullet in their own mouths. Sometimes wives and girlfriends killed their men.

If a person turned up in a suspicious death, their lover was always the prime suspect, and that bias on the part of the detectives rarely turned out to be wrong. When couples didn't fight about sex and jealousy, they fought about money. Sometimes a slap became a kick became a bullet. Cops themselves were no different. They offed their exes and then ate their guns. Cops also slept with a lot of other cops' spouses or girlfriends or boyfriends, and then things went lethally bad.

Most victims and suspects came from the same socioeconomic class, and, in a city like Cincinnati, from the same race. Most were black, living in the poor and forgotten neighborhoods

overrun by drugs and offering no jobs. The cops knew the suspects and victims already. In most cases, the homicide had been
only a matter of time.

Hold-ups went wrong. Some kid with no impulse control
wanted to play gangsta. He thought pulling the trigger was no
different than what happens in a video game. Concepts like
mortality, forever…forget it. It wasn't wired in their brains these
days. Try to get ahead of it and the ACLU and the ministers
and all the do-gooders who never spent a night in the ghetto
would be all over you. But the same things happened in the
white-trash neighborhoods like Lower Price Hill. The really
lurid stuff occurred out in the suburbs, but don't try telling that
to the average Cincinnatian.

Cops burned out of homicide. Not because of blood or gore
or being outwitted by criminal masterminds. No, because of its
monotony: The same easy suspects, the same filthy apartments,
and same kinds of people doing the killing. The pressure from
the brass to clear cases. And the paperwork. And that forever
part, dead, gone completely… if they let themselves think about
it too long.

The younger cops didn't know much about real investiga-
tions because DNA solved everything, or so nearly everyone was
convinced. The really gifted homicide investigators were mostly
retired or close to it. Then, the endless time with the D.A. and
in court, and a sentence that never seemed like justice. Traffic
division was much the same but the stakes weren't as high.

It's not that serial killers weren't out there or that some
homicides weren't true mysteries. It's not even that criminal
masterminds didn't exist. A person could get away with it, if he
was really careful, disciplined, and, especially, didn't know the
victim. But that wasn't the day-in, day-out of working homicide.

The truth is, most murder is boring. Except when it's not.

Chapter Five

The murders caused the campus to go on alert. Classes were canceled for the day, and that included Cheryl Beth's meeting. Students were told to stay in their dorms, faculty to remain in their offices. Cheryl Beth's office was at the Hamilton campus, so she walked into town, past the cordon of police at the university's entrance, and ordered coffee at a bagel shop on High Street. An *Enquirer* was sitting on the table, and she absently thumbed through it. "Couple arrested after flagging down cop," a headline on an inside page read.

It went on, "A couple who flagged down police to report that they had been robbed at gunpoint early Saturday evening got more than a sympathetic ear from a Cincinnati police officer. According to Detective Will Borders, Karole and Stephen Sweigert, both 27 and from Cleves, were arrested because the couple drove from Cleves to purchase drugs on McKeone Avenue with their three children in tow." Cheryl Beth drummed her fingers on the newsprint and sipped the coffee, scalding the inside of her mouth. She popped the lid off to let it cool.

When her cell phone rang, it showed a number she didn't recognize. She keyed it to voice mail and drank the coffee, re-reading the news article. In a moment, the message icon appeared and she listened to a male voice, exuding authority. The coffee lost its taste.

The voice identified itself as Detective Hank Brooks of the Oxford Police Department. He took the time to spell his last name. Would she please come to the station as soon as possible? He gave her the address and his number. "Please come to the station, ma'am," he reiterated. As a nurse, she had been calling women ma'am for her entire career, and came from a small town where "sirring" and "ma'amming" were as expected as church attendance. But now when she heard it, she felt old. The pretty young woman behind the counter had called her that when she had poured the coffee. Ma'am. It was a vain thought, she knew. Hearing it from Detective Hank Brooks—B-r-o-o-k-s— rekindled the dread in her stomach.

She could carry it off well. A bystander would see a woman in a black pant suit, pleasant face, idly watching the street through the window, tapping her fingers on the newspaper, slowly sipping her coffee. Cheryl Beth locked all her crises deep inside. Her training had taught her to mask emotions when necessary, to do the job. That was the way to be effective, the way to help people. But inside, she could feel her stomach muscles trembling.

Two girls dead in the Formal Gardens, hidden by a blue tarp. One of her students arrested. A crime so lurid it made her friend, the campus cop, look as if he were going to vomit. She thought more about Noah Smith. He seemed dependable and smart. He was getting good grades. A nice guy. Good-looking with an easy smile—too young and too skinny for her tastes—but he seemed popular with the women in class. He made them laugh. But she didn't know him. Did you really know anyone? She couldn't say she really knew her own mother. The blackness of her drink stared back at her. She pushed it aside and stood to go.

The Oxford Police Department was a short walk, sitting beside the quaint city hall at High and Poplar streets with its pitched roof, small tower, and white columns in front. The flowerbeds were blooming violet and white. The station itself was simpler, a squat addition with two windows and a door facing the street. She walked through the door and asked for Detective Brooks. She started to sit, studying the department's shoulder patch with its American flag and eagle, "Police, City of Oxford, State of Ohio, Est. 1810."

"Ms. Wilson?"

A man stuck his head out of a doorway and beckoned her inside. He was short and solid, somewhere around forty, with wavy brown hair and a bushy moustache. His handgun stuck out from his sport coat when he shook her hand. Hank Brooks mostly looked her in the eye, but also he gave her an appraising once-over. Up close, she realized he was only a little taller than her five-feet-five-inches. He moved with nervous energy barely contained.

"Come back, please. Thanks for coming in so soon."

She said something polite. Then, "Is Noah here? Is he all right?"

"He's fine," Brooks said, walking ahead of her down a hallway. "They've taken him to the Butler County jail."

He led her into a room with a table and modern wheeled office chairs, upholstered in black. Bulletin boards and white boards lined the walls. She didn't take the time to study their contents. He invited her to sit and left the door open.

"Did you know Noah Smith well?" Brooks asked. "How long did you know him?"

She told him all she knew. Noah was a third-year student, in her NSG 362 class, Nursing Care for Adults with Health Alterations. She typically team-taught with a woman with more academic experience. They made a good pair, Cheryl Beth bringing the real-world experience, leading the clinical part of the course that took place in the hospital. Noah was in his second semester with her.

"Was he moody? Did he have a temper?"

"Never that I saw."

"Ever seem to be on drugs?"

Cheryl Beth shook her head. As a pain-management nurse, she was very good at spotting that kind of behavior, and Noah had never displayed it.

"What about with women? Was he hostile?"

"Not at all," she said. "He got along well with the women students."

"I guess that's one reason to become a male nurse." Brooks leaned back, stretched, and cradled the back of his head into his outstretched hands.

"We call them all nurses," Cheryl Beth said. "It's like not calling out gender differences between police officers." That was the stress in her stomach talking. She tamped it down and smiled. "But, sure, men are still outnumbered by women in the program, and Noah is a good-looking guy."

"Think that's why he did it? To meet women?"

She couldn't stop herself from making a face. "How about a personals ad in *CityBeat*? These students who have reached this level have worked very hard and they want to make nursing their career."

He nodded, leaned forward, and opened a beaten-up brown portfolio. A yellow legal pad was filled with handwriting in blue ink. He flipped the page and began making new notes. Outside the door, she saw police officers walk past but the station seemed oddly quiet.

"What about you?"

She felt the sudden defensiveness of a driver going the speed limit who sees a patrol car behind her. "What about me?"

"You're new to Miami."

So he had checked on her. She wondered why.

"I was at Cincinnati Memorial Hospital. When it closed, I decided to try something new."

"You're not from Ohio, not with that accent."

"Where I come from, it's not considered an accent." All those years in Cincinnati and she couldn't get Kentucky out of her voice.

"So you're what, an adjunct?"

She nodded. The money wasn't great, but she had some saved and had welcomed the change of teaching. She could get a new nursing position again any time.

"No tenure," he sighed. "That's why they call those jobs, ad-junk." He didn't smile. "That was where they had those murders. Cincinnati Memorial, right?"

"That's right."

He made more notes.

"Why did Noah Smith call out to you, Ms. Wilson? Do you prefer Ms., Mrs., Miss?"

She was fine with "Cheryl Beth," but something about Detective Hank Brooks didn't sit right with her.

"Miss is fine," she said. "And I have no idea. I was standing there…"

"Why was that?"

"I was going for a morning walk to the Formal Gardens." She worked to keep the irritation and anxiety out of her voice. "He saw me and recognized me. He asked for my help. He seemed afraid."

"I might be afraid if I had murdered two girls and was caught napping at the crime scene with blood all over me, Cheryl." He stared at her and stroked the edge of his moustache with his right index finger. His shoulders were a straight line of tension.

"Is that what happened? You found him there asleep?"

Brooks sat back straight and hesitated. She knew he had told her more than he had intended. But that only made her want to know more.

"The Formal Gardens seem like a pretty public place." She looked at him evenly and let the silence fall between them.

Finally, "You don't know the campus very well, do you, Cheryl?"

"My name is Cheryl Beth."

She didn't like him well enough to tell the story of how in the first grade, the teacher had been confronted with three girls named Cheryl, so she called them by their first and middle names: Cheryl Ann, Cheryl Sue, and Cheryl Beth, and how the name had stuck and she liked it. If she were back at the hospital, back in her position as pain nurse, she would have added: *Are you trying to piss me off?*

"Sure, okay, Cheryl *Beth*," he said. "There are times of the day when parts of the campus can be very isolated. All the trees and shrubbery and open spaces. Even so more at night and in the early morning."

"So the girls were killed overnight?"

"I can't discuss the details," he said, but she got the point: The killings had not occurred soon before she arrived.

"And Noah fell asleep in the bushes, naked?" she said. She raised her hands to calm him. "I know, you can't tell me anything."

"I can't get over him calling to you and asking for your help." He leaned forward on his elbows and stared at her. She looked back at him, wearing her pleasant face.

"That's what happened. Actually, he seemed disoriented. I don't really get your point, Detective Brooks."

"This is a small-town department, but we're not idiots, Cheryl Beth."

"I didn't say you were, Hank."

He flipped back a yellow page of handwriting and studied it.

"I don't think you told me where you're from with that accent? Originally."

"I didn't tell you. Corbin, Kentucky."

"Corbin, Kentucky," he said, neutrally. "Never been there."

"I haven't lived there in twenty-five years." She realized she was nervously playing with her hair. She forced her hands back to the top of the table.

"Noah Smith is from Corbin, Kentucky."

"What?"

"That's right, Cheryl Beth. And you're telling me you don't know him? Must be a pretty small town."

Noah had never told her that. His accent was as Midwestern as most of her students.

Brooks persisted. "Want to tell me more, now?"

She took a deep breath but maintained her composure. "There's nothing to tell, Hank. I don't live in Corbin. I haven't lived there in a very long time. I didn't know he was from there.

Lots of people named Smith in every town, probably even Oxford."

She ran through her mental Rolodex. In fifth grade, she had a crush on Billy Smith. His family moved away. She knew Donna Smith all through school; Donna had brothers but none was named Noah. Joe Smith owned the filling station on Main Street before it was shut down. It was an impossible task.

"You still have family in Corbin?

She hesitated. "Yes, a brother."

"Noah Smith doesn't," he said. "He claims he has no living relatives. Did you know that?"

She told him that she didn't.

"He was a loner, I guess." He leaned back and the chair gave a creak that seemed at odds with its newness. He started shaking his right leg.

"Kept to himself in class?"

"No, he was quite outgoing. He seemed normal." She heard herself talking too fast. She slowed down and added: "I know that's what people always say." She smiled, the insincerity of it hurting her facial muscles.

"Mmm-hmmm."

"He was never disruptive," she said. "He never missed a class. He was good with his clinical work. Don't tell me he has a record or something."

"That doesn't tell anything," he said. "Lots of killers have never had a parking ticket."

He wiggled in his seat, reached into a file, and slid two plastic bags onto the table. Each contained a small card. A driver's license.

"Do you know these girls?"

The shock radiated down her legs. One license showed Holly Metzger. The other was Lauren Benish. She tried to keep her breathing even.

"Are they the ones who were killed?"

He nodded and stroked his moustache. If it were a little longer, he could play Simon Legree.

"My God." Her hand went involuntarily to her mouth. "They were in my class."

"With Noah Smith."

"Yes."

He pulled back the licenses and slid them back into the folder.

"I can't believe it," she said.

He swung the portfolio closed and slid his pen in his shirt pocket. He stared hard at her. "What I can't understand is why he was calling for you out there. And you happened to be there."

She stared back at him until he spoke again.

"The thing is, Cheryl Beth, he's asking to see you."

Chapter Six

The quick movement caught Will's eye as he was crossing the wide expanse of Central Parkway headed into downtown. On the far corner, a man was down on the sidewalk. Another man, twice his size, was kicking him. Will instinctively hit the siren, a quick blurt, called for backup, and parked his unmarked car at the edge of the curb, partly blocking a traffic lane. The bumper was five feet from the fight. He swung himself out, pain and spasms clinching his strong right leg. He raised himself to his full height and used the car door and roof as support.

"Police, step back."

The assailant was huge, with baggy black jeans and a dirty Reds cap. His pockets, embroidered with what looked like sequins, drooped nearly down to the backs of his knees. He looked over at Will and mouthed a profanity, again swinging his leg hard into the other man's side. He was in his mid-twenties, wearing heavy black boots, with thick toes and heels, and silver buckles and chains ornamenting the tops. His rap sheet was long.

"I thought you was dead, Borders."

"You're going to be if you don't step back, Junior," Will said.

"Motherfucka' owes me money. He gotta pay!"

He said this as if it were a rational justification. Another day at the office. "Ain't that right, cocksucka'? You give me my money!" He raised the boot to stomp the man's head.

Before the surgery, Will would already have been out of the car, at the sidewalk, and had Junior, Clarence Kavon James Jr., prone on the pavement. But he couldn't do that now. And he didn't have time to pull out his cane and walk with difficulty the short distance to the crime. As if that would allow him to control the suspect. A small crowd was gathering, encouraging the beating.

Will unsnapped the holster on his belt and in seconds had his pistol aimed across the car roof.

"I said stop, asshole." His voice, at least, was still commanding. The gun was leveled at the man's chest.

A wide brown angry face stared at him with the usual empty sociopath eyes. It was dusted with darker freckles on either side of a wide nose. Will and Dodds had put his father in prison seven years ago for murder. The rotten apple didn't fall too far from the rotten tree. With his leg cocked in the air, he looked like a malevolent drum major. He slowly lowered his boot halfway to the concrete.

"What, Borders? You gonna shoot another unarmed black man?"

"Yes, Junior. Did I say police? There, I've identified myself. You people, move away now so I can shoot this unarmed black man!" The dozen onlookers backed a few paces away.

"I'm a man of color!"

"You're assaulting a man of color, Junior. Get on the ground, now!"

"This is a G thang, Borders, none y'all's bidness."

"It's a police thing now, Junior. Lower your foot or lose it."

Junior glowered at him. Will didn't know what the hell he would do if the suspect didn't comply.

The look of defiance seemed to last an hour. Then he spat in Will's direction and lowered himself to the pavement with studied dignity.

"Hands! Spread out your arms and show me your hands."

The man did as ordered. The victim, wearing layers of old clothes and agony on his face, lay in a fetal position on the sidewalk, moaning.

"Stay there." He continued to lean on the roof, keeping the gun on the man. He whispered to himself. "Now, if only the cavalry will arrive." Traffic went by on Central Parkway. The road had been the Miami and Erie barge canal in the nineteenth century. Underneath it was Cincinnati's never-finished, never-opened subway. Now it was only a spacious dividing line between Over-the-Rhine and the central business district. Will was sweating, the wet spring air starting to fill the sky.

He saw the white paint of the cruiser out of his peripheral vision and a uniformed officer sprang out and handcuffed the kicker. Another unit arrived and two more unis walked to Junior, lifting him to his feet.

"Police fucking brutality! You gonna let The Man do this to a brother!? We need another riot!"

The onlookers walked away quickly in every direction.

Junior was far from done. "Every man has his boiling point! His boiling point, bro! You, too, Borders! Every man has his boiling point!" The yelling was muffled when he was placed in the prisoner compartment of a cruiser and the door was shut.

Will holstered his firearm and sat heavily in his car, using the radio to request a fire department medic unit. The dispatcher acknowledged his request as his cell rang. He swiveled into the seat, using both hands to lift his weak left leg inside, and answered.

"Good morning, Specialist Borders." It was Amy Garrett, the chief's secretary, using the department and union's technical term for his rank. She usually gave this greeting in a voice where you could almost see her smile, high cheekbones, and tasteful-but-short skirt. Amy could almost make you look forward to a visit to the chief's office. All the cops wanted to sleep with her. She was happily married. Imagine that, Will thought, happily married. Today she sounded different. "Busy morning, huh?"

He assumed she meant the homicide that Dodds was working. He had already used his iPad to type out the preliminary report for the police department Web site, not naming the victim, saying that Cincinnati homicide detectives were investigating. The iPad was easier to use for such tasks than the clunky police laptop mounted between the seats. Now he said, "You don't know the half of it," as he felt his heart rate start to go down and he could still hear Junior shouting at him from inside the prisoner compartment of the squad car.

"There's been an incident in Kenton County."

He waited.

"You need to go down there."

His trouble meter was registering high. Kenton was Covington, right across the river from downtown, but another state, another county, another jurisdiction, and, thank God, another public information officer.

"What's up, Amy? What aren't you telling me?"

Her voice lowered to nearly a whisper. "It's Kristen Gruber. She's been found dead. Probable homicide."

"What do you mean?" He blurted it in exactly the same way he had heard countless family and friends of dead people do, back when he was a homicide detective delivering bad news.

"Will, she's been killed. Are you hearing me?"

"Yes." He let himself exhale. "Was she on the job?"

"No. We don't have a lot of details yet. She was found on a boat."

"Who knows? Anybody in the media?"

"Nobody yet. But you'd better get down there. This will be national news."

"What am I supposed to do? What's the plan? Is a homicide team coming?"

"It's only you," she said. "Go down and find out what they have. Then the commanders will hold a press conference. This is direct from the chief, Will. He wants you to begin an investigation."

Will hesitated. "Amy, I'm the PIO."

"You're a veteran homicide detective, Will. You'll be the liaison officer between this department and the Kentucky cops. As far as the chief is concerned, you're the lead detective on this for us."

The lead.

She added, "Now be nice to them down there."

"On my way."

"So are you going to…" A tall young uni stood at the car door. Then he saw it was Borders. The one who walked with a cane.

"He was kicking the other guy," Will said. "Clarence Kevon James Junior. Street name of Junior. He's on probation. I'll add to your incident report later."

"Great," the kid said sarcastically. "You have powers of arrest, detective."

"Paperwork comes with the job, son. I've got to go." Before the uni could protest further, Will slammed the car door, backed up, and raced toward the Ohio River.

Kristen Gruber. Officer Kristen Gruber. He could see her face as he raced past Piatt Park, the Netherland Plaza Hotel, and the dense cluster of buildings that lined both sides of Fourth Street. The intense blue eyes, easy smile, and the blond hair worn in a pixie cut. But she was no pixie. She was one of the most gung-ho cops he had known. He even remembered her badge number.

In a roundabout way, Kristen was responsible for him having this job. She had been the public information officer. With her girl-next-door good looks, athletic build, and perfect television presence, she was ideal for the department's makeover after the riots. She had set up the Web site and the Twitter account that Will now had to feed like a machine. Transparency, the chief said. She could have remained the PIO forever if it hadn't been for the show.

LadyCops: Cincinnati was a reality TV show featuring three female officers, but Kristen was the star. She always had the first segment. Of course, the show was heavily sanitized, the calls routine and low-priority, the department always appearing business-like and professional. It was great publicity. Virtually every suspect was black, but nobody involved mentioned this fact. They had to sign releases for their faces to be shown, and many did so happily—such was the power of television.

As a result, the PIO job came open at precisely the time Will was able-bodied enough to return to work, at least to a desk job. Years before, he had been one of her instructors at the academy and she recommended him as the new PIO.

Will had a cop's dislike of the media. He didn't trust reporters. They got in the way and their stories could send a case sideways. The exception had been an old hand with the *Cincinnati Post* who smoked cigars, knew when to withhold detail, and had earned the respect of both Will and Dodds. The man had been on the police beat for twenty years and knew more about the department than most of the officers. Otherwise, about the last thing Will wanted was to be the department's face to the media.

But the chief liked the idea—Will thought cynically because it would get the Cincinnati Police points to have a disabled cop in front of the cameras. He hadn't been shot and wounded. But the cameras didn't know that. Still, being PIO got him back on duty. He learned that most of the reporters were very lazy: they would take what he posted on the Web site or recorded on the information line and simply put it on the air or in the newspaper. *The Post* had closed and the *Enquirer* rotated through a string of rookies, none of whom had time to learn their jobs—this when the last newspaper in town wasn't laying people off. The television stations only wanted "visuals," as they called them.

It would have made for an easy job if the department wasn't still living with the fallout from the riot: a class-action lawsuit, Justice Department intervention, and federal court oversight of reforms. Will was no different from most of the cops, who felt the politicians, the media, hell, even the police commanders had sold out the working officers, had no idea of conditions out on the streets. But when the issue reared up again, Will read the statements given him by his masters and drew his paycheck.

Now he crossed the Roebling Suspension Bridge, hearing the metal grates under his tires, feeling them rubbing against his brain. The riverfront had undergone a dramatic transformation in his lifetime and now it was all devoted to pleasure. The old rail yards were gone, as were most of the gritty multistory brick warehouses. Even the flying-saucer-shaped Riverfront Stadium had been supplanted by two showy and expensive replacements, one each for the Reds and Bengals. Even as the city lost population, it gained new development close to the water. The National Underground Freedom Center was new, and a fancy mixed-use project called The Banks was going up.

Will barely appreciated any of this at the moment. He was thinking too much about himself. There was always a danger that someone video-recorded his encounter with Junior and on television it would be made out as a new sign of racial insensitivity. That would land him in an internal investigation or worse, charges of racial profiling and excessive use of force. What really happened didn't matter. The cop was guilty until proven innocent.

That led to brooding on his limitations, too. His weak left leg's muscles were now in fierce spasms from the effort of standing. He pushed his left foot into the floor of the car, barely stopping the limb's protests. What had happened on Central Parkway was an intense reminder of what he could not do.

Yes, he was lucky to be alive—he told himself that every day. And the surgeons had removed the rare tumor inside his spinal cord in time so, with much work, he could walk again. Only a few months ago, he had been in a wheelchair. Now he could stand and walk. The tumor hadn't been cancerous. All lucky things, miracles even. But they couldn't return him to what he was: a fully functional man, a real cop. They couldn't take away his feelings that he had been allowed to return to duty out of a sort of professional pity rather for than the skills he still possessed, even if he couldn't run and jump. That he had been allowed back in no small measure because his father's name was on the wall: the memorial to police officers killed in the line of duty.

He pushed the thoughts aside, passed through the 150-year-old masonry of the bridge's southern tower, and then he was in Covington. Except for the expanse of river and different tax rates, it was really a contiguous part of downtown Cincinnati. Before the new building done on the southern bank, Covington's street grid exactly matched up with Cincinnati's. He passed the new high-rise hotels and the wild black-and-white curve of the Ascent condos facing the Cincinnati skyline, then the hulk of the Internal Revenue Service, before he was on the familiar streets lined with their vintage buildings. In ten minutes, he reached the police station in the southern end of the little city.

He had a dead cop. And he was the lead.

Chapter Seven

The drive to the Butler County jail took a long half hour, past the thick cornfields and sleepy rural crossroads that gradually gave way to the shabby outskirts of Hamilton. Like so many smaller blue-collar cities in the Midwest, it had been suffering for decades and looked it. Cheryl Beth didn't care for the town, but that might have been because the Miami University extension, where most of the nursing classes were held, was located in soulless new buildings separated from downtown and fronting on a huge a parking lot.

The main part of Hamilton had good bones even in bad times, the old buildings built for a hopeful future that came and went. Even the huge empty factories with their dead smokestacks held a mysterious grandeur. When she had been younger, most of these plants had been operating. No longer. The big recession in the early '80s had started the process and manufacturing jobs lost to Mexico and then China had pretty much finished them off. As a result many who lived there were taking classes for jobs in health-care or commuting long distances to work in Cincinnati or Dayton.

Hank Brooks drove in silence. Cheryl Beth looked out the car window. It wasn't until they crossed the white arched bridge across the Great Miami River and started down High Street that the apprehension again gripped her middle. She distracted herself wondering how many Ohio towns had High streets.

The jail was sterile and sprawling, sitting beside the railroad tracks. It was one of the few things in the little city that appeared new and successful. He led her through the reception area, which was empty save for one young woman sitting watchfully on a bench.

"You ought to see this place on the weekends," Brooks said as he signed them in. "Packed with families to see inmates. Thing that breaks my heart is the kids. You have kids, Cheryl Beth?"

"No."

"I've got two, girl and a boy. They make life worthwhile."

She ignored him and showed her driver's license to a deputy. He searched her purse. Brooks handed his gun over and it was locked in a steel cabinet. Then she heard a loud buzz, and Brooks led her through a glass door, which led to more and heavier doors, more guards, and a gathering sense of isolation.

They moved through white corridors with neatly spaced banks of fluorescent lights overhead and shiny white floors with wide dark stripes on the outer edges that encouraged you to walk in the middle. She wondered again what she was doing here. The long walk led them to a room, which a deputy unlocked. It had a metal table with metal chairs. Noah wasn't there.

"You're sure you want to do this?" he asked, beckoning her to sit.

"No."

"Then why do it?"

"You want me to, don't you? I'm a pleaser."

"A sarcastic one."

"And this involves my students."

Now it was his turn to say nothing, merely open his portfolio and turn to a fresh sheet of lined yellow paper. She looked at him, wondering what angle he was playing. He looked like a man of hidden agendas, but one was pretty obvious: He thought Noah was guilty, and she was sure he'd be on her during the long drive back to Oxford. Why hadn't she brought her own car?

The room echoed with a loud metallic sound and two deputies led Noah Smith in, pulled out a chair across from them, and sat him down. One deputy left, closing the door. Noah was in loose-fitting prison stripes, shackles on his arms and legs, a chain around his middle and an ashen expression on his face.

Brooks introduced himself, spelled his last name. He read Noah his rights.

Noah ignored him.

"Thank you for coming, Cheryl Beth." He reached a manacled hand across the table toward her and a female deputy instantly intervened. "Prisoner! Hands in your lap."

Noah cringed and dropped his hands. He looked shrunken in the inmate garb. She searched his face: Noah Smith from Corbin. Somebody's son, brother, cousin? Nothing. He didn't look like anyone she had known there. And it was a place she had tried very hard to forget.

"I don't need to tell you that you're in a lot of trouble, Mr. Smith," Brooks said. "You can make things easier on yourself if you tell me what happened out there."

"I didn't…"

"Noah," Cheryl Beth said. "You'd better not say anything until you talk to a lawyer." She didn't look Brooks' way, felt his cosmic annoyance flooding her.

"I didn't do anything." His voice shook.

"Tell me about the two girls, Holly and Lauren?" Brooks asked it in a confidant's voice. "I can help you, Noah, if you'll help me. Lawyers are going to get in the way of that. Now's the time to work with me, before things get more complicated. Tell me about the girls."

Noah swallowed hard enough that his Adam's apple, his laryngeal prominence her interior voice said, bobbed up and down. He said, "We were drinking in town and went back on campus to party some more."

"Noah!" Cheryl Beth stared at him. "Wait for your lawyer before you say anything."

He shook his head. "I've got nothing to hide."

Brooks said, "You all were together?"

"Sure. We were together at the bar." He gave the name of the place, a popular hangout for students.

Cheryl Beth wanted to slap him silly. He was a fool to be talking or to trust Hank Brooks.

Brooks asked, "Why?"

He looked bewildered.

"My point is, did you all have plans? Did one of them go there with you on a date? Did you pick them both up? What?"

Noah said they had met up at the bar. "We were drinking and having fun. First Holly and me, and then we saw Lauren and she joined us."

"Drank too much?"

"Maybe"

"And you expect me to believe these two good-looking girls, both of 'em, left with you."

"They did."

"Must be nice," Brooks said. He made some notes. Noah's eyes beseeched her, but all Cheryl Beth could do was give a small, soothing smile she had perfected over the years. At the moment, she was doubtful of its comfort. She mouthed the words: "shut up." He looked away.

"You're kind of old to be hanging around campus bars, Noah," Brooks said. "My information says you're twenty-five. These girls were both twenty."

"I was in the Army," he said. "After my discharge, I went back to school."

"An honorable discharge?"

"Yes, sir."

"We'll check on that." Brooks put down his pen and stared at the young man. Then his voice resumed its friendly tone. "What time did you leave the bar?"

"I don't know. Maybe around midnight."

"You're sure of that."

Cheryl Beth turned to Brooks. "He already told you he wasn't sure." She turned back to Noah. "You should shut up."

"I'm innocent." He said it, looking incredibly boy-like and vulnerable.

"Then how do you know it was after midnight?" Instantly she wished she hadn't asked it.

"I got a call around midnight, let it go to voice mail. I saw the time then. We left awhile afterwards. The place was getting pretty crowded."

"Who called you?" Brooks twirled his pen in his fingers.

Noah hesitated. "A friend."

"Female friend?"

Noah nodded.

Brooks stood and paced toward the wall, his shoes squeaking on the waxed floor.

"You're a popular guy," Brooks said. "So you and the two girls walked to the Formal Gardens? Did you do drugs?"

"Noah," Cheryl Beth said.

"It's okay," he said. "We did some E."

"Ecstasy," Brooks said. "You always bring that when you're out with women?"

"Lauren had it," he said. "We took one each, watched the stars, and talked."

Brooks sighed. Then: "Did you hook up?"

"Sure. That's kind of the idea."

"With both of them?"

Noah nodded.

"Man, you are a lucky guy," Brooks said, circling around behind Noah. Cheryl Beth noted again how short he was, how he radiated short-man insecurities. It reminded her of certain doctors she had known.

Brooks said, "What made you kill them?"

"I didn't!"

The deputy stepped closer and Noah slumped in his chair. Brooks leaned in behind Noah's left side.

"You own a knife?"

"Probably. Yes, I do. I have a couple from the service." Noah leaned back and turned his head, but Brooks had switched sides. He spoke into Noah's other ear, barely a whisper.

"What about handcuffs?"

"No, of course not."

"Those girls had abrasions on their wrists. Somebody handcuffed them, Noah. I think that somebody is you."

He shook his head, saying "No" over and over.

"We're going to find the knife that killed those girls, Noah. We're going to find the handcuffs. And when we do, we're going to find your fingerprints on it. So why don't you tell me what really happened."

"I'm trying to tell you the truth. Somebody hit me from behind."

"Somebody?"

He nodded and Brooks sat back down. Some anonymous sounds came from back in the jail, and Brooks leaned in, baring his teeth.

"You like to hurt women, right?"

"I never…!"

"You're really sick to have done this, Noah. Carve up those girls that way."

Noah shivered and sobbed.

Brooks' tone shifted again. In a quieter voice, he asked, "Did the girls see this somebody? Did they warn you? Did they scream?"

"No. They were passed out. I was about to wake them up so we could go."

"Passed out?" Brooks cocked an eyebrow and stroked his mustache. "I didn't think ecstasy made you pass out. I thought it made you feel all full of peace and self-acceptance and shit like that."

"We'd had a lot to drink."

"But not too much for you to have sex with them."

"We had sex."

"Your DNA's going to be in those bodies, Noah. Why did you kill them?"

"I didn't kill them!" His face was red and he was crying.

"Because somebody hit you."

"That's right. When I came to, I felt like hell. Holly and Lauren were gone. It was raining, but I passed out again. The next thing I know was when you guys… Wait. Holly and Lauren were gone because I wasn't in the Formal Gardens when I woke up. I was off in some bushes. Like somebody dragged me over there."

"That 'somebody' again," Brooks said.

"Noah," Cheryl Beth said, "When you three were together, were you alone in the gardens? Did you notice anyone else?"

He hung his head, shaking it slowly. "I don't remember."

His story seemed implausible. But Cheryl Beth also knew that many of the behaviors Noah exhibited, from the loss of focus, impaired attention, and even paranoia were after-effects of Ecstasy, otherwise known as MDMA.

She turned to Brooks: "Did you notice any marks on the grass as if he'd been dragged?"

Brooks glared at her.

"Has anyone examined the back of his head?" she asked.

"This is bullshit," Brooks said,

"May I?" She stood. "I'm an R.N."

The deputy seemed unsure.

"Go ahead," Brooks said. "What the hell."

She walked behind Noah and felt above his neck into his hair. There was no bleeding but a noticeable lump. "There is a hematoma there," she said. "A big bruise. A blow from the back could have made it. He needs to be checked for a concussion."

"That's what I'm telling you." Noah said.

"It could also have come from the arrest," Brooks said. "Or maybe you fell. Killers are stupid that way." He stood and walked to the door.

"I'll see you in the lobby, Cheryl Beth. You," he pointed at Noah. "You and I are going to have more talks."

After the door shut, Cheryl Beth faced Noah. His face was wet with tears. He didn't dare raise his hands to wipe them away.

"Why did you ask for me?"

"I don't have anybody," he said. "You seem kind."

She watched him carefully. Was he manipulating her? She couldn't be sure. He seemed sincere. "Who can I call for you? Parents? Brothers or sisters?"

He shook his head. "I don't have anybody."

She thought about bringing up Corbin, but didn't. The place held too many ghosts and heartbreaks. That he was from there unsettled her further. She made herself look him in the eye. "I don't know how to help you. I could ask around about lawyers.

"I don't have any money. I'm over my head with student loans. You've got to believe me. I didn't kill them." After a long pause, he spoke again. "Do you believe me?"

"Yes." Cheryl Beth felt the lie burning her throat.

Chapter Eight

The press conference began at five minutes after four at Cincinnati police headquarters on Ezzard Charles Drive. The city was under a tornado watch. When Will had reached the station two hours earlier to brief the brass, the air was thick with humidity and enormous thunderheads were advancing over the Western Hills. Kristen Gruber's parents had retired to Myrtle Beach, South Carolina, and the chief had called them personally, hoping to reach them before they heard about the murder from the media. Now the briefing room was bright with television lights whatever the sky outside had to say. All the local stations were there, plus a crew from Indianapolis and a freelance team. Half the room seemed to be sneezing and sniffling. Sinus Valley.

The chief stood at the center of the podium flanked by the lieutenant colonels that commanded different bureaus in the department. All wore black mourning bands on their badges. All were in full uniform, including the dark dress jacket. This was a good thing in Will's mind, not only because the white uniform shirts of CPD overly reflected light and drove the television people crazy, but also because they made the cops look like ice-cream men. That, at least, had been Cindy's joke. Will's ex-wife had disapproved of his career choice with increasing intensity as their marriage went on.

White shirts and television lights. Will had learned about such arcana when he was sent to a special school for law-enforcement media officers. He had been drilled in how to handle the parry and thrust of difficult press conferences. Still, he felt ill at ease before the cameras, and today especially he was happy to stand off to the side of the brass, the only one in a suit. He gripped the edge of a chair with his right hand, subtly he hoped. His body was exhausted from the day and standing now was taking all his effort. Chest up, shoulders back, lats pulled down, diaphragm tight, all the things he had been taught. Still, his left leg was reliably thumping every eighteen seconds. You could set a stopwatch by it. He desperately wanted to hyper-extend the leg and let all the pent-up energy out, but he had learned the hard way that doing this would cause him to be in danger of falling down from the resulting spasm. So he put weight on it hoping the leg would calm itself.

He badly wanted to sit down.

The chief had served his whole career in the department. Like most officers, Will's opinion of him was complicated. What was not in question was that he was very much a Cincinnati product: coming from old German stock west of the "Sauerkraut Curtain," a graduate of Elder High School, and a cop who came up through the ranks. He stuck to his roots by bowling in a league at Heid's Lanes. His trim figure looked good in a uniform, his sandy hair combed precisely into a style out of the early 1960s, his face still youthful for fifty-eight. Now he faced the cameras and gave a stoic account.

"Officer Kristen Gruber was found dead on a boat tied up on the Licking River this morning. We're working with our colleagues at the Covington Police Department and the Kenton County Sheriff and treating this as a homicide. I can tell you she died of multiple stab wounds. I'm not going to go into details…"

Will knew the details. He stared into the lights and recalled the photos he had seen in Covington. Kristen had been handcuffed, hands behind her, and placed on a bench in the cabin of the boat. The assailant had used a knife to rape her. The genital mutilation was the worst Will had ever seen. At some point in the attack, the femoral artery in her right leg had been slashed and she had been left to bleed out. It appeared that bleach had been poured around her genital area, perhaps to corrupt DNA testing. Her face was untouched. Had she screamed out there? Would anyone have heard it? The blood volume was so high that it was still pooled when the first cops came aboard.

"...We intend to expend every resource in the department to find the vicious killer of a Cincinnati Police officer...," the chief went on.

The boat was tied up on a deserted tract of the Covington riverbank. A kayaker had found it early this morning. The time of death was sometime between Saturday afternoon and Sunday morning; the medical examiner would narrow it further. The kayaker had been home with his wife during that time. Tracing ownership of the boat was easy: it belonged to Kristen. Other than the blood, the crime scene appeared surprisingly tidy. No bloody footprints or fingerprints were immediately found. Crime-scene techs from both CPD and Covington were still there when Will drove back downtown. The adjacent riverbank showed no recent tracks. Whoever killed her had probably come from the river.

Will heard a thunderclap from outside as the chief kept talking.

"...We will spare nothing to capture the killer or killers. We definitely want them badly..."

No knife was found on the boat. Divers had spent the day searching the river bottom, although Will was not optimistic. The lead diver told him what he'd heard before when evidence was being sought in the Ohio River: You can't even see your hand in front of you down in that water. A search a mile above and below the crime scene along the riverbank hadn't turned up anything but garbage, especially beer bottles.

The chief continued: "...I'll take some questions now, but I'll warn you that we won't discuss details or anything that might jeopardize the case. I'll close with an appeal to anyone who might have been on the Licking River on Saturday night or Sunday morning and might have seen anything suspicious, or seen this boat, to call us at this number on the screen behind me." He read out the phone number, too.

Will was astonished that the first question was what would happen to the new season of *Lady Cops: Cincinnati*?

After the chief called an end to questions, the reporters obediently filed out one door, the commanders another. Cincinnati was that kind of town. People still played by certain rules. Will finally sat in the blessed chair, careful as always to make sure he was really centered because he couldn't feel every part of his butt. The light returned to its normal unhealthy fluorescent glow, the four walls containing nothing but silence. His right leg jumped up violently. He forced it down with his hands and shook it, like someone with nervous leg syndrome instead of a spinal cord that had been chewed up by tumors and surgical instruments. He dry-swallowed his five p.m. Baclofen pill, tried to generate some saliva, swallowed again. Within a minute, the right leg settled down.

He felt the hand on his shoulder.

"How you feeling, Will?"

"Good, chief. I'm okay."

The chief pulled up another chair and sat, an alert posture with his back straight and his hips near the edge of the seat. Will was finally full-back in his chair, grateful for the furniture under him, the weight off his legs, and a stable surface beneath him.

"How are our friends in the Commonwealth treating you?"

"Good. How can you not love a department who has a lieutenant colonel named Spike Jones?" Receiving not even a hint of a smile, he hurried on. "They have six detectives on this, between Covington and the Kenton sheriff. But they understand we're going to want a big role. The dive team's been in the river all day. I've sent crime-scene over to work with them. We should know more about the boat by tomorrow."

"Good, good." He nodded, looking Will in the eye. "You'll tell me what you need from us? Resources, manpower. I talked to the mayor and city manager, and overtime won't be a problem."

Will nodded. He kept his own doubts and fears to himself. He wasn't in good enough shape to be the lead detective, certainly not on such an important case. But he didn't dare say no, didn't dare show weakness. The city was struggling with budget cuts and Will knew he was lucky to have a job. He intended to keep it.

"Gruber was a good cop," the chief said.

"Yes, sir."

Will hesitated. "We're going to need to talk to her boyfriend, if she has one. Ex-husband. The usual. I can coordinate all that. I'll get a timeline of her past few days, see how often she went out on the boat and with who. But I also want access to her emails, work and home, phone records. She was on national television. She might have had stalkers. The other officers on the show, you might want to give them an extra heads-up. This might be a one-off killing, but you never know."

The chief nodded. "You follow it wherever it leads, but get this son of a bitch."

"Yes, sir." He said the words, but wondered if the commanders really wanted to know wherever the truth might lead. What if Gruber wasn't a good cop? What if it was a typical sleazy domestic violence or romantic triangle gone wrong? His paranoia kicked in: Why was he sent alone to Covington this morning—why not a real homicide team? Maybe command wanted to keep things discreet; cop gossip traveled fast. Maybe he was being set up.

The chief leaned in an inch. "There's one more thing. And I know you have a lot on your plate."

Will waited.

"The D.B. this morning. The one in Over-the-Rhine."

"The cellist."

"Exactly. You still have season tickets to the symphony?"

"I do." Will figured he was the only officer on the force who did.

"That'll help. The symphony board is climbing down my throat on this one." He sighed. "As if one headliner isn't enough right now. Maybe you'd be willing to go over tomorrow, meet with the president, and make sure they know we're doing all we can? These are some powerful people. You'll know precisely the right touch in this kind of situation. It's one skill your friend, Dodds doesn't have. You know what I mean."

Will knew.

Chapter Nine

Cheryl Beth was back in Cincinnati by five, curled up on her sofa at the little bungalow she owned in Clifton, which sat at the end of Sauer Avenue on a bluff. In the winter, you could look south out the kitchen window and see Over-the-Rhine and downtown. In spring and summer, it was as if those vistas had never existed. A tree canopy ran from her small backyard into Bellevue Hill Park and all she could see was green. She was on her second glass of wine and she had the band Over the Rhine on the sound system. The songs were as pensive and mournful as her mood. Her mind still back at the jail with Noah Smith. He looked impossibly frightened, alone, and innocent. But was he? Hank Brooks was convinced he was a killer.

It didn't track for her. How could Noah alone have killed two fit young women?

Then her concern over him switched to guilt: her own. It wasn't only about Noah. Holly Metzger and Lauren Benish were dead. Two bright young women who would have made fine nurses. Dead.

A too-familiar dread washed over her. The spike of ice grew in her abdomen. She saw the blue tarp again, could only imagine what lay behind it. When the murder happened at the old hospital, she had been followed and spied on by the killer, and this lovely old house, her sanctuary, had become a domicile of fear. She had pulled the curtains tight all those weeks, triple-checked the locks, especially after she had seen the footprints in her flowerbeds. Another policeman had saved her then, a man very different from Hank Brooks. She missed him.

Sitting still and stewing was not an option. She tended to fill any vacuum that appeared. It made her a good nurse. Sometimes it made her supervisors crazy. More than once an evaluation had used the words "bull in a China shop."

She shut off the music and dug through her class files to find the information cards she asked each student to fill out at the beginning of the semester. They included emergency contacts. She sipped the glass of Chardonnay too fast, carefully studying Holly and Lauren's cards, putting them on the side table, picking each up in turn. She walked to the kitchen, poured another glass, came back to stretch out on the sofa, and picked up the telephone.

Holly's mother answered on the eighth ring. Cheryl Beth identified herself and told the woman how sorry she was. Nursing had taught her to be a master of the difficult conversation: the terminal diagnosis, the failed surgery, and the too-many things that went wrong in hospitals. When the doctors had said their lines and left, it was up to the nurses to stay with the patient and the family, pick up the pieces of mortality. Still, this was inexplicably difficult. She told the mother what a good student her daughter was, what a fine person, quick to help her classmates, and to make a joke. By the end, they were both crying.

Lauren's parents lived in Kettering, a suburb of Dayton. When the phone was picked up, the voice on the other end sounded young and businesslike.

"My name is Cheryl Beth Wilson and I'm calling for Mr. or Mrs. Benish."

"They're not available and you news people are horrible for harassing us at a time like this."

"No, I'm not with the news. I know this is a terrible moment for you all." She heard her voice lapse into y'all. "I was one of Lauren's nursing instructors at Miami, and I felt I should call.

I wanted to let you know how sorry I am, and ask if there's anything I can do. Anything."

After a pause, the woman's tone softened. "I'm sorry. The TV people have been calling nonstop. I won't let mom and dad pick up. I'm scared to death they'll just send a camera crew to our front lawn. Cheryl Beth, my name is April and I'm Lauren's big sister." She choked a moment. "Was."

"April, I am so sorry. Lauren was such a joy to have in class. I wish I would have had a chance to get to know her better."

"Thank you," the woman said. "At least they caught the monster who would do such a thing. Thank God."

"Yes."

They made small talk for ten minutes. April inevitably asked about the origins of Cheryl Beth's accent. Then, "I've been so afraid something like this might happen. I told myself not to over-react, not to be the overbearing big sister…"

"What do you mean?"

"Lauren thought she was being stalked."

Cheryl Beth sat upright.

"It started about a month ago. She told me this creep came onto her in a bar and she tried to give him a nice brush-off and he wouldn't go. She finally ended up leaving, getting in her car, and driving off with the guy standing on the curb watching her. Then she started seeing him on campus. He'd follow her at a distance, but she knew he wasn't walking there by accident, if you know what I mean. It wasn't a coincidence. This happened twice."

"Was he a student?"

"I don't know. Lauren said he definitely didn't fit in with the college crowd in the bar. He was older, she said, but he was in good shape. Oh, he was completely bald. She said he looked like Mister Clean, you know?"

That didn't describe Noah Smith.

April said, "In the bar, he'd been all friendly and funny, but when he wanted to take it further and she said no, he got all weird. Then the stalking."

Cheryl Beth asked if Lauren had notified the police.

"No," April said. "She was forever blaming herself for things. She was afraid she's been too provocative and flirty in the bar. Then she thought maybe she was imagining that he was really following her. But she was afraid. I can tell you that. I was about to come down there and make her go to the campus police when this happened."

"Did you tell all this to Detective Brooks?"

"I don't know who that is," April said. "My parents got a call from the university and had to go down and…" A sniffle broke her control, "…identify Lauren's body. They didn't know about this. Lauren wouldn't tell them. They're very protective and she wanted to be independent. It makes me want to throw up."

When the phone rang a little after seven, Cheryl Beth thought it might be April calling her back. She answered on the first ring and could hear the anxiety in her own voice.

No one spoke. She could hear a background of voices and telephones ringing, then a hand muffling the receiver. The peculiar dread of a mysterious call sanded her nerve endings.

Finally: "Cheryl Beth?" A man's voice. A nice baritone, vaguely familiar.

"Yes. Who's this?"

"I'm not sure you remember me. My name is Will Borders. I was a patient at Cincinnati General when you were the pain nurse…"

She felt a catch in her throat and hesitated. Then, "Of course I remember you, Will. Tell me how you're doing?"

"I'm doing well. I'm back at work, on the force."

"I've seen your name in the paper and hoped you were all right." She could hear more voices and phones in the background. "Where are you?"

"I'm in homicide right now. Detective Dodds sends his best."

A deeper voice called, "Hello, Cheryl Beth!" and laughed.

"Tell him 'hi' back."

She heard a rustling and Dodds came on. "Are you still as beautiful as the last time I saw you?"

"Hello, Detective Dodds." She laughed. "The last time you saw me I was beaten up and bloody."

"You were the most beautiful beaten up and bloody I've ever seen. Anyway, I'll give you back to Mister President."

"Sorry," Will said. "He gets very enthusiastic."

"I can see that. Why does he call you Mister President?"

"Long story." He paused. "Anyway, I'm walking. I use a cane. But I'm walking."

"That is so great. I prayed for that, Will." She blurted that last part out suddenly and then worried if she had gone too far.

After a long pause, Will said, "I hope I'm not calling at a bad time. I've wanted to call and check in. There's no excuse for not doing it sooner."

She smiled and said nothing.

He said, "I wonder if you'd have a drink with me sometime? It's okay if you say no. I understand. I know this out of left field…"

"Will," she interrupted, "I'd love to."

Chapter Ten

"God damn you."

Will glared at Dodds as the entire homicide unit erupted in applause and laughter.

"I didn't even know who you were dialing at first."

"You may call me J.C. the matchmaker," Dodds said, a smug grin on his face. "You were too much of a chickenshit, so I had to do it for you."

"Asshole. And stop that 'Mister President' shit. Now where do I take her?"

"Palm Court," came one suggestion behind his back.

"Too formal," Will said. "What will that make her think?"

"I dunno," Dodds said. "Like you have class? How about the Precinct? Historic old police station, cop motif, all that."

"Across the river," Lieutenant Fassbinder said. "Nice view of the city."

It felt good to be back in homicide again, in the fifth-floor offices leased from the county in the art deco tower at 800 Broadway that once housed the *Cincinnati Times-Star* newspaper. The old energy, the familiar faces, now everyone fueled with the adrenaline to catch whoever killed Kristen Gruber. Her name was written in red capital letters on the big white board that tracked the progress of the year's homicide cases: unsolved. Immediately above it, also in red, was Jeremy Snowden, the cellist. That call early that morning seemed like a lifetime ago. In fact, the board had half a dozen names in red. All unsolved cases. The unit was already stretched.

Still, everyone was eager for a piece of this case. It was a murdered cop and, thanks to the television show, also a dead celebrity. Will went through the same briefing he had given the commanders before their press conference. Much was being held back, including that Gruber's purse or wallet, cell phone, badge, and gun were not on the boat. Her keys were missing. The divers brought out sonar to search the river bottom for the firearm. Her clothes were aboard, neatly folded, but her panties were missing.

"Maybe a trophy taker," Slamowitz theorized, picking his teeth as usual.

"Maybe she didn't wear panties." This from Kovach, who was one year from retirement and smiling for the first time Will could remember.

Fassbinder told LeAnn Skeen, the only woman in the unit, to be on the first morning flight to Myrtle Beach to interview the parents. Will knew he was reasoning, from experience, that a female detective would be better at coaxing information out of a grieving mother and father.

"Take your bikini," Dodds said.

"I'd use one of yours, J.C., but your man-boobs are too big," she said.

"Meet me at the Hustler store, baby." He smiled lasciviously.

"Stop it, children," Fassbinder said, "or I'm going to have a sexual harassment claim on my hands, probably filed by Dodds."

"Always keeping the black man down," Dodds said in mock severity.

For these minutes the unit had the snug feel of the old days. Amazingly, his old desk across from Dodds was empty, too, as if waiting for him. Dodds still had the homey needlepoint sign on the cluttered desktop that said, "Our Day Begins When Your Days End." But everything had changed. Will had spent ten years in this office and now he felt like a stranger. He was off homicide and his real desk was over at headquarters. And even though he had received a round of applause when he walked in tonight, his first appearance there since getting out of the hospital, he knew they no longer really considered him one of them. He was the PIO, the guy on television, the one who walked with a cane. He sensed that at least some of his former colleagues wondered why the hell he was the lead on this case. He wondered the same thing. But he had cleared too many murders for this to be anything but an awareness leavened deep in the collective consciousness of a group used to working together.

With Covington detectives checking Gruber's phone records, Fassbinder sent Kovach and Slamowitz to interview the other two officers featured on *LadyCops*. "Find out if they know whether she had a boyfriend," Will said and regretted it. They knew that.

Schmidt was dispatched to the Seven Hills Marina, where Gruber moored the boat. Would her car be in the parking lot? Someone would need to look into cases she had worked. Will volunteered. But first, he set off for the home of a dead cop.

Kristen Gruber lived in a high-rise condo at the end of a long cul-de-sac that ran off McMillan Street. It was on a palisade overlooking the Ohio River at the edge of Walnut Hills, a short drive east from downtown. Walk a few blocks and you'd be in the heart of a ghetto. But this street was quiet, empty and framed by trees, the remnants of the thunderstorm still dripping off the leaves. The storms had moved east, leaving the air smelling of rain. Will sat in his unmarked car, driver's window open to the damp night air, waiting for the Covington detective. Cheryl Beth Wilson was way too much on his mind. He had been so nervous he hadn't even asked what she was doing now that the hospital had closed. Did she think he was rude? And what if something did develop between them? His body was different now. Could he perform as a man? He gently pushed her face out of his mind, flipped on a flashlight, and began reading Kristen's personnel jacket.

She was thirty-four years old, five-feet-seven, one-hundred-thirty pounds, single. She had joined the force ten years ago after graduating from the University of Cincinnati. After four years on patrol, she had joined Central Vice, then became PIO. The jacket held a slick folder used to promote *LadyCops*. Inside that was a color eight-and-half-by-eleven photo of Kristen, wearing a black T-shirt, black flack vest emblazoned with "POLICE," and a smile with perfect teeth and seamless confidence. The other two officers on the show were uniforms, one white with brown hair, the other black and average-looking. Neither had the fine looks of Kristen.

Gruber's record looked almost too clean: No excessive force complaints, no shootings, not even an accidental firearm discharge. She had plenty of commendations. Will flipped through the supervisor reviews: "proactive," "highly effective," "diffused dangerous situation," "dedicated," "tough," "unrelenting." Will knew some of these sergeants and lieutenants, and a few were still back in the Stone Age about female officers. They would be much more likely to grade her hard. Yet she uniformly won them over. That and the all-American-girl face: an Ivory Soap complexion for Ivory's hometown. He remembered her from the academy: even then she seemed like a comer.

He was not. His body was giving out on him after working the longest straight shift since he had gotten out of the hospital. He usually took a break in the middle of the day and laid down. Not today, and even the gift of adrenaline was starting to run out. His back was catching fire with pain. His right leg felt wrapped around itself with muscle spasms. He had been off pain meds for months now. Nothing to do about that except take Advil back at home. He popped his two Neurontin on time, washing them down with bottled water, and wished he could go upstairs by himself. But jurisdictional niceties must be observed.

"Can't quit," he mumbled, waiting for the pills to kick in and lessen the spasms.

He saw the headlights behind him and a dark Ford Crown Vic slowed. He waved and started the car, pulling up to the building's main entrance. The Covington detective met him at the door. Her name was Diane Henderson, and she was also a thirty-something strawberry blonde, but she was shorter and lacked the youthful dazzle and fit build of Kristen. Henderson was still in the black jeans and white top she had worn when he had first met her and the other Covington cops that morning.

"You have a search warrant?" she said.

Will nodded. With a murdered police officer, the Hamilton County judges had been lined up to sign.

They approached the concierge, a middle-aged black man in a blazer and tie, who exuded a studied dignity. He examined Will's badge and identification a long time. Will's shield still lacked the black band of mourning. He'd have to fix that later. Then he read the search warrant. They asked if he had a master key.

"I'll let you in," he said. "Terrible thing, what happened to that girl."

"Yes, sir," Will said, and asked if the concierge worked there regularly. He did, every night except Monday and Tuesday. All visitors had to check in at his desk. Unfortunately, a log of names wasn't kept. The concierge called the tenant and then the visitor was allowed to go up.

"Did Ms. Gruber have a boyfriend?" Will asked.

"Hmmmmm. Couldn't really say, detective."

"Which means?" Henderson said.

He stared at his shoes. "Which means, ma'am, that she kept male company, but I don't know which were her boyfriends. I'm not paid to pay attention to things like that. She was a good tenant."

"I don't doubt it," Will said. "So you're saying she had more than one boyfriend?"

"She was a normal young woman," the concierge said.

Will asked, "Did she have a lot of men or a few men? Regulars?"

"She was young and attractive. She was burnin' rubber, if you know what I mean. And I don't mean anything more than that. She was a good tenant, like I said. I can remember some men who came a few times. Some once or twice."

They started toward the elevators, Henderson and the concierge sprinting ahead of him, or so it seemed. Will walked as fast as he could and they slowed down. "So they stayed the night? These men?"

"Some did."

"Five in one year?" Will asked.

"Sounds about right." He stared at Will. "Detective, I don't get paid to keep track of tenants' personal lives. In fact, I get paid to do the opposite, as long as they follow the rules."

They stepped in the elevator and started to the fifteenth floor. Henderson spoke. "What about women?"

"She had women visitors, if that's what you mean."

"Any stay the night."

He paused. "I noticed one. Not my business to know more. Kids today are different."

The elevator doors slid open with the sound of a whoosh and an electronic bell, and they stepped out into a carpeted hallway.

"We may be back in the next few days to show you photos," Will said.

"I'll try to help, but to be honest all you people look alike to me."

Nobody laughed.

"So her visitors were all white?"

"That would be so."

He led them to a door and used the master key. It didn't open easily. He had to jiggle it and pull the door up slightly before it opened.

"It automatically locks, so please close up when you're done." The concierge disappeared quickly.

"'All you people look alike to me.'" Henderson let out a low laugh.

The condo was spacious, with hardwood floors and new contemporary furniture.

"I don't think I've ever had a neat-freak who was a vic," she said, and it was true. They turned on lights, and the place looked immaculate. Everything was in its place. The kitchen seemed unused. The refrigerator held three bottles of Chardonnay and half-a-dozen individual containers of plain yogurt. The cabinets had a few dishes, pots, and pans, but this was not a woman who cooked.

"So is your leg injured, Borders?"

"It's way more complicated than that," Will said. And she left it alone, motioning. "I'll start in the bedroom."

He slipped on latex gloves and wandered around the living room, which had two walls of windows facing south and east. Traffic on Columbia Parkway shot by silently far below, and the view of the big bend in the Ohio River must have been spectacular in daylight. As it was, he could see the lights of Newport across the wide darkness of water. A large framed photo of the Riverfest fireworks dominated one wall. Another held a sizeable flat plasma television facing a cream sofa and chairs. There were no books. One shelf held a photo of her parents, another of her in uniform on graduation day from the academy. No boyfriends. He opened drawers and cabinets to a chest below the TV: carefully catalogued DVDs of *LadyCops* episodes, a few movies, a new DVD player. No knives or threatening letters.

A smaller bedroom held a desk, chair, and computer. Two pens sat neatly spaced next to the PC. Six inches away, a cordless phone sat charging in its dock. Beside the desk, a shelf contained half a dozen black boxes, the kind you bought at a home organization store. He sat down and began opening them. The first held office supplies. The next two were filled with letters, all neatly filed with tabs indicating months. He slid one out at random and began to read. It was addressed to her, care of CPD headquarters. A thirteen-year-old girl from San Diego watched Kristen on every episode of *LadyCops* and wanted to become a police officer "like you." At the top, a neat hand had written in red, "replied 2/23." Will was amazed a teenager would write a real letter, but then Kristen's email address wasn't easily available. He slid it back in its place and opened another. The Cleveland NAACP was complaining that the show only had African-American suspects.

"Fan mail." He looked over his shoulder at Henderson standing in the doorway.

"Jeez, Borders, how many?"

"Hundreds. At least."

"Do you know how many man hours that is? My captain will go berserk."

"We haven't even started on her email," Will said.

"You guys can do that. You have more resources."

"Yeah, yeah. My lieutenant would disagree with you."

"This is more fun." She dangled a pair of black panties. "Officer Gruber favored black lace." Will followed her into the master bedroom and sat heavily in an upholstered chair facing a king-sized bed. Henderson held up more contents from Kristen's underwear drawer.

She saw Will's expression. "That's called a merry widow, or a corset," she said, replacing the garment. "She's also got garters and stockings. Black and white, depending on the mood, I guess. In the closet, she's got three little black dresses. Must be nice to have had the body to carry that off."

"Any firearm?"

Henderson shook her head. "Not a damn one. No badge or ID. No cell phone. She's got birth control pills in the bathroom. No other prescriptions. Nothing else out of the ordinary."

Will pushed himself up and walked over to the bed that faced the wide window. On a side table, another telephone handset sat in the main charger, but it showed no messages. That seemed strange, but he made note of it in his mind.

A tall, modern wardrobe sat against an interior wall. Inside were uniforms, neatly hung on stainless steel hangers. All had been taken out of their dry-cleaning bags. Suddenly his left leg, which he had hyperextended back at the knee, shot forward, kicking the heavy piece of furniture.

"Sorry," he said, regaining his footing. "It does that."

Henderson bent down. "Good move. Check this out."

Will had accidentally unhinged a hidden drawer beneath the wardrobe. Henderson pulled it out. The contents were arrayed with the same obsessive neatness as elsewhere in the condo, but they were two pairs of handcuffs, a blindfold, a ball gag, leather shackles, some other restraints he'd never seen before, and a couple of very large black dildos.

"No offense to a fallen sister officer," Henderson said, "but our girl seems to have liked it rough."

An uneasy feeling flooded Will's body, something he had been dreading ever since he had been assigned to the case. The Ivory Soap girl was not who she seemed.

He sighed. "We'll bag it all, I guess."

"That'll make me popular in the evidence room tonight." She pulled out clear plastic evidence envelopes and a set of latex gloves.

Metal on metal.

An alert shot silently through Will's head.

Someone was trying the front door.

They both walked quietly in that direction. The floors were solid and didn't creak. But with the lights on, there was a chance whoever was outside might see their shadows under the door. The sound continued. Will heard Henderson unsnap her holster.

Someone was inserting a key in the door.

"How do you want to play it?" Henderson whispered.

"Let him come in."

Henderson took up a position in the kitchen to the right of the front door. She now had her semi-automatic out, held down at her side. Will unholstered his own weapon and retreated into the hallway. He switched his cane to his left hand, held the gun in his right, but the adrenaline coursing through his system made him feel steady on his feet. He turned off the light in the hall, so he would have the advantage of darkness. There was nothing to be done about the lights already on in the living room.

Maybe Kristen had a roommate. The concierge hadn't said anything about that. Still, they would have to be careful when the door opened. They would anyway. The key in the door was most likely the one missing from Kristen's boat, and the hand holding it belonged to her killer.

The key was all the way in, but once again the lock resisted. Click-click, click-click. He didn't know the trick the concierge had used to open the door. Click-click, click-click.

Then, silence. Henderson looked back at him.

"Go." He mouthed it silently. She walked five feet to the door and looked through the fisheye.

She shook her head. By that time he was standing there, too.

"Open it." He had his gun up now, aimed toward the door.

The sound was unmistakable: the key was sliding back out. It took a good ten seconds of pulling to get the warped door to unlatch. By the time she opened it, the threshold was empty. They moved quickly into an empty hall.

"This is bullshit," she said. "I'll take the fire stairs. You take the elevator to the lobby."

Will strode as fast as he dared, his right quads screaming their silent protest. In less than two minutes he was back in the quiet lobby. He holstered the gun and approached the concierge.

"Somebody come through here in the past ten minutes?"

The man shook his head. "Only you and the woman."

A sound indicated a door opening and Diane Henderson trotted up. Will told her what he knew.

"What about visitors tonight, earlier," she said. "Maybe he hid in the fire stairs or on a different floor."

"Only residents tonight, ma'am."

Will knew they were both wondering if the killer was a resident.

He said, "Do you have a garage?"

"Yes, sir. It's indicated on the elevator. P-1 and P-2. It's secured by a door to the street. Residents have a card key that opens it."

"So our guy could have Kristen's card key," Henderson said.

Will tried again. "Is the garage entrance on camera?"

"It is," the concierge said. "But that camera's been down for two months. The homeowners' board hasn't kicked loose the money to get it fixed."

Chapter Eleven

Will noticed the car parked in front of his townhouse when he turned onto Liberty Hill. Otherwise the street was deserted. He parked, heaved himself out, and came up behind the other vehicle. One male occupant. For a second, he thought about unsnapping the trigger guard on his holster before recognition let his heart rate go down.

He tapped on the car window and the driver jumped.

"John?"

The door opened and his stepson got out.

"Hey, Will."

"Sorry if I startled you."

"I wasn't startled."

"Are you all right?"

"Yeah, sure…"

"Well, come on in."

The young man followed him as he unlocked the door and turned on some lights. They made small talk about the townhouse, which Will had bought from a Procter & Gamble employee who had completely redone it: 1870 on the outside, bright and new on the inside. All the furniture was familiar to John because it had been at home before Will moved out and Cindy decided she wanted to redecorate, and then remarry. John wore jeans and a black T-shirt with an elaborate drawing involving skulls. He seemed nervous and tired. His eyes were red.

"Have you been crying?"

"No," John said, a little too emphatically. "These allergies drive me nuts." He asked if Will was practicing his piano and Will had to admit he wasn't.

"Beer?"

"For me, too?" John seemed surprised. "Sure, Will."

"There's Christian Moerlein in the 'fridge. Open a couple of bottles and let's go upstairs." It still made Will feel strange that John called him by his first name. He had married Cindy when John was a baby and he was the only father the boy had known growing up. But once he was in high school, Will was no longer "daddy" but Will. He wondered what John called his real father in Boston.

They tramped up the stairs, through the bedroom, turning on lights as they went, and Will led him out on the small deck.

"Wow," John said.

It was a "wow" view. This side of Liberty Hill was high enough that they could see over the rooftops of the townhouses across the street and into downtown. Directly in front was a vacant lot, enhancing the vista. The air had turned cool and the skyscrapers floated in the liquid black sky above the trees. The city brooded around them on its hills and inside its ravines beneath the green abundance of the changing season. The Queen City of the West, but the West had moved on. It was still a beauty. The night was quiet except for the steady distant rumble of Interstate 71.

Will set his cane against the railing and eased into one of the two chairs. The weight of the day was full on him now and he had been looking forward to the chance to actually sleep tonight. It would be a rarity. At the moment, he didn't know if he could even get up again.

"How do you handle it down here?"

Will sipped his beer. "I like it."

"The riots were right over there. And all the blacks..."

"Oh, John, there's all sorts of people in this neighborhood. You weren't raised that way, and as I recall you didn't like it out in the suburbs." He took a deeper pull of the Christian Moerlein. "So are you going back to Portland after the summer?"

John said he didn't know if he would return. He had liked the city but thought college was boring. Will might not have been his real father but he couldn't stop worrying about this baby who had become a man in the quick-time that was the dark gift of getting older. He had been such a sweet little boy. Then adolescence, and they had lost him. He was aimless and angry, an indifferent student except for music and art classes. This, even though Will and Cindy had skimped to put him in a good high school before Cindy started to make real money at the bank. Will blamed himself. Cindy was gone more and more with work. Some of her positions required travel, and then there were her serial affairs. Will should have done more, but he, too, worked long hours on homicide. John had often been left to raise himself.

"There are good schools here, too," Will said.

"I hate Cincinnati."

"Miami's right up the road. Live on campus. You'd never know Cincinnati existed."

"Still pimping for your alma mater. You went there with all those preppy snots and became a cop. How the hell did that happen, man?"

Will laughed and John did, too, stretching out his legs and relaxing a bit. Will thought about offering some fatherly advice about college and careers. He wanted to ask about his friends and find out what his plans were, but he thought better of it. He was grateful for the company, and had been the designated bad guy in John's life for so long that he didn't want to spoil the moment.

"I've partied up there," John said. "But the kids are so stuck up."

Will knew that could be true at one of Ohio's "Public Ivies." Time to change the subject.

"Those are nice shoes."

"You think so?" John said. "I bought 'em in Portland. They're called Drainmakers." He pointed to the lime green soles.

"How are you?" John asked.

"I'm okay. It's been a long day."

"But the cancer's gone, right?"

Will wearied of explaining the betrayal his body had carried out a few months after he turned forty-one. The doctors had discovered a tumor inside his spinal cord. It was a very rare condition. Luckily it had not been cancerous. They called it "malignant by location": it would have left him paralyzed. Fortunately, they seem to have gotten it all. He ran through it for John patiently. There was no reason to expect Cindy would have told John the details.

"So it won't come back, right?"

"Unfortunately, there's no guarantee of that. Every day's a gift."

"You've turned into one mellow dude, Will. Letting me have a beer, not even ragging my ass about the pot."

He was trying to get a rise, but Will remembered being that age, when small things loomed so huge, when a young man's pride was everything.

"Come on, John," he said gently. "That was a long time ago. Your mother and I were concerned for your well being, doing the whole parent thing. You'll be there someday." He took a deep breath and let it out slowly. "I guess you heard about Kristen Gruber."

"Yeah."

"You remember meeting her?" Will had taken John to the party thrown by the show's producers to mark the completion of filming for the first season of *LadyCops: Cincinnati*. It was the last time Will had attempted to draw John out of his shyness. Kristen had worn one of those little black dresses that night.

"I remember."

"I'm the lead detective on the case."

"Back in homicide? Good for you," John said.

They fell into silence and Will's mind was back on the case. Henderson had taken her evidence back to Kentucky and Will had stopped by a Skyline Chili to grab a late dinner and update the online police blotter. *The Enquirer's* Web site had a long story about Kristen, but also another one about a double-homicide on the Miami University campus. A suspect was in custody and a knife had been used in the attack. He made a mental note to call the police in Oxford in the morning.

"It's really bad," John said in a low voice. "Her being killed."

"Yes." Will never talked about the ugly details of his work with his family.

"So you like doing the whole TV thing? 'Police spokesman.' You're a celebrity."

"Not really. It's the job they let me do. It's not like I can chase the bad guys any more. So I'm grateful for it." Will shook his right leg and wondered why John was there. He hadn't seen him in months. Coming by to check on him was a mature thing. That was good. Will set aside his suspicious cop thoughts, looked into the lights of the Kroger Building, and let his mind swim across memories of Cheryl Beth.

"So are you seeing anybody?" he asked.

John started to speak but only shook his head. Then: "I've tried to do scamming, but the girls don't really go for me. They, like, want to be friends. Not friends with benefits, you know? Like 'friends' means get lost. Don't want to dance with no pants. They save that for the dangerous ones, the alpha dudes. Then they complain because they turn out to be pricks."

"I've been there," Will said, wondering what "scamming" meant. "At your age. It'll change."

"I don't know." John chugged the beer and put his feet up on the railing. Metal clattered onto the floor. It was a folding knife.

John scrambled to retrieve it and slipped it back in his pants pocket.

"Why are you carrying a knife?"

"Because."

Will waited.

"Things are dangerous in this city," John said.

"Make sure it's not used on you. And make sure you tell a police officer you have it if he ever starts to search you."

"Yes, sir," he said, with sarcastic emphasis.

"Relax, John. I'm not your enemy."

John sat upright and fiddled with his pants. "Check this out, Will. Now that you're cool and all…"

John unzipped his pants and pulled out his penis. Even in the ambient light, Will could see something like a small carabiner attached to its head. No, it was more like a crescent or curved barbell.

"What is that?"

"They call it a Prince Albert piercing," John said. "This is what the chicks dig."

"That looks like it hurts. Can you pee?" Will stopped looking.

"Not a problem," John said.

"You can put it away now," Will said, and John did. Will wished he had something stronger than the beer. He started to ask if his mother knew he had done that with the money she gave him, but stopped himself.

They drank in silence until John spoke again.

"How did you handle seeing all those dead bodies over the years?"

"You get used to it," Will said. "Or you get another job. You try to think about doing your job, finding the bad guy."

"I gotta go." John stood up. "I'll put the bottle downstairs. Want another one?"

"No, I'll fall asleep. Can't drink like I once could."

In a minute, he watched John walk to his car and drive away.

As the quiet returned to the street, Will wondered why John had visited him, had chosen tonight, and had waited for him outside. Why had he put a piece of metal through his penis and felt the need to show it? Will was a man whose training and experience had made him a skeptic, even with his own family, perhaps especially with his own family. But John was no longer a boy and had long ago slipped the influence of his parents. Maybe John merely wanted to see how his stepfather was holding up.

"How are you?" John had asked. That commonplace greeting was always given in the expectation of a simple return: "fine." The person asking it didn't really want to know how you were.

Will had done the same thing a hundred thousand times in his life before his surgery. Now he dutifully said, "fine," even if inside he thought, "how much time do you have to hear my answer?"

How was he? His latest MRI scan had shown the area inside his spinal cord where the tumor had chosen to do its damage to be "stable," the doctor said. That was good news. It meant no new tumor. But the neutrality of the word carried incredible weight. How was he? He couldn't really feel touch on his belly or trunk below the tumor zone. The same numbness appeared in unpredictable patches on down his legs and feet. Thank god he could feel his right foot to drive a car.

He was usually constipated. His right leg was as strong as before. His left leg could barely make a step; he used the swing of his hip to compensate as he walked. That, and the inside muscles of both legs, which he had developed thanks to time with a kinesio-therapist, endlessly raising and lowing himself, knees pointed inward, with his back held straight against a concrete post. He walked with a cane and some days were better than others. After the activity of today, there would be hell to pay tomorrow. That's how it went. Every. Step. Is. Hard.

How he was: it very much involved the spasms that ruled both legs now. Impulses to and from the brain and legs were scrambled by the damage inside the spinal cord. The result in the right leg centered on his quads. *Quadriceps femoris*—he had even learned the Latin name. As a normal man, it would have been the strongest muscle in his body. Now, the confusion between brain and muscles, and the fact that the right leg did most of the work walking, left it constantly clenching. The left quad were not so ambitious, simply jumping and thumping as it became tired. He took the maximum dose of Baclofen and Neurontin to make it bearable. Right at the moment, his right quads felt as if they wanted to tear themselves free from the bone, rip the confines of his skin, and fly out into the night like a wild creature.

How did you explain this to anyone?

This was how he was. He hadn't been shot or otherwise injured in the line of duty. He hadn't ended up in neurosurgery because of a crackup on a Harley he had foolishly bought to fend off middle age. Will Borders had bad DNA. Instead of a helix, it was the shape of a bull's eye. Now he qualified for a handicapped placard. People asked him if his leg was getting better. What could you say? He had seen the MRI scans showing the inside of his spinal cord after the surgery: where once the cord had run thick and true, he now literally had threads.

And for all this, John was right: He was mellower, strangely so. It was more than the anti-spasticity drugs. His wife had left him, his body had, well, stabbed him in the back. But, most of the time, he was strangely at peace. He couldn't understand it. Had he been the victim of an on-the-job injury, he probably would have spent many hours discussing this with a police shrink. As it was, he had the Christian Moerlein, nearly drained, the city skyline, slightly diminished as banks of lights in the towers were turned off. It would have been enough if he didn't have a murder to solve.

He looked out on his city, wondered who had been on that boat with Kristen Gruber. He wished he knew who had tried the door to her condo. The doorman had been downstairs. They interviewed the neighbors on the floor: Two old ladies. One other condo was empty, on the market. He felt not a little pressure from the chief's benevolent encouragement earlier that day. If he were really suspicious, Dodds-like suspicious, for Dodds had spent time in police-union politics, he would have worried he was being set up to fail. But that qualm didn't find purchase in his mind or his maniac quads.

Maybe part of it was the "wow" view. He couldn't keep his eyes from roaming to the left, into the little jewels of lights on Mount Adams, to Theresa, to her needless death. They had become accidental lovers, yet he wasn't there to protect her when she needed him most. The weights on his heart that were never gone pulled painfully. Somehow, he let himself think again of Cheryl Beth, without anxiety and regret, and as he did, he fell asleep.

As his legs started quivering, he found himself with his father. They were both in uniform, their shirts incandescently white against the darkness of the narrow alley. Dirty brick walls of tenements hemmed them in. The only light besides their uniform shirts was a yellow streetlight half a block away: it backlit a shadow that approached slowly. Will reached for his service weapon but his holster was empty. He shouted to warn his father, "get down!" "take cover!" but his mouth seemed sewn shut. The words would not come out, instead being half-born primal sounds trapped inside him. The shots came as long fingers of flame from the shadow's hand. Then the shadow was gone and his father was gone and only John was left standing in the alley, watching him.

When Will's eyes came open and he was still sitting on the balcony, chilled from the post-midnight air, staring at the skyline, it still took him a full minute to know for certain he was awake.

Tuesday

Chapter Twelve

At a quarter past six that morning, Cheryl Beth stepped off the elevator at The Christ Hospital to begin her clinical day with the nursing students. Fortunately, this was only a few blocks from home. It was probably the best hospital in Cincinnati and it actively recruited her when Memorial Hospital closed. She might still come here permanently, on staff. She was impressed with the people and the facilities, and it always felt good to be back in her soft scrubs with her white lab coat. The rhythms of the hospital morning were in high gear. She was in her element.

The usual routine began: checking the patient census for new patients, surgical schedule, tests scheduled, and discharges. She also did a quick look at the in-service classes scheduled that the students could benefit by attending. Then she had a conversation with the charge nurse, asking a couple of questions to clarify the situation of one patient. The overnight shift was eager to get home. As the clinical instructor, Cheryl Beth reviewed the nurses coming on duty and which students would be working with them. She walked down the hall to find two new patients, introduced herself, and asked if they would be comfortable being treated by student nurses. Some patients would refuse to have a student care for them, not realizing that they would get even better care and more attention from the student considering how stretched the regular R.N. staff could be. Especially if they were treated by *her* students.

Classes had resumed at Miami, so she expected all her students at the hospital for their clinical. And by 6:45, all were there. Cheryl Beth met them at the nurses' bay. She was proud of her group, having watched them grow in skills and confidence over the semester. Each one was now good enough to care for as many as three patients at once.

Yet now everyone was subdued and the absence of the two girls, even of Noah, was an unspoken weight as they gathered in a semicircle. She thought about leading a prayer, but settled for a moment of silence. It wasn't much silence, with all the hospital sounds around them, but it would have to do. That only brought her back to her conversation last night with Lauren's sister: an older bald man was stalking Lauren. The students had been here all semester for their clinical work. Was there any way he had first seen her here?

After the silence, she handed out assignments for the day. Then they listened to report, as the off-going shift briefed the oncoming shift. She tried to concentrate: what went on overnight, what of note occurred the evening shift before, the status of IVs, when the last pain meds were administered, which post-op patients had voided or eaten or been ambulated. The status of wounds. Anything to be expected this shift. She watched the young faces and knew they were struggling to focus, too. She would have to keep a close eye on them today.

She was happy to have heard from Will Borders. That was the best news of the past twenty-four hours. He sounded so shy and tentative, this man who had been so good in the worst situations. It was an attractive feature, considering the usual demeanor of doctors who hit on her and especially of the one she had foolishly had an affair with. Was it an affair? It lacked the fun of a romp. Maybe a fling. Whatever, it had been bad news. With doctors, there was always the undercurrent of power and class when they had relationships with nurses. On the other hand, she knew friends who had dated and married cops. Those hadn't always worked out happily, either. But this man seemed different. And she realized she was getting way ahead of herself with Will.

She cocked her head at one student to make sure he was listening. They had all heard her lecture. Report was a sacred rite and a critical issue that was too often watered down or violated. When that happened, it was a sure path to get misinformation or no information or to miss vital clues about a patient's condition. As the quality of care had deteriorated at Memorial, she traced much of it to sloppy report. But she was a stickler.

At Christ, high-caliber report wasn't a problem. The charge nurse, a stout black woman with very short hair and blowsy purple scrubs, went methodically though each patient's name, room number, age, reason for hospitalization, current status and vitals, and what was expected for the new shift. IV fluids were done right here. It was always bad karma for the rest of the day to tell the oncoming shift that there were still 200 cc's in the IV fluid bag, then only to have the light come on and the patient say over the intercom that the bag was dry and the machine was beeping.

"You have to run and take care of that and the rest of your planned day goes up in smoke," Cheryl Beth had lectured her students. They couldn't count on landing jobs at the best hospitals, but they could improve what they found by giving and insisting on getting a thorough report.

The status of wounds: the term referred to post-op patients, but it made her think of Lauren and Holly. Then she had seen the newspaper that morning, with a page one story about the murder of a Cincinnati policewoman. It said she was the star of a reality television show, but Cheryl Beth had never seen it. She was more attracted to *Masterpiece Theater* kinds of shows, *Sherlock Holmes, Inspector Morse,* plus some gardening and cooking shows. The title of the reality police show sounded demeaning, but the woman herself seemed very accomplished. Found in her boat on the Licking River, dead of multiple knife wounds. Cheryl Beth's hands had turned cold as she read this. Could there be a connection with what happened in the Formal Gardens or was she reaching? Was Will Borders involved in this case? Unlike the typical crime story, his name wasn't mentioned.

Focus on report, Cheryl Beth.

Afterward, she huddled with the students once again, being a nag about their nursing care plans.

"NCPs are the work of the devil…" one of the charge nurses said, laughing.

"Don't listen to her," Cheryl Beth said in good-natured dudgeon.

Her students chanted in unison: "It is a tool designed to identify the needs of the patient based on a physical assessment, the medical diagnosis, any treatments or surgical interventions past, present or future. Family, social, psychological, and spiritual needs, and the most important, the nursing interventions to meet the needs."

Cheryl Beth laughed hard for the first time in two days. "I'll expect them from you at the end of the week. And remember, I want one in-depth NCP on one patient of your choice at the end of semester. That's coming right up."

Everyone groaned. As they went off, her smile faded and she thought: what happened in the Formal Gardens is the work of the devil.

She turned to begin her day of perpetual motion when the elevators opened and a familiar figure strode purposefully in her direction. It was one of those out-of-place moments and she didn't immediately recognize the silhouette, one the shape of a small refrigerator, coming her way.

"Hank?"

"Glad I caught you." It was indeed Hank Brooks of the Oxford Police Department. "I need to talk to your students."

"What do you mean?"

"You know, talk? To all your students."

"Well you picked a damned bad time, Hank."

"You're pretty when you're angry."

"That's a cliché," she said, frustrated that it showed. "And you're an oaf."

"So others have said. Did anyone ever tell you that you look like Jodie Foster?"

"Only all my life, Hank. I don't see it."

"So where are they?"

"Hank, they're attending to patients, and I need to be checking on them. You can't barge in here."

"I can and will." His nose was three inches away. He really was about her height. "I want to interview each student. Did they know the dead girls? Did they know Noah? Yes. I need their statements."

"Why?"

"Because this is a homicide investigation."

Cheryl Beth put her hands on her hips. This was her environment, not his, and in a moment the reality caused him to let out a long sigh.

He steered her to a corner by the code cart. "Cheryl Beth, this guy is a bad dude, get me? He was Army Special Forces, served in Iraq. I suspect one of his specialties was knife combat. We searched his apartment and found two different knives there."

"So was one of them used in the attack?"

"No." He stared at his feet like a little boy caught doing something wrong.

Her phone buzzed and she checked it: A text from one of her students: a patient was complaining about his pain meds.

"I've got to go, Hank."

He held her shoulder in a firm grip. "Goddamnit, Cheryl Beth, I'm going to have to kick this guy loose by Thursday morning if I can't get some evidence. Maybe sooner."

"What?"

"You heard me. There's not evidence enough to hold him. I'm going to get my ass handed to me by a public defender, no less.

"I saw the police catch him right there."

"Yeah, I wish the real world worked like one of those TV shows, but that's not enough. He claims he was attacked, too. He was a decorated soldier. You very helpfully found that goose egg on the back of his head. We don't have a weapon. We don't have a motive. The D.A. won't file on him. So they'll probably release him for now. And while we're trying to make a case, this bad dude is going to be out on the street, maybe coming to a place near you."

"Maybe he didn't do it."

"You know he did!" He whispered it harshly, slapping a fist in the other palm. "Do you know how those girls died? He raped them with a knife. That's right. He cut them to pieces down there and let them bleed to death."

Cheryl Beth visibly winced. "But these were two strong young women. I don't understand. Could there have been more than one attacker?"

"Lauren was also stabbed in the back. My guess is she tried to get away while he was attacking Holly. It's not unheard of for two women to be raped by one man armed with a knife. They're both scared. They want to live through it. When Lauren realized what was really happening, she tried to make a break, he ran her down, and stabbed her."

Now it was her turn to look at the floor. She was hardly a novice to gore, but this…

"You need to know this, too," Brooks said. "These girls were arranged after he killed them. Like…like some kind of sick art-work. He wanted us to see what he had done. He wanted to make sure, I don't know, that we understood he was in total control. That they were his toys, his conquest. I'll tell you something else. I had a talk this morning with a Cincinnati detective. That policewoman who was murdered on the Licking River? The one who's on TV? She was raped with a knife, too, and handcuffed. Sometime early Sunday morning." He stared at her with a red face. "I need your help."

She ran schedules and logistics through her head. "All right, we can set you up, uh, maybe at the Café on A, and I'll bring each one down separately. But you're going to have to be patient. They've got work to do, it's close to the end of semester, it's the start of the shift, everybody's busy."

"God, you don't make it easy, woman. Fine. Show me the way."

"I'll tell you the way. I've got to go down the hall right now." She gave him directions to the café.

She added: "Did Lauren's sister call you?"

"What?"

"Her sister, April. I talked to her last night and she said Lauren thought she was being stalked. She described a bald man, older, nothing like Noah."

"Are you working my case, Cheryl Beth?"

"No, Hank. I told her to call you. Now go down there to the café and I'll bring you a student when I can break her free, and I'll give you April's number. In the meantime, unless you're an R.N., I've got work to do here, and you're in the way."

Chapter Thirteen

Will parked beside the imposing Victorian edifice on Elm Street that was Music Hall and limped into the offices of the Cincinnati Symphony Orchestra. Music Hall itself looked like a great red-brick cathedral to music with a grand pitched roof and circular window, guarded on either side by sharp-topped towers. It had been built in 1878 on top of a pauper's graveyard, where the dead had been buried without coffins. The stories went that during construction, onlookers would play around with the disinterred bones before workers could toss them into barrels set aside for that purpose. When a new elevator shaft was built in 1988, more remains were found. Ghost stories were as much a part of the building as great music. The offices, reached by a side entrance, were far plainer. Instead of the staid elegance of the concert hall, they formed a clutter of cubicles and little rooms added over many decades, half renovated, half modern, slightly shabby.

Even so, Will knew that of all the city's arts organizations, the Cincinnati Symphony was the kingdom and the power and the glory. It was fiercely protective of itself. This would be a difficult meeting.

He showed his badge and was greeted by a wren of a dark-haired woman from the marketing department, looking fine in a navy blue suit with a skirt slightly above the knees. She led him back to the president's office.

"Forgive me if this is too personal," she said. "But I hope you're not in pain."

The damned cane again.

"Not much," Will said.

"My husband had an accident on his motorcycle," she said. "Since then, he's been in terrible pain, and nobody can really help him. He's afraid of getting addicted to Oxycontin or something like that. But…"

"If you like, I know someone who might be able to give you a referral. My friend, Cheryl Beth Wilson…"

They were almost there when a tall man threw open the door and nearly slammed it. Will was paying more attention to the wren and the daydream of Cheryl Beth, but the movement ahead caught his attention. The man bent over, tied a shoe, and then fiddled with the back pocket of his baggy jeans, producing a ball cap, which he slapped on. Then he stalked toward them, looking down, and shaking his head. His long-legged stride covered the ten feet that separated them in seconds. Will stopped walking and stood.

"Excuse us," the wren said.

The man looked up and halted abruptly. He had a face young but rutted with creases, and set off with a wide mouth, and strong jaw. At the moment, it held an indignant expression. He stared Will in the eye. Will was past dancing with anyone who was in his path. He couldn't move that fast any longer, so he continued to stand there. The man glared harder, then sidestepped, and brusquely walked on. Under his breath: "Get the fuck out of the way."

Will thought about making something of it, but stopped himself. He wondered if his stepson would act any better in the circumstances. Hell, he remembered his old, impatient self when facing someone with a disability. He wouldn't have cursed, but he might well have wondered why this person was in his way. He was no better than anybody. In any event, he was on a peace mission from the chief.

"Sorry," the wren said. "That's the president's son. He can be a bit abrupt."

"Those aren't the words I'd use."

She smiled uncomfortably and led him into more spacious digs.

In two more minutes he was sitting in a deep comfortable chair facing the desk of Kathryn S. Buchanan, president of the CSO. He hoped he could get back out of that chair without too much trouble. His legs had awoken him after an hour's sleep and he was still sitting on the balcony. He had gotten, maybe, four hours of sleep last night, his new normal.

Buchanan was somewhere north of fifty but looked at least ten years younger, with features as delicate and poised as her son's were large and emphatic. Will guessed her suit and shoes cost as much as a month of his salary. Cindy dressed that way now. He pushed his ex-wife away and tried to sit at attention, properly representing the department. After his back could take it no longer, he sank back into the cushions, and admired the large portraits of famous CSO conductors on her wall: Leopold Stokowski, Thomas Schippers, and Paavo Jervi.

"Your chief tells me you have season tickets to the symphony," she was saying. "That's highly unusual for a police officer, if you'll forgive me seeming to stereotype. But, hey, I'm extremely grateful. And you enjoy the symphony apparently, not only the Pops."

"You can thank my mother. She started bringing me as a kid. She thought I was a piano prodigy. I wasn't, and my dad was having none of that anyway. He was a cop and I was no prodigy. But I came away with a love of classical…"

"Men are a difficult demographic, even ones without a blue-collar background, no offense," she interrupted, already unimpressed with him. "Their wives drag them along." She had been here only two years, having come from Atlanta. He wasn't sure she fully understood what classical music meant to Cincinnati, but she had absorbed the subtle Indian Hill snobbishness well. He had no doubt that she had also learned the aggressive defensiveness of all who loved the symphony.

She shrugged and leaned toward him. "Now, to this tragedy. Jeremy Snowden was one of our rising stars, as you probably know. He was pure Cincinnati. Born here. Studied at CCM with Stephanie Foust..." Will also knew Foust was the principal cellist for the orchestra, even knew she held the Linda and David Goodman Endowed Chair, because he read the programs. "...who studied at Julliard. As for Jeremy, the whole world was before him. I could list the prestigious competitions he had won, the orchestras trying to steal him away...oh!" She shook her head and seemed on the verge of tears before quickly composing herself.

"I'm counting on you to understand this, Detective Borders. You know the deep history of this orchestra and what it means to the community. The May Festival is coming right up. And these aren't easy times for even an orchestra of our caliber." She held her palms up as if everything should be perfectly obvious.

"How may I help, Ms. Buchanan?"

"That man Dodds. He's very unpleasant."

"You're telling me. He was my partner for eight years."

Her perfect small mouth didn't register even a millimeter of amusement. It was as if he had let out a loud, long fart at the Queen City Club.

"He wants to talk to members of the orchestra," she said. "That's unacceptable. These are world-class musicians. Their time is simply beyond price. And we're a family grieving over this tragedy."

"Detective Dodds is the finest homicide investigator in the state, maybe even the nation," Will said as calmly as he could. "It's normal to speak with coworkers. We need to know if Mr. Snowden had enemies..."

"Enemies!" Her calm demeanor vanished and Will saw a bit of that raw anger from her son's face. "It's perfectly obvious what this is! Some...some...ghetto youth from the ghetto murdered him. They deal drugs right out in the open, you know, right out in Washington Park. We warn our musicians about this neighborhood. My god, I'm sometimes afraid here in the middle of the day."

"We can't be sure of who did it, I'm sorry to say. He wasn't robbed. His cello was still in the car. The murderer could be anyone. It could be a crime of passion..."

"That's absurd. He had become engaged to be married only a month ago!"

"It would be the first place I'd look for a suspect. Discreetly, of course." His brain told him not to say it, but now he was getting pissed. "The cello is a sensuous instrument, played between the legs." Her eyes shot open and she flushed. Will continued: "It could also be blackmail, or a case of mistaken identity, wrong-place-wrong-time, a kidnapping gone wrong."

"This is unbelievable." She shook her head but not a strand of expensively maintained hair moved.

"We'll still have to talk to the musicians, ma'am." Will used his best respectful-but-firm voice. Inside he was disgusted with the sense of privilege and haughtiness. *It's never about the victim. It's always about the reputation of their companies and organizations and rich Cincinnati tribes.* He could never get used to it.

"So you're not going to help." Her voice was flat and seething.

"I am, ma'am. And you need to do your part, as well."

"I have friends on city council," she said, her voice no longer heated but now almost languid. "I have friends beyond that. This is not the end of the matter, Mr. Borders. Now, I have an important meeting."

He used every trick he had learned in months of physical therapy to stand in one fluid motion. Somehow he did it. "We'll handle this investigation with tact and confidentiality. But our detectives will talk to your people."

For several seconds she stared as if her brain had stopped processing. Then her eyes found him again. "Very well. But I expect you to put a stop to the media's incessant calling."

He laughed. He couldn't help it. The phone call to the chief about him was coming anyway. "The First Amendment is beyond my control, Ms. Buchanan. Don't get up. I'll find my way out."

The wren in the short skirt was gone, so he wandered through the hallways for a moment. He had actually heard Jeremy Snowden play several times with the whole orchestra, once as a soloist on Beethoven's Cello Sonata No. 1. Snowden was indeed very gifted and now the gift was dead, murdered. But he, not Kathryn S. Buchanan or the CSO, was the vic.

A custodian recognized him from the television and offered to give him a tour backstage, even take him into the attics "where the ghosts hang out." Will regretfully turned him down.

He was back in the car when his phone rang: Dodds.

"Where are you?"

"I'm at Music Hall trying to do damage control because of your winning personality."

"Ah, fuck 'em. I got an arrest."

"Do tell."

"Black male, twenty-five, tried to rob a motorist with a knife this morning two blocks from where the cello player was killed. Motorist maces him and drives away, dragging the suspect two blocks until he falls off, thanks to the intervention of a mail box." Dodds was laughing the entire time. "So he's in custody. And the sweetest little thing of all? We've got his fingerprint on the door of the cello player's Lexus. Case clearance, my brother. So you, PIO, need to put out the news."

"You get to do that, Dodds. The chief has given me leave while I work Gruber."

"So I heard." His voice changed. "I hate talking to the media."

"Welcome to my world."

"I can do it, though. Give a handsome African-American face to the department."

"I'll tweet it," Will volunteered.

"Fuck you. Let me give you some friendly intel, partner. Not all the brass was happy when the chief let you come back, and they're sure as hell not happy now that you're the lead on Gruber. They don't know why you didn't take disability and go away."

Will had suspected as much, but his stomach churned anyway.

"Fair enough," he said. "And if I were you, I'd show around some photos of that expensive letter opener. In case your suspect isn't really a…ghetto youth."

Dodds was cursing him when the connection ended.

Chapter Fourteen

The setting sun painted the clouds pink as Will sat in the parking lot of the Montgomery Boathouse. It wasn't a real boathouse but a popular restaurant selling ribs and overlooking the Ohio River. Will had been to a dozen police retirement parties here over the years. Now, he was waiting for someone. A someone who had instructed him to sit in a parking spot as far as possible from the front entrance. Will only accepted this instruction because this someone was a partner in one of the city's most powerful law firms. His cell number had shown up on Kristen Gruber's recent calls in the hours before she was killed.

It had been another long day, and while Will waited, he stood, sandwiching himself between the car and car door. His legs were not cooperating with this long day of too much sitting interspersed with too much walking. He needed the relief of simply standing for a few moments, stopping the thumping in his left leg and easing the mammoth tightness of his right quads. He said out loud: "Ahhh." But he was so tired that he couldn't stand for long. He was tellingly leaning on the car roof and door.

He had spent the day with the Covington police. Although Kristen's cell phone was still missing, techs had found her cellular phone bill on her computer, and the phone company had provided records. The detectives ran through phone numbers. Much of it was dull and tedious: calls to the dry cleaner, the producer of *LadyCops: Cincinnati*, her parents in Myrtle Beach, and her sister in Phoenix. Finally, Will called the number that led him to this meeting.

A hand tapped brusquely on the passenger window. The door opened and a man got in. He was wearing a navy pinstripe suit far more expensive than anything in Will's closet and he folded long legs into the well of the car and closed the door. With his executive build and tan, he looked pretty much as Will had expected for a senior partner at Briscoe, Hayne, and Douglas. Along with Baker Hostetler, Taft Stettinius & Hollister, and Keating, Muething, and Klekamp, it was one of the city's most prestigious law firms.

What stood out most was his fine head, with a fringe of close-cropped iron-gray hair and creeping forehead, with two dramatic slashes of eyebrows amid uniformly strong features. He had barely a wrinkle even though he seemed at least Will's age or older. In fact, he looked younger than the son who had nearly run down Will at Music Hall that morning.

The patrician head swiveled around, looking to see that no one was watching them. He didn't offer his hand and neither did Will.

"I'll see your identification, please."

Will handed over his badge case.

"I called your chief." He closely examined Will's identification. "And I assume he called you."

"He did."

"How does that make you feel, Detective Border?"

"It's Borders, and I don't follow you."

"How does it make you feel? Does it make you feel small? It should. I've only been in this city a short time. I didn't go to Moeller or Elder or any of that provincial crap I hear all the time. Who gives a shit where you people went to high school? If I hadn't had to move here with my wife, I wouldn't even have flown through your airport. I don't care about Cincinnati. I don't speak Cincinnati. So don't expect me to be impressed by you or your badge."

"Fair enough," Will said. "But I warn you, people move to Cincinnati and dislike it, but after two years you couldn't pry them out. They fall in love with the city."

"I'll keep that in mind. What did your chief tell you, Borders?"

"He said to do what I felt needed to be done, counselor. So let's cut the bullshit. I have a murdered police officer. I suspect they take that seriously even where you come from. It so happens that your cell phone called Kristen Gruber at 2:21 p.m. Saturday, a few hours before she was killed. Those are the facts, unless you want to tell me your phone wasn't under your control during that time, and then we can have a different conversation."

He handed back the badge case and sat in silence for a good five minutes. Will was happy to let him stew.

"I called Ms. Gruber," he said. "She berths her boat next to mine. I wanted to ask her a question about the marina management. They can get pretty sloppy."

Will watched him lie smoothly, not even a blink to his eyes. He said nothing, letting the silence do its work.

He finally couldn't stand it. "Are we done, Detective?"

"No, we're not done. We have records of you calling Kristen Gruber more than a hundred times in the past three months. You must really have issues with the marina management."

He sighed. "Off the record?"

"For now."

"Look. Do you have any idea who my wife is?"

"Actually, I do. I was talking with her this morning, Mr. Buchanan."

He sat up straight and stared ahead at the trees and, beyond them, Riverside Drive.

"It was about another matter," Will said.

"And you say these phone records showed a call from me Saturday?"

"That's right. Did you make it?"

Kenneth Buchanan hesitated, ran a hand with long fingers across his face, and pinched the bridge of his nose. The dark eyebrows inched together.

"I had an affair with Kristen," he said. "It started about a year ago. I'm willing to cooperate with the police, off the record, but my wife can't know about this. I want your guarantee."

Will looked at the man. He might have been old enough to be Kristen's father, but he supposed that was one of the perks that came with money and power.

"I can't make that guarantee, sir. All I can say is that I'll do my best."

"Well, I was golfing with friends on Saturday, then I went home, where my wife and I had a quiet dinner and spent the evening and night together. So this should cover the entire period you're talking about, if what I read in the newspapers is true."

Will watched for tells that he was lying, saw none.

"So why did you call Officer Gruber? What did you talk about?"

"I got her voice mail. That's it."

"It was a six-minute conversation. Want to try again, counselor?"

He made fists out of his hands and put them in his lap.

"I didn't kill her. I didn't even see her, haven't seen her for a month. We broke things off."

"Because you were afraid of being found out?"

He rearranged himself to face Will, leaning against the door, and trying to stretch out.

"Let's say I was tired of competing with other men, all right? Kristen was not…faithful."

"As a mistress."

His mouth crooked down. "You're in no position to judge me, and I can walk away."

"But you won't," Will said. "I got enough sense of your wife to know you really want her kept out of this."

"And you're an asshole."

"So I've been told." Will smiled without humor. "How did you meet Officer Gruber?"

"She moored her boat next to ours, like I told you. My wife doesn't really care for the water, so usually I was there alone.

She flirted. A man can tell. At least, I can tell. Things went from there."

"Tell me about things."

"Things? I don't get you."

"Did you have sex at her place?"

He angrily pursed his lips and nodded. "Sure."

"Five times? Twenty times?"

Kenneth Buchanan laughed. "Obviously you didn't know Kristen. A hundred would probably be more like it." His eyes glowed with the memory.

Will used the ensuing quiet to study the man. Was a murderer sitting next to him? He looked physically powerful enough to have inflicted the brutal knife strokes that tore apart Kristen's vagina. His hands were large, their backs showing engorged veins. But not one knife knick was showing on a knuckle or finger.

For someone who had been Kristen's lover, who had been intimate with her so many times, he was strangely calm, actually cold, about her death and the way it came about. It was very close to being "no affect," as the cops and shrinks put it.

"Did she like rough sex?"

He turned his head slightly and his mouth created small dimples. "Yes."

"Nice memory, huh?"

The dimples went away and he readjusted back into the seat, facing forward.

After a while, he spoke: "I'm not really into that kind of kink, understand. But she liked it."

"Liked what?"

He cleared his throat. "She enjoyed being handcuffed and, well, taken. She got off on a rape fantasy. The rougher the better. This was what she wanted, understand? Sometimes she wanted to be blindfolded. Sometimes she wanted... Why the hell am I telling you all this?"

"So you don't have to explain it to your wife," Will said.

"She wanted me to call her a little slut who deserved it. A cunt. Those were her words, not mine. She wanted to be choked, but I wouldn't do it."

"Did you ever role-play with her using a knife?"

"God, no!" His reaction seemed genuine.

Will asked if he owned a knife.

"A knife? Like kitchen knives?"

"A combat knife. A pocket knife?"

"No, detective. I haven't had a pocket knife since I was a Boy Scout."

"She had other lovers, you say. Did this make you angry."

"Sure," he said without hesitation. "Wouldn't you be angry?"

"Did you fight over it?"

"Some." He ran a hand over hair that no longer existed. "But, hell, I was very attracted to her. We kept on until I broke it off. I didn't want to run the risk of taking some S.T.D. home. Anyway, other men made things…complicated. I needed her discretion."

"So it made you angry, her playing around."

"Yes, it did," he said, without irony.

"When you fought, did you call her a little slut who was deserved it and a cunt? Did you ever hit her?"

His face struggled to maintain its composure. "No. She was promiscuous. She liked sex. She was a television star with lots of opportunities."

"Any idea who these other men were?"

He shook his head.

Will had a few more routine questions. When was the last time he had been intimate with her? In March. But they had talked since then; he had admitted as much. He said she had called him at his office several weeks ago, he couldn't be precise, asking if he wanted to come by. He had declined.

"And why were you calling her Saturday?" Will asked.

"I missed her," he said. "She was a very passionate woman. And remember, we're talking off the record. I'm nothing more than a cooperating citizen, trying to be helpful to the police. You haven't even read me my rights."

Will paused. "I'll only do that if you're a suspect."

"Then I'll ruin your life, detective." He said it calmly, at the end of a pointed finger, his face set, but the tendons in his neck visible with tension. "I'll sue your department for harassment. I'll have your badge. I'll get a settlement that will drive this city into bankruptcy. I'll fuck you over, Borders." He opened the door and stood.

"Oh, Mr. Buchanan…"

He stuck his head back in, the same look of barely suppressed rage on his face.

"What?"

"Seems like you have an anger-management issue, sir. That makes you seem less like a cooperating citizen and more like a suspect. And even if I can't place you on that boat Sunday morning, I'll check your alibi. Very indiscreetly, if you get me. Then I have a lot of ways to let your partners know about your little hidden life. And what you think about Elder and Moeller. They won't like any of it, especially that last part. So be careful I don't fuck you over. How does that make you feel, counselor?"

Will stuffed down his own anger as the door slammed hard and Kenneth Buchanan stalked over to a new Mercedes Benz. It was amazing, watching this man walk fast with no effort, no thought to it at all.

He started the car and his phone rang. It was Diane Henderson.

"How's the lawyer?"

"Pissed and full of threats." Will gave her the rundown.

"Do you like him for this?"

"I don't dislike him," Will said. "He claims he's got an alibi, but my gut says he's hiding something."

"Trust your gut. They were lovers. They broke up. She was seeing other men. Jealousy is a great motive."

"He's got powerful connections. He called the chief."

"And what did the chief tell you?"

"Handle with care."

"I have some news," she said. "Crime scene found some hairs that didn't belong to Gruber. And they have a partial shoeprint."

After she hung up, he realized he was an hour late taking his Baclofen. He dry swallowed the white pill. Only the realization that he had missed the dose caused the right quads to get angry. He hadn't felt any discomfort during his confrontation with Kenneth Buchanan.

Such a strange thing, this mind-body connection.

Wednesday

Chapter Fifteen

She left home and flew down Ravine Street, her favorite in the city. It inclined down the hill toward downtown at a steep angle, offering splendid views. Then she drove out Madison to the Joseph-Beth Bookstore in Rookwood Pavilion. It was this or spend the afternoon in her closet agonizing over what to wear tonight when she went out with Will Borders. A short skirt wouldn't do, but neither would pants. Men liked her legs. But she didn't want to come off wrong on a first date. It was a date, right? Cheryl Beth hadn't been on a real date in a very long time. Maybe on the way home she would get a pedicure.

She was turning the corner of the poetry section when she almost ran straight on into Noah Smith.

"I'm sorry I gave you a start," he said.

It was true. Her heart rate was still over one-fifty when she asked him what he was doing there.

"I was released this morning. Brooks sure didn't like it."

Noah looked gaunt and pale, but still handsome in khakis and a blue long-sleeved shirt. His big smile that must have attracted the girls was gone. "The truth is, I followed you."

Pulse back up. "You what? You know where I live? How do you know where I live?"

"You can find things on the Internet."

She took another step back. "Now you're really creeping me out."

"You don't…" He stepped closer and this time she held her ground. "You can't think I had anything to do with Lauren and Holly getting killed."

"Keep your voice down."

"I want to come back to class," he whispered.

She told him all the ways that would be a bad idea, impossible even. She couldn't imagine having him as student right now, and the university had suspended him pending the investigation.

She looked around. The store was crowded even on a Wednesday afternoon. She was safe. Except for the fact that he knew where she lived.

"I need to graduate. I need to get a job."

"I can't fix that, Noah. You can't take the NCLEX until you're cleared of this, anyway." The national licensing examinations.

"Cheryl Beth, I need something to do. To keep my mind off this. Brooks is going to do everything he can to put me in prison for something I did not do." His eyes were suddenly older, exhausted.

"What happened out there that night, Noah?"

"I keep trying to remember." He carefully touched the back of his head. "They said I had a mild concussion, but I keep having headaches. It still burns where they used the Taser on me, and I don't feel right. It's hard to keep it all in my head."

"You screamed something like 'hostiles! I have wounded!' What were you thinking?"

He leaned his hands against a shelve and stared at the floor. "I don't remember. Sometimes, after my deployments, I have flashbacks…"

He seemed sincere. But she pressed on: "Did you have a knife with you that night?"

"No!"

"But you were in the Army, right? You're good with a knife."

"That doesn't mean I would kill those girls. I was crazy about them."

"Nothing but an an innocent boy from Corbin, Kentucky," she said.

"You don't believe me." He roughly ran his hands down his face. "If you don't believe me, I'm sunk."

"Do you know I'm from Corbin, Noah? Is that something you found on the Internet, too?"

"You are? Good lord."

"It's a small town. Tell me somebody I might know."

"I'm a lot younger than you," he said. "No offense. You're very attractive." He shook his head. "Shit, I can't say the right thing here."

"Corbin." She heard the sternness in her voice.

He stared beyond her. She was about to walk away when he spoke again.

"When I was three years old, my father killed my mother, okay?"

She stopped and watched him again. He seemed to age before her eyes.

"My earliest memories are their fights. Both of them screaming as loud as they could. Him slapping her. He finally used a shotgun. I saw it happen. The whole thing. I saw her brains and blood against the wallpaper of the kitchen. I didn't know that's what they were, I remember the colors and textures and her head was…" He stopped speaking and the muscles in his neck tensed.

He was breathing heavily, holding his hands tightly at his side. "Then he killed himself. I remember everything. Forget anything you've heard about little kids not remembering trauma." He fought tears as he gave the date, his parents' names and where they lived, a couple miles out of town. "You can look it up. After that, I was sent to live with my uncle and aunt in Lexington. When I was eighteen, I joined the Army."

"I'm sorry," she said. The year he gave was long after she had left Corbin. "I don't know what to say."

"Well, Hank Brooks thinks I have my daddy's homicidal bloodline. That's the way he put it."

When he had composed himself, he said, "On Monday, I keep remembering waking up in the grass, then seeing Lauren and Holly. They were maybe twenty feet away, but I could already see the blood. I got to my feet and went to them. I checked their pulses but they were both dead. Cold. Oh, god…"

"What about before?"

He stared at the carpet. "We were pretty drunk and feeling mellow. We were making out. They were making out with each other. Everybody was laughing. We stripped and had sex in the grass. Afterward, we all got dressed again and sat around talking…"

"But they were found nude."

"I know. But that's not the way they were when I was hit."

"And you didn't see anyone. You didn't hear anything at all?"

He shook his head. She remembered all that Hank Brooks had told her and she didn't know what to believe.

"I've got to go, Noah. And please, don't contact me again. I can't help you."

"Fine," he said. "I've always been on my own. Now it's me, nobody's got my back. Only Hank Brooks is following me."

"You're being followed, or you're being paranoid?"

"I'm being followed."

She angrily tapped her hand on the side of her forehead. "Great, Noah. So Detective Brooks is watching us right now. Smart." She wheeled and walked out.

She was almost to the front doors when she felt a pull on her sleeve. He was right there again. Now she was on the edge of afraid. Half a dozen people were at the registers, checking out. Nothing could happen right here, could it? Her short, shallow breathing wasn't so sure. She reached into her purse and took hold of her keys, placing one between her fingers and making a fist around it. If he came any closer, she would call for help. If he did more, she would use the key on his face.

"Noah…"

"Wait. I do remember."

"Take your hand off me." She said it loud enough that an older man slowed as he passed and stared at Noah.

His hand dropped but he spoke urgently. "What you said. You brought it back to my mind. When we were making out by the Formal Gardens, it was really dark. But Holly thought somebody was watching us. I remember it now! She said it out loud. She even made a show of standing up and taking off her blouse and bra, like a strip tease."

Cheryl Beth was dubious. "Somebody was watching? Did you notice anything?"

"No."

"You were trained in the Army and you didn't notice anything?"

He shrugged. "I kind of had other things on my mind, if you know what I mean."

"So Holly says somebody's there and you go ahead and have sex together, not thinking a thing about it?"

"We thought it was hot if someone was watching us."

Chapter Sixteen

Will took Cheryl Beth to Zip's Café for burgers and beers. The talk was easy and relaxing. It helped him forget the anxiety dreams of the night before, where he got his usual four hours of sleep. They knew much about each other already from the time in the hospital. She looked radiant. It was the first time he hadn't seen her in scrubs. Now they could laugh about the terrible night when he, she, and Dodds had been trapped with the hospital killer. Dodds was knocked cold and Cheryl Beth beaten. That was when Will launched himself out of his wheelchair into the killer and nearly strangled him to death. He only stopped when Cheryl Beth pulled at him, telling him, "I need you." He wondered if she remembered that?

She told him that she was teaching nursing now. He filled her in on his public information job, with a bit about the case he had been assigned. It was nice not to have to explain his physical condition. She already knew it.

Afterwards, they walked into Mount Lookout Square and watched the traffic go by as the bells from Our Lord Christ the King Church tolled the hour. The night was warm and dry, with a hint of a pleasant breeze and flower scents. Here he learned that the two girls who had been murdered at Miami were her students. So was the prime suspect.

"For once, I'd like us to have some time when a murder wasn't involved," she said.

He tried to change the subject, but she wanted to talk, particularly about her questions concerning Noah Smith and her unpleasant encounters with Hank Brooks. Will assumed as much about Brooks from their phone conversations: his gruff defensiveness came through.

Brooks' case against Smith seemed weak; it was no surprise the man was released. The case had tantalizing similarities to Gruber: use of handcuffs, genital mutilation. The killer had taken their panties as trophies. Now Cheryl Beth told him something that Brooks had omitted: that a bald man was stalking one of the Miami victims, a man who looked like Mister Clean. That description could easily fit Kenneth Buchanan.

Still, he knew from experience not to move too fast to lock in on a hypothesis. Would Gruber's killer have struck the next night, and be so bold as to take on three people, including a man? He would probably need to drive up to Oxford and also get the autopsy results on the murdered students. All this and keep fielding calls from the national media about Kristen Gruber, even though he was supposed to be getting backup as PIO.

Later, they drove over to Aglamesis Brothers in Oakley Square for ice cream. There were two kinds of people in Cincinnati: those who liked ice cream from Graeter's and the ones who preferred Aglamesis. It was like Gold Star vs. Skyline Chili. Will was definitely among the latter, and he was delighted that Cheryl Beth was, too. He brought the conversation back to light things, telling her about his days as a student at Miami. "Let's say I'm not one of the really successful alumni they name buildings after," he said.

"Well, they should," she said.

He was happy to be off the clock, had even turned off his cell phone. He had briefed the chief late that afternoon and felt safe in being gone awhile. The case was spooling out, if too slowly for the chief. Will wasn't happy about it either and felt the pressure. But it was what it was. Some homicides went that way. Woe to the detectives when it was this high profile.

Kristen Gruber's phone records had turned up two more boyfriends. One was a thirty-five-year-old patrol sergeant in District 2 on the east side. The other was a diving instructor who lived in Butler County. Both were cooperative. Will was able to keep internal affairs away from his talk with the sergeant, so that smoothed things out. Both were tall, good-looking, and muscular; both single.

Neither knew about the other, or about the attorney she was also seeing. Both said she liked rough sex, where she would be bound or handcuffed during the act. It didn't go both ways, however. She didn't handcuff the men. Both voluntarily gave DNA samples. The sergeant had been with her on Friday night. The diving instructor wanted to take her out on Saturday night, but she said she had plans: she was going to take her boat out.

News stories were starting to say "the police are baffled" by Kristen's murder. The chief and Lieutenant Fassbinder would love that. Will was not baffled. He was beginning to wonder if the killer was random, not someone she knew. That would complicate things.

This far into an investigation, you knew some victims like they were brothers and sisters, mothers and fathers. Others were like Kristen, cloudy at best. She had grown up on the West Side, the daughter of a mail carrier and a teacher. She was a tomboy, a star athlete in volleyball, swimming, and lacrosse at Seton High School in Price Hill. It was the female equivalent of Elder High, right next door. Her grades were good. At Ohio State, she majored in sociology and came back to join the force. Her parents said she had always wanted to be a police officer, even being a police Explorer in high school.

She always loved the water. Her father owned a boat when she was growing up, and she had bought the Rinker Fiesta 300 five years before.

Her parents said she had married when she was twenty-six and had divorced two years later. They had not approved, being pious Catholics. It had caused a rift between them that had taken some years to heal. The ex-husband was remarried and living in

Los Angeles. He, like all the potential suspects, had no criminal record. He told a detective that it had been five years since he had even spoken to Kristen.

Cincinnati and Covington detectives went through the laborious task of sifting through Kristen's cop life. Her record was better than clean, but that didn't mean she hadn't made enemies. Five years before, she had been the first officer on the scene in Sayler Park, where a couple was arrested for starving their baby daughter to death. The crime had shocked the city. Although the ten-week-old was barely alive when officers arrived, it weighed half what a normal infant its age should. At his sentencing, the father, a young white-trash hood, had threatened to rape and kill Kristen when he got out of prison. Such threats weren't uncommon, but this one, so specific, would have to be checked out. At the same time, they were going through her emails for threats: so far, nothing was panning out.

The false-confession nuts were unchained by the crime. Most were well known to the police and regularly owned up to crimes they didn't commit. That this was the murder of an attractive woman seen on national television only ramped up the lunatics. Their stories could be easily shot down by the information they couldn't provide. But it all required detective time, and Will knew his colleagues resented it.

Kristen. She had lovers, many acquaintances, but no close friends, no real boyfriend, as far as he could tell. Work was her life, with sex and her boat to relieve the tension.

Kristen's timeline also had unfortunate gaps. She had withdrawn a hundred dollars from an ATM downtown on Saturday. She made no calls that day. No one saw her leave the marina. So far, no one had seen her on the river that day or night.

Now he drove Cheryl Beth back home and they fell into silence. But it was a comfortable one. At the little house in Clifton, he pulled into the driveway, opened her car door, and walked her to the porch.

"Thank you for a nice evening." He held out his hand.

"Oh, Will, come here." She raised her head and they kissed. It lasted longer than five seconds and less than five minutes, then he held her close to him with one arm as he balanced on his cane, feeling every part of her against him.

He felt normal.

"May I see you again?"

"I'm counting on it," she said. "Good night."

Back in the car, he turned on his cell. One message: he listened to his ex-wife. He was way past her, but hearing Cindy's voice, and the intonations and emotions behind the words he knew so well, battered his tranquility. Why would she be calling? He thought about ignoring it. Then the phone rang.

"Hello, Cindy."

"Will, I'm sorry to bother you, but I need to talk. It's about our son."

Our son. As their marriage had fallen apart, piece by piece like a cursed dwelling, she would refer to John as *her* son. Tonight it was *our* son.

He sighed. "Give me the new address." He wrote it down and backed out of Cheryl Beth's driveway.

Cindy was now Cynthia Morrison, or Mrs. J. Bradford Morrison. She had remarried quickly and moved to her new husband's house in Hyde Park. This somewhat surprised Will. Cindy disliked the city. Her insistence several years ago that they move to a new house out in Deerfield Township, such a long commute up I-71, was one more crack in their marriage. But, then, he couldn't give her a home in the city's most exclusive, leafiest, old-money neighborhood. Still, on the drive over he was smiling from his time with Cheryl Beth. He was past being hurt by Cindy. It was merely interesting now.

The address went with a massive Tudor behind a sweeping, immaculate lawn, and basking in ornamental lighting. An alarm company sign was prominently stuck into the grass. This was what J. Bradford Morrison had been able to buy as a stockbroker. He and Cindy at least had something in common to talk about: money.

Three steps up. No railing, of course. Will pulled down his lats, and carefully mounted each step, then up the walk to the wide front door.

"Thank you for coming." She was already waiting. "Brad is out of town."

Cindy had gone blond, an expensive color job and cut parted on one side and swept over her head. She was about as far as she could get from the twenty-year-old brunette bank teller he had met as a young patrolman. There had been a bank robbery. He impulsively asked her out. She had a baby son, had been abandoned by his father. Will and Cindy married too young. They weren't the people they would become, and they became those people largely apart. He helped her finish her B.A., then later an M.B.A., as she rose in the bank. Sometimes she slept with her bosses. But she didn't have to. She was smart as hell.

She led him past the expansive entry hall with its dark, hardwood floor, and into a living room that appeared as if no ordinary humans had ever been inside it, only interior designers. It was flawless. It was larger than his entire townhouse.

He sat in a broad cushioned chair, keeping his Lazarus tasselled loafers off the vast Persian rug, and she settled across from him on a cream-colored sofa, draping one aerobicized leg over the other. She had become a stick person with breasts.

"About our son," Will prompted, moving quickly past the uncomfortable small talk.

"Something's wrong with him," she said, sitting upright with her hands carefully folded in her lap, as if she were talking to a client.

"He's a young man," Will said. "I've always thought you should lock up the young men until they were thirty. The young women you can let out at twenty."

Not even a smile.

"He's so aimless," she went on. "He wanted to go to Portland State, for god's sake. So, okay. He ended up dropping almost every class so he wouldn't get a failing grade."

Will was tempted to say something about Cindy continuing to give him money, letting him live at home. He held the head of his cane tighter.

"He was out all Saturday night," she went on. "Dragged himself in at eight the next morning. Thought I wouldn't even notice! Wouldn't say where he was. But I knew. I got a call around midnight from Heather Bridges' mother. She had a date with him. We talked later, on Sunday, after Heather came home. Her mother said they were out on the river all night with some other kids from Summit."

Atomic particles in Will's brain wished he didn't know this information. But hundreds of young people were on the river this time of year.

He said, "What does he do with his time?"

"He still reads all the time. He rides his bike."

"Does he have a job?"

She shook her head.

"I had to work my way through college."

"Kids are different now," Cindy said. "They take longer to grow up. You can read it anywhere. Anyway, he doesn't need money."

"That's part of the problem."

Her voice rose. "You have no right to judge!"

"Okay."

"Will, I'm afraid he's into drugs again." She leaned forward. "I want you to talk to him."

"He came to see me the other night," Will said.

"Did he say anything?"

Will shook his head. "We only had a beer and watched the city. If he had something to tell me, he kept it to himself."

"William!" It was that familiar voice, harsh and frustrated.

"What do you want me to do, Cindy?" Everything was transactional with her. He felt the old toxic feelings returning.

"Why haven't you talked to him? Have Brad talk to him. What about his real father?"

She stood. "You are so...so much the same."

He stood and left without another word. The walkway was slanted down. He was extra aware of it and wished he hadn't enjoyed that second beer with Cheryl Beth. Next came the steps. Those would be more dangerous: Not even a shrub to hold onto. He did all the things he had been taught to steady himself and made the first step down.

Then he was down on the sidewalk, a sudden, scary vertical rollercoaster dip that was over before he even knew what was happening. He reflexively put his hands out and avoided mashing his face in the concrete. His blood was pumping too fast to feel any pain. One second he was upright, now he was down. For a long time, he took in the quiet of the street and the plain black tires on his car. A small bug walked beneath his gaze. He got to his knees and then the agony seared through him. Somehow the rewiring of his spinal cord made being on his knees especially painful. He couldn't stand the normal way. He thought about turning around and using the steps to get up. But he was in too much pain, and too angry. He used his strength to crabwalk until his body bent in the middle, and then he could push himself up with his hands until he could use the cane to help lift the rest of the way. It hurt like hell. Then he was upright again. His pant legs looked in good shape. His hands weren't bleeding. He felt his phone vibrating and let it alone.

On shaky legs, he walked around to the driver's side. Looking up, he saw that Cindy had long since closed the door. Maybe if he had gone on to law school, as he had intended, he could have given her this pile of rocks. It never happened. The more he got to know lawyers as a cop, the less he wanted to be one. He could have stomached being a prosecutor, but there was no money in it. Prosecutors didn't live in Hyde Park. Cindy never understood how he liked being a police officer. Every day, no matter how shitty, you could come home and know you had actually helped someone. On good days, you got the bad guys. That sensibility never left him. He was so much the same.

He listened to the voice mail: "Will, it's Diane Henderson, Covington P.D. We matched the shoe print that we found on the boat. It's a size ten-and-a-half Columbia Sportswear Drainmaker."

Thursday

Chapter Seventeen

Cheryl Beth visited her daughter early that morning. Eighteen years old now: past childhood that went so fast and nearly an adult. She had Cheryl Beth's face, hair, and eyes. They were nearly carbon copies. She could do anything she wanted, live adventures her mother had never experienced, give her so much to be proud of. Someday give her grandchildren. Cheryl Beth imagined the years of pink dresses and stuffed animals and squeals of laughter over the most trivial delights. She was not like *her* mother had been, telling Cheryl Beth all that she could not be, subtly upending her dreams at every corner. At eighteen, her daughter would be confident and kind, full of wit and decency, so intelligent it would continually astonish Cheryl Beth.

If only she had lived.

As she had for fifteen years, Cheryl Beth sat on her daughter's grave, arranged fresh flowers for her birthday, and wept. Time did not heal some things.

Time did not heal this gaping hole in her heart. It did little better than, very slowly, to dull the pain from losing her father when she was nine, that big, rough-handed, laughing bear of a man she had so loved. She had been a daddy's girl. He had a good job on the L&N Railroad until the day it killed him. She still heard his voice. She still felt that anguish beyond words. Time didn't heal.

The best you could do was try to take one step forward, then follow it with another, and try to go on. For years, this had been a day Cheryl Beth would take off, even calling in sick if necessary. She could now at least function enough to go to the hospital after saying a long prayer for all the lost children, all the lives that were never lived, the eighteenth birthdays that were marked on the dewy grass of graveyards until they could see each other again at God's table.

She used her index finger to trace the name on the headstone. The green and gold of the newborn grass mocked her. The trees flaunted their beauty, unconcerned with her cares.

She had lied to Will last night when he asked if she had children. This honorable man and she had lied, as she always did. *No*: That was always her response. Ask a little more and she would say, *the timing didn't work out.* Damned straight. Fifteen years and she still couldn't talk about it. The only people who knew were her family, and the family of her ex-husband. Their marriage hadn't survived the death. Cheryl Beth had barely survived. Oh, so many years she had cried an angry prayer of *why didn't you take me?* Even now, she could work in any unit of any hospital but peds.

She was put together again by the time she arrived at the hospital and the intensity of the morning shift let her put that one foot forward once again.

At lunch, she had to get out. So she walked up and down the broad lawn that ran from the main entrance to Auburn Avenue. The groundskeepers probably wouldn't like it, but the spring sunshine and the shade of the trees was healing, these and her fast stride back and forth. Across the street, the occasional car would pull into the William Howard Taft National Historical Site, honoring the only president from Cincinnati. She wasn't hungry.

On her third circuit, she noticed Allison Schultz watching her.

The funeral for Cincinnati Police Officer Kristen Gruber was held at ten a.m. at St. Peter in Chains Cathedral. It was a grand, Greek revival building with a tall, slender steeple at Eighth and Plum downtown. It sat across the street from the brick Victorian mass of City Hall and the delicately Moorish-Gothic Isaac M.

Wise Temple, home of Reform Judaism. Church and state in the Queen City. Inside the cathedral was a magnificent pipe organ. Cops from three states came, all in their finest dress uniforms. Will would later learn that 1,200 mourners filled the church. He wasn't among them. Instead, he sat in his car and watched the crowd. Another detective was concealed among the television crews, filming the people as they walked up the steps. The process would be repeated when Kristen's coffin, an American flag tight across the top, was carried back out, a police bagpiper in front, on its journey out to St. Mary Cemetery.

Will despised the sound of bagpipes. He had barely slept the night before. It was even worse than usual. He sat in the chair at the foot of the bed, shaking his tense right leg until what he called "shift change" caused his left leg to start its own little hell. Then he would have to walk on it. His back hurt from the fall in front of Cindy's house. His hands were raw. He didn't want to know about Drainmaker shoes. Tens of thousands must have been sold. But then there was that knife in John's pocket, that damned knife. And his odd visit to Will's townhouse. His instincts told him something was wrong.

Calling Cheryl Beth to thank her for a nice evening—that was the good thing on his mind. But he might seem to be coming on too strong. In any event, he had to watch carefully. He didn't know exactly what he was looking for, but this was S.O.P. It didn't surprise him that Kenneth Buchanan wasn't there. Her lover the sergeant walked by in dress uniform. From another direction, several minutes later, the diving instructor mounted the steps and disappeared inside.

"You're mighty inconspicuous."

Dodds climbed in and sat, momentarily tilting the car. He slid Will's cane out of the passenger seat.

Will said, "And now I've got a fat black man in his band uniform to complete the picture."

"Anything happening?"

Will shook his head.

"I'm sorry, partner. I tried to fight for you."

Will's stomach turned sour. "What?"

"They didn't tell you? Fuckers. Fassbinder's made me the lead on Gruber. You know how he can get. You never feel the knife until it's in your back."

"The chief put me on this case."

"I know. But it's a done deal. The case is moving too slowly for command. They want somebody in custody. Hell, Kristen's face is on the cover of *People* magazine, all over the blogs, and the Cincinnati Police can't solve the murder." He sighed. "I was able to keep you as the liaison detective with Covington."

Will fought to control his emotions, without much success. "It's not one of her boyfriends, unless it's the lawyer, Buchanan. And he'll sue us if we push too hard. You know how these things go."

"That's why I fought for you," Dodds said. "I told them you were the best homicide investigator in the department…"

"But all they see is this goddamned cane."

Dodds was silent as Will thought about his father's full-dress funeral. That day it had rained.

His call sign came over the radio.

"Meet the officers, Spring Grove Cemetery."

He told the dispatcher he was on special assignment. To Dodds, "Is this some PIO shit work for me?"

Dodds shrugged.

"Break away from that," the female voice came back immediately. "Respond code three."

"You coming?"

"Why not?" Dodds said. "Hey, isn't that your boy?"

Sure enough, John was walking up Plum Street, wearing a dark suit. He didn't see Will and walked quickly up the steps into the cathedral.

"It is." Will was thankful that Dodds didn't ask more. He started the car, made a U-turn, and rolled away from the curb, only hitting the siren when he was a block away.

Allison Schultz was the student Cheryl Beth worried about. Her bookwork was perfect and she was competent clinically. But she was so shy, so unsure of herself. It meant she had a difficult time communicating with patients. She wouldn't have the confidence to push back on a doctor, question a dosage, or find a mistake. Now she was slowly walking toward Cheryl Beth.

"Do you mind if I talk to you?"

"Walk with me," Cheryl Beth said, and they started out toward the street.

"Are you all right?" Allison asked.

"I'm tired."

"They think Noah killed Lauren and Holly."

"That's right."

"They're not going to let him come back, are they?"

"I think it's unlikely, Allison. I really can't discuss this with you."

"He's got his whole life aimed at becoming an R.N." She mustered more assertiveness than Cheryl Beth had ever seen her show. She started to say that class and his career were the least of his troubles, that Hank Brooks wanted him on death row. But she walked on.

"He saw things in the wars, you know," Allison said. "He was deployed five times. He has nightmares. Sudden loud noises make him afraid. But he's a good man. I don't care what they think they know, there's no way he could have done this."

Cheryl Beth remembered the way Noah had reacted when the police were trying to run him down in the grass. It was a classic post-traumatic stress disorder response. But how did Allison know any of this?

"He was my boyfriend," she said simply.

Cheryl Beth stopped and looked at the ordinary, slightly chubby, pale brunette with out-of-style eyeglasses and a ponytail standing beside her. Noah and Allison? Lauren and Holly were young thoroughbreds. Allison was like a doorknob next to their polished jewels.

"I'm sorry." Cheryl Beth sighed heavily. "Have you told this to Detective Brooks?"

"I was afraid," she said. "And I was angry. That he would be with Lauren and Holly. They could have their pick of any guy, why take mine? I called him Saturday night and he never called me back. But, then, he was with them, wasn't he? He did this to me, cheated. I was sick about it, and I was so mad at him. He betrayed me! I thought he could rot in jail and think about the damage he did. But then I calmed down. I knew he was innocent of murder…"

"So maybe you didn't know him as well as you thought. Maybe he could also be a killer. There are PTSD incidents like that all the time. Soldiers come home and kill their families."

"No." Allison spoke softly but with finality. Then she started sobbing and wrapped her arms around herself awkwardly until Cheryl Beth hugged her. She said, "I don't believe he did it. I've seen how Noah reacted to things, loud noises, things like that, and he was never violent. He was scared."

"He was Special Forces?"

"No, he was a combat medic. He was assigned to a Special Forces base once. But he was there to help people. He watched his friends get blown up by I.E.D.s. He saw a lot. Too much."

"Why didn't he call you from the jail?"

Another sob, and then: "Would you call your lover after getting caught like that?"

"I guess not."

The men and women who built Cincinnati were under the sod of Spring Grove Cemetery. Like so much else in town, it was a National Historic Landmark. Amid the trees, flowers, ponds, and chapels were the monuments and mausoleums carved with names such as Kroger, Procter, Gamble, Chase, Lytle, Fleischmann, and Taft. This morning, beyond the oxidizing statue of a Civil War soldier with a bayonet attached to his rifle, there were also five CPD patrol cars. Will parked behind the last one and they walked up the sloping drive.

Dodds, who had a solid sense of dignity, straightened his dress uniform and precisely placed his cap. He uncharacteristically slowed his pace to match Will's.

"Detectives." A female sergeant met them. "Thanks for getting out here. There's something you should see. Over here."

A body was sitting against a large marker overseen by a statue of a weeping angel. It was a male in his twenties, completely nude, with bloody wounds between his legs, his clothes neatly folded in the grass, and more gore around his mouth. The sudden knowledge about what was in his mouth made another observation secondary. A piece of paper was attached to his chest.

"Fuck me…" Dodds whispered.

The newly dead was leaned precisely against the monument, so it appeared as if the angel, its head down and wings drooped in grief, had discovered him that moment.

His penis had been cut off and stuffed in his mouth.

His hands were cuffed behind him.

A sheet of white paper was attached to his chest by the large safety pin run through his right nipple. It was encased in a clear plastic sheet and looked like ordinary printer paper, with large typed letters in a single paragraph.

Both Will and Dodds were slipping on latex gloves.

Dodds bent forward and read aloud:

"Detective Borders, meet Noah Smith. I had planned to kill him along with the women, but things didn't work out. It spoiled what would have been a masterpiece. I couldn't let the police give him credit for my art, now could I? Kristen was easier, but the result was beautiful. I cut them where they get their pleasure and I watched them die. Don't think I'm bragging. I have a lot to learn. But you probably won't hear from me again. Serial killers don't know when to stop. My deathscapes are rare and executed with discipline, like all great art. I wish we could have spent time together, detective. On my terms, of course. I've seen how you struggle to walk, how your affliction keeps you up all night. But I know you would fight and it would be beautiful. I think about this temptation…"

Dodds turned back and faced Will. "Looks like you're still on the case."

Chapter Eighteen

"Okay, Devil, advocate."

It was one of their procedures when they were partners and Will happily took the cue.

"He's a copycat claiming credit for all the other murders."

"Nope," Dodds said. "He said he 'cut them where they get their pleasure.' The genital mutilation is information we held back and they also held back in Butler County."

"Maybe the killer is law enforcement."

"That can't be ruled out."

"These are still separate murders. The same subject who did the two nursing students killed Noah Smith. But Gruber is separate, another murderer. This killer is claiming credit for her."

Dodds thought about it. "You've got the same problem with him knowing that Kristen was mutilated. Lucky guess? Maybe. The scenes weren't exactly the same. The two female nursing students' clothes weren't neatly folded, like with Smith and Gruber. Their purses and wallets were still there. Their panties were gone. Unlike Gruber, he took the handcuffs off the bodies."

Will leaned against another gravestone. It was as tall as he was and green with moss. He tried to choreograph it. "So the killer is watching the three of them get it on…"

"How come I didn't have a college life like that?" Dodds complained.

"I hear you, but stick with me. They're screwing and making out. It's arousing the killer, enraging him. One of the girls said she thought someone was watching. At some point, when they're mellow from the Ecstasy, he comes behind Noah and hits him with something, knocks him out. He threatens the girls with the knife."

"Why don't they try to outrun him?"

"Maybe they're worried about Noah. Maybe he's got a gun, too. But they submit. They're scared. They want to live. Happens all the time in rape cases. 'I'm only going to rape you. So if you want to live, go along with me.' Or, 'go along or I'll kill your friend.' So they do, until it becomes clear he's a killer and the one girl makes a break for it, he runs her down and stabs her. It's also pretty isolated up there where these killings took place. So that would add to their terror. Anyway, either the girl trying to escape or even something else, like car headlights or somebody walking nearby, threw off his timetable for arranging things."

"Why did he take the handcuffs?"

Will thought about it and had no good answer. "We'll have to ask him."

"Consistency is the hobgoblin of little criminal minds." Dodds shrugged. "So keep going. Argue me out of the logical conclusion."

"It's more than one person, a gang, claiming to be a single serial killer."

"Could be," Dodds said. "That would explain how a trained police officer was overpowered and how the three students were successfully attacked up at Miami. It would make it more likely that one would turn on the other." He sighed. "But my golden gut says it's one guy. Strong as hell, too. Try again."

"Smith killed himself," Will said. "He killed Kristen. Oxford already liked him for the murder of the nursing students. He was driven crazy by remorse, so decides to off himself."

"Cold-blooded, man," Dodds said, admiringly. "But when you think about it: you've cut your own dick off, so what do you have to live for? Case closed. But you'd have to be one disciplined dude to pull it off. I couldn't cut my own dick off if I'd killed everybody above the rank of sergeant, and don't think I haven't thought more than once about doing it."

"The problem is no knife," Will said. "And no confessing suicide note." He limped over to the clothes: blue jeans and a cotton short-sleeve shirt, and examined them. "His wallet and keys and underwear are gone. Trophies. I think the guy who wrote the note is the real deal." He returned to his trusty headstone and again rested against it. "I think he's the one who stuck the key in the door at Kristen's condo the other night. Fuck, we were that close!"

The sunlight gleamed off Dodds' immaculately shaved darkbrown head. He indicated blood spatter with a gloved finger. One long strand of dark red reached under the angel's wing. "It happened here. The vic wasn't killed elsewhere."

Will took it in and agreed. Birdsong and wind through the trees were the only sounds. They had caught a break: All the media were covering Kristen's funeral.

"How'd he overpower a well-built young man?" Will asked.

Dodds stood, the three medals of valor on his dress uniform jangling. "I would have carried a gun. Ordered him to disrobe, get on the ground, and handcuff himself. Maybe I'd make him think I only wanted to scare him or suck his dick, whatever. Then get out my blade and take care of business."

"Okay, so you're the vic. Why wouldn't you run if you knew you were going to die anyway? Why would you handcuff yourself and take away your last chance to escape or fight?"

"Nobody knows how they're going to react on the business end of a gun," Dodds said. "Anyway, look." He leaned back and yelled for the sergeant. "Did you folks make this?"

"No, detective." She was huffy about it.

The grass was pulled up a few feet from the body, with fresh dirt exposed. Next to it were indentations on the grass.

"Maybe he did try to fight."

"Quiet part of a quiet cemetery," Will said, halfway to himself. "A fight or calls for help wouldn't be heard. Killer could have gagged him at first. Actually, you can probably get a lot of noise from the trains at Queensgate Yard, especially in the middle of the night. Maybe you can build on the respectful relationship you've started with the sergeant and get some unis canvassing the houses across on Winton Road, see if anybody heard anything. We should talk to the groundskeepers, see what kind of security they have here. Looks like a place where anybody can jump the wall and be easily hidden."

"Smell that?" Will said.

"Bleach." Dodds pointed to the gore of Smith's groin. "He poured it down there."

"Exactly like with Gruber," Will said. "When I first heard about that I thought the killer might have thought he would mess up the DNA analysis, that he had left semen inside her. But this tells me…"

Dodds completed his thought: "He did it to torture them. Let it burn in the wounds as they died."

They looked over the scene silently for several minutes.

"This guy's got balls," Dodds said. "The killer, I mean, not the vic. He does this guy in public, in one of the most prominent landmarks in the city. If his note is accurate, he set out to kill three healthy young people in one shot. Thinks he's the god of murder."

"Those are the ones I like to take down," Will said. "I'd love to know where the lawyer was over the past twelve hours."

"You think this Kenneth Buchanan is really the one?"

"I don't know," Will said. "He had a connection to Kristen. A motive, too, if he was jealous of her other lovers. A crime of passion, however twisted. But maybe the asshole is really a psychopath? So he kills the girls up at Oxford for the fun of it and then has this guy for dessert."

Will drifted into thinking again about John, about his stepson's visit earlier in the week, and about the shoeprint found on Kristen's boat.

Dodds said, "You don't like his ass because he reminds you of Cindy's new husband. Don't get me wrong, I'd love to send a lawyer to the express lane at death row. But we're going to need more before command will let us lean on him."

"We can still ViCAP his ass," Will said, referring to the FBI's colossal Violent Criminal Apprehension Program database. "He came here with his wife from Atlanta. It will be interesting to see if they have some unsolved homicides with this kind of mutilation."

Five days, four victims. Will said, "Now we know they were all tied together, but we still don't know how or why he chose them. Kristen's a cop on national television. The two vics at Miami were nobodies. Same with this guy. Not only did they have different hair colors and body types, they were different genders. Did you know Cheryl Beth was one of the instructors of those dead students? And Smith asked her to come out and talk to him at the Butler County jail?"

"No shit?" Dodds' back was to him, as he closely examined the body. "So how was your date?"

"It was nice."

"How many positions? What does she look like naked? Tell an old married man everything so I can live vicariously."

Will felt his face flush. "We had dinner and beers and talked. It was nice."

Dodds simply shook his head.

A uni brought up a middle-aged man who had found the body an hour before. He was a gardener. They went through the usual: Did you touch anything? Was anyone else nearby when you found the body? Was anything amiss elsewhere on the grounds? They got nowhere.

"If I found some guy with his penis stuck in his mouth, I'd run like hell and call the cops, too," Will said.

"Shit, it's beautiful here," Dodds said, snapping off his gloves, rolling them inside each other, and sticking them in his pocket. It was an understatement. A person could spend days wandering the lanes, taking in all the architecture driven by grief and vanity, reading the history carved in stone, and loving the nature. "All

these important dead white people, and I'm-a walkin' on 'em."
He laughed, but not loud enough to attract attention.

"I keep going back to the note," Will said. "He addressed
it to me. How did he know I was investigating this case? That
information isn't out there."

"Again," Dodds said, "could be a cop and maybe somebody
we know. Who else knew you were investigating Gruber?"

"Buchanan," Will said. "Otherwise, I don't know. I was on
the other side of the levee when they brought Gruber's body up.
There was a little group watching, looked like locals."

"So how do you want to play it?"

Will cocked his head.

"I thought I was the PIO again."

"Quit feeling sorry for yourself. I need your brain here, partner. This guy's obviously into himself."

It was an understatement. He wanted all of Cincinnati to
know that a dangerous murderer was loose, somebody who had
made fools of the cops, and had gotten away with it.

"We could report minimal information," Will said. "Uniden-
tified body found in Spring Grove Cemetery. Cheryl Beth said
Smith didn't have any relatives. So no relatives are going to be
interviewed on television. We can order the gardener to shut up.
This killer wants to be famous. He wants everybody peeing in
their pants wondering where his next 'art show' will be. Notice
how he types and prints out this note, then puts it in a plastic
cover, in case it rains. He wants attention. We could take it
even further and say we don't know whether it's a suicide or a
homicide, or even the cause of death. That'd mind-fuck this
master criminal back."

"I like it," Dodds said. "The only problem is, he might be
tempted to send the note to the newspaper. Hell, he might be
tempted to try another killing."

"So?" Will said. "He addressed the note to me. Who do you
think his next victim would be?"

Dodds studied him and raised his eyebrows. "I hope to god
you sleep with Cheryl Beth before he cuts your dick off."

Chapter Nineteen

Cheryl Beth was finishing up the post-shift conferences with her students when she saw Will walking down the hall. He looked handsome, but he was holding one shoulder too high, and his face looked exhausted. She complimented him on how he looked in his suit.

"Can we go somewhere?"

"Yes." She steered him into a family waiting room that was remarkably empty and they sat down.

"What happened?" She took his hands. They were well-shaped and warm, but had fresh abrasions.

"I fell last night." He smiled. "You swept me off my feet."

"Are you hurting?"

He shook his head. "Cheryl Beth, Noah Smith is dead."

Somewhere deep inside she had somehow been expecting this news. Still, it felt as if the end of a baseball bat had been driven into her stomach. "Oh, no. Suicide?"

"No. He was killed like the others."

"What?"

As he gave her the details, she was first slightly nauseous, then frightened. She was good at controlling herself, but she knew this showed all over her face. She could hear her mother's voice: "You're an open book, Cheryl Beth."

"And he left you a note?"

"It was addressed specifically to me," he said. "Otherwise, they were going to take me off the case. Goddamned cripple." His face was a mask of disgust.

"Stop that. You're not a cripple. You only walk with a cane. It adds character. I think you're very attractive."

He let himself smile. "That's funny, because I think you are, too." After a pause: "I used to be good at flirting, but I'm way out of practice."

She patted his arm. "You're doing well, detective. I don't understand how this could happen. I saw Noah in the bookstore yesterday. He actually tracked me down. Kind of surprised me, but he seemed desperate for someone to believe him. He thought Hank Brooks was following him."

"Oh, hell," Will said. "Give me a minute." He pulled out his cell phone and had a brief conversation—with Brooks, it was soon evident. After he hung up, he said, "I hate these multi-jurisdictional cases. I forgot to tell him about Smith's body being found. Now he claims he never really thought Noah did it. And he denied following him."

"But Noah was certain he was being followed," Cheryl Beth said.

"Maybe by the killer."

The chill returned to her bloodstream. "The killer who writes to you personally. Oh, Will…"

"I want to show you some photographs," he said. "Let me know if any of them are familiar. Anybody you've seen hanging around campus or the hospital. Anybody who might have seen these three students."

She ran through ten photographs and none looked familiar. One was a bald man, although he looked distinguished in a suit and tie. She went one by one again, trying to remember. She finally shook her head.

"I'm sorry."

"You lingered on one," he said.

"Only because he was older and bald. I keep thinking about what Lauren's sister said, about how Lauren was afraid she was being stalked by an older bald man."

"Something's got to tie them together. Three separate attacks, sixty miles apart from each other. One was on a trained police officer, and I can vouch for her toughness. Another was on a well-built young man. And this guy went after two young women at the same time, and after knocking Noah Smith out. Then he comes back and kills him. Thinks he's an artist. Now we know all these killings were done by the same guy. But we don't have the key that connects them."

"Aren't there random murders?"

"Sure," he said. "But this random is very rare. It's common to read about supposedly random murders, but the victims are all prostitutes, sometimes all working on the same strip. Or they're dark-haired women who remind the killer of someone in his life. Anyway, whoever wrote that note was taking credit, as if he specifically chose his victims. They're going to bring in an FBI profiler. But I already know what he'll say. White male. Narcissist, sense of grandiosity. Probably had a screwed-up childhood. Maybe impotent: none of the autopsies showed the presence of semen. Noah and the girls used condoms, and the killer took them. He's very precise. He's done it before…"

"Hold that thought." Cheryl Beth stood and sprinted into the hall, catching up with Allison. She brought her back and introduced her to Will.

"Allison was Noah's girlfriend," she said. The girl sat, but upright in apprehension, and Cheryl Beth thought about breaking the news to her easy, she was very good at that. But, no, she would trust Will.

"Allison, I'm a detective with the Cincinnati Police," he said, his voice even and friendly. "I'm working on some cases that are related to what happened to Lauren and Holly."

"Yes." A little girl voice.

"Were you friends with them?"

"Only school friends," she said.

"Ever hang out together?"

Allison shook her head.

"How long have you been seeing Noah?"

"About a year," she said. "Ten months."

"Did you ever feel like anything wasn't right?"

She clenched her hands. "If you mean do I think Noah did it, the answer is no. There's no way. He's gentle and kind and…"

"It's okay," Will said. "I meant something else. Did it ever seem like anyone was following the two of you? Anonymous phone calls? Anything creepy?"

She was silent, and then shook her head.

"We were normal. We went to movies. We rode our bikes together. Noah's in a lot better shape than I am."

"Does he have any enemies?"

Cheryl Beth was struck by how Will used the present tense to refer to Noah.

"No!" Allison shook her head adamantly. "He made friends so easily." Then, tonelessly, "Especially women." She raised her head and spoke more forcefully. "Do you think someone is trying to frame him for killing Holly and Lauren? Please tell that awful detective from Oxford."

Will nodded. After a silence, He produced the same file folder. "I want to show you some photographs. I'm not saying these are suspects. But they might be. I want you to take as much time as you like, and really look at each one. Ever see any of these men."

He handed her one photo at a time. She took the each one and slowly ran her fingers over it, then handed it back. He was very patient and Allison was diligent. It took a good fifteen minutes. Cheryl Beth was impressed that Will was eliciting information now, before Allison knew the worst and would probably fall apart.

She handed them back. "I'm sorry, Detective Borders. I've never seen any of them."

"I know this seems out of left field, but did you guys ever watch *LadyCops: Cincinnati*? The reality TV show?"

"No. There's not much TV time when we have a slave driver like her." She smiled fondly at Cheryl Beth.

Will smiled slightly and let a couple of beats pass. "Did you ever go to the bar where Noah met Holly and Lauren that night."

She pursed her lips. "Yeah, we used to party up there…"

Cheryl Beth watched Will's expression subtly change. The color momentarily left his face. Then he rearranged himself and leaned forward.

"Allison, there's no easy way to tell you this, so I'm going to say it…"

Chapter Twenty

Will was usually aware of every difficult step, but the long walk from the hospital floor back to his car was over before he even realized it. His mind was in a bad place elsewhere. Back in the car, he filed the mug shots in his brief case. The photos had included Kenneth Buchanan—taken off his law firm's Web site—the sergeant and diving instructor who were also Kristen's lovers, along with three other cops and four sex offenders. He pulled out his iPad, logged into the department intranet, and posted what he and Dodds had agreed on to the publicly available police blotter.

```
Body found in Spring Grove Cemetery

By Detective Will Borders
   A man's body was discovered at approxi-
mately 9:30 a.m. Thursday in Spring Grove
Cemetery. The unidentified male was white,
between the ages of twenty-five and thirty.
Cincinnati Police Department homicide detec-
tives responded, although the cause of death
was unknown and may be suicide. A routine
autopsy will be conducted. Anyone with infor-
mation in the case should contact Cincinnati
Police or Crime Stoppers.
```

He clicked "post" and the system responded immediately.

Then he sat back and digested the words of the mousy little nursing student: *We used to party up there…*

Those were almost the same words John had said to him when they were sitting on Will's balcony, talking about Miami. Will hadn't thought about it much at the time, but why would John be hanging around Oxford?

Why did John have the same brand of shoe that left a print on Kristen Gruber's boat? For that matter, why had John gone to Kristen's funeral, a woman he had met once? It's not as if John was deep into the life of the city or looking for an excuse to dress up.

Will stared at the steering wheel, feeling numb inside. If he were examining this evidence about anyone else than his stepson, *his son,* he would think this is the only person he had encountered who had a connection between Kristen and Oxford. John had met Kristen. He had partied up at Oxford. It was circumstantial, so far. But circumstantial evidence could be the building blocks of a homicide case.

He laughed mordantly. Cindy was afraid John was involved with drugs. Right now that would be a relief.

John had wanted to tell Will something when he stopped by on Monday night. Did he intend to confess? The memory made Will angry and woozy at the same time. He should have pushed him.

All Will needed was some of John's DNA to test against the hair found on the boat. Matching the shoe-print could also be probable cause. So would getting Cindy's permission to enter the house, where he could search John's room, and find Kristen's badge, gun, wallet, and keys, as well as the underwear of all the victims. Right that moment, he should pull out his cell phone and call Diane Henderson or Dodds. Then he should call the police in Oregon and find out if they had any unsolved homicides from the time John was in Portland, especially ones involving a knife.

He left the phone in his suit-coat pocket.

Maybe that female nursing student—Allison?—was a potential suspect. She would have a motive to kill two rivals being screwed under the stars by her good-looking boyfriend, and then coax him to the same fate. She didn't have the strength for it. And how did she know Kristen? He was reaching to the moon.

He and Cindy hadn't been the best parents, but had they raised a killer? The thought crowded out all his body's other complaints. John had never killed an animal—that Will knew of. He had a Siamese cat for fifteen years while he was growing up, and was nothing but affectionate toward it. Would he write that kind of letter? The language sounded more mature. John didn't even know Will had been the lead detective on the Gruber case. But he could also hear Dodds' voice in his head: "Who the hell knows why or when somebody becomes a monster." Killing at his stepfather's alma mater, killing his famous and attractive colleague, addressing a note specifically to Will. If he stepped back, all of this would make him one thing: suspicious as hell.

The sound of a car's tires squealing on the concrete made him jump. Here he had a killer at loose, taunting him with a note pinned through a dead man's skin, and he's in a reverie in a deserted parking garage.

"Smart, Borders," he said, and started the car.

Before he drove out, he checked the *Enquirer's* Web site. What he wrote was already there, as a brief, with his headline. The only editing was to attribute the information to him, rather than giving him the byline. He thanked God that the tough old police reporters who dug and worked closely with the cops had all retired, and now the people down at the paper pretty much only took dictation.

Chapter Twenty-one

Heather Bridges lived in an apartment in a turreted three-story brick building off Hamilton Avenue in Northside. It was a neighborhood above the split between Interstates 74 and 75, and sandwiched between Spring Grove Cemetery and Mount Airy Forest, and Will was amazed how quickly it had gone from down-on-its-luck Rust Belt to Bohemian trendy. Cincinnati had plenty of such districts, but only a limited number of Bohemians, especially with money.

He had gotten rid of his police tail with some difficulty, telling Dodds that he had to run an errand for his ex. Now he was telling lies for John. They called that "accomplice" in his business. But he didn't need Dodds or some other detective following him up here. He was bait now. The letter on Noah Smith was addressed to him. With luck, good or bad, the killer might come after him. He successfully argued against wearing a constant wire. But he had a hand-held radio with him at all times. Now he carried it in his left hand as he used the right, as always, for the cane.

A girl's voice answered the intercom after a long wait. "Cincinnati Police" was enough to get him buzzed in. Oh, for a day without a long stair climb. He made it. She was waiting on the second floor, with the door cracked and the chain on. He showed her his badge, now draped in black, and identification.

"You're John's dad."

"May I come in?"

The chain slid off and he stepped inside a high-ceilinged living room. It held a few pieces of expensive new furniture and art posters on the wall. He didn't take time to read the details of galleries and dates, although one prominently featured the avant-garde Contemporary Arts Center downtown.

"I'm only living here through the summer. Until I go to college. But I didn't want to be stuck out at the parents' house, if you know what I mean, nothing wrong with parents, mine are cool, but I love this area…"

The chirping young woman was tall, with reddish-brown hair falling in tendrils over her shoulders, high cheekbones, and shapely legs shown to advantage in shorts. He could see why John was attracted to her. Still, she was mussed and out of breath.

"Let's sit down," he interrupted. She sat quickly and nervously. He turned down the radio and set it on the cushion beside him.

"We need to talk, Heather."

"About what, Will?" A smile to light up a city. The sense of entitlement he had expected from her parents' bankbook.

"Let's get off on the right foot," Will said. "I'll call you Heather. You call me Detective Borders."

"Okay." A pout descended over her lovely face.

"I know you and John were on the river Saturday night and early Sunday morning…"

The pout was turning to unconcealed alarm when a closed door fifteen feet down a hallway was thrown open and a man angrily strode toward them. He was only wearing boxer shorts.

"What's going on, Heather? This dude bothering you?"

Will made no effort to react. If the guy got in his face, the steel shaft of the cane would make an excellent impression on his nose. As he came into the light, Will saw how young he was. He was John's age, maybe a year or two younger, and his stride was all confidence. He was lean and fit in an untested way, with stubble on his pretty-boy face, stubble on his head, and no hair on his chest. Beyond his belligerent posture, he wore a sleepy expression. When the fly of his boxers came open as he walked,

Will could see the piercing. Lord, he didn't understand this. But that was a reflection deep inside. His face was all cop.

"Who the fuck are you, kid?"

"I don't have to…"

"Actually you do, asshole," Will said, flashing his badge. The young man was momentarily deflated. Long enough for Heather to say, "This is my friend, Zack."

"Go put on some clothes, friend Zack."

The young man stared defiantly, then padded back to the bedroom, cursing under his breath.

"What's Zack's full name?"

She meekly complied. "Zachary Paul Miller."

"Is he your boyfriend?"

She shrugged. "We hook up. Friends with benefits, you know. Or maybe you don't…" She glanced at the cane, and for a nanosecond he wanted to beat her to death with it. The urge passed quickly.

"So is John an F.W.B.?"

Heather smirked. "Oh, my god, no."

"But you went to meet him on Saturday, for a date?"

"Not a date." She fluffed out her hair and smoothed it down. "He's sweet. But…"

Zachary Paul Miller stomped back and sat next to Heather. His jeans were so low on his hips that Will didn't know how they didn't fall to the floor.

"Stop talking." He looked like he was going to slap her. To Will: "We don't have to tell you anything, Borders. I've got the family lawyer on speed dial." He dangled his iPhone. "Kenneth Buchanan. Ever hear of him, cop?" He laughed, a surprisingly high-pitched sound.

Will lifted himself up and walked two paces. He shifted the cane to his left hand. Then he delivered a hard jab to the young man's abdomen, where it would hurt the most and leave no trace.

He was a tough-guy, at least in his own mind, but he let out a sound between a belch and a pig squeal. Tears came to his eyes as he struggled to breathe.

"Oh, I'm so sorry I fell against you, sir," Will said. "It's this whole cane thing. I get unstable. Damned cripples, and we get all the best parking places."

Will returned and sat down again. "Now listen to me. You may be the king stud of Summit Country Day School, but if I make one call you're going to be nothing but another jailhouse chicken who'll get sodomized all night by very muscular men below your social class. They'd love to get hold of your virgin ass and your Prince Albert piercing. Only one night in lockup, you know, before the lawyers can sort things out. Jeez, I've seen it happen so many times to the East Side kids." Will shook his head in mock sympathy. Zack's eyes widened with terror.

Will continued. "I've already talked to Mr. Buchanan." Technically true. "I'm hoping we can settle this without trouble: the kind that would keep you from your Ivy League future. This is a homicide investigation." He paused and watched the color return to Zack's face and quickly flee again. "I know you want to cooperate, Mr. Miller."

For perhaps the first time in his life, the kid hadn't gotten what he wanted. He shut up and nodded, his eyes down, his mouth open, and struggling to refill his lungs.

"So why don't you tell me what happened on the river last weekend."

Zack started talking, gradually regaining his voice.

"I was out in my dad's boat. We picked up some ladies. Your kid tagged along. We went up the Licking to party. No big deal."

Will watched him. When the silence was starting to make him uncomfortable, Will said, "You want to try again?"

The young man jutted out his chin, then dropped his head. "We saw the boat, okay? Where the lady cop was killed."

"When did you see it?"

"First when we went up-river."

Will wanted the time: around three that afternoon. He started making notes.

"It didn't look like anybody was aboard," Zack Miller said. "It was tied up. I didn't think anything about it. Then it was still there when we came back."

"What time?"

"I have no idea. Way after midnight. We slowed down, thought maybe we could pull a prank. I ran the spotlight over the boat. We called over and nobody called back. So we pulled alongside, and I was going to check it out, make sure everybody was okay. But John went over. I guess he was trying to impress the girls. When he comes back, he said there was a dead woman in the cabin."

Will suddenly had a headache. "John got onto that boat?"

"Yes, sir, he did."

"How long was he there?"

Zack shrugged. "A few minutes. Then he came back and told us."

"Why didn't you call the police?"

"I wanted to, but John said not to do it. He made us get out of there and I let everybody off at the Serpentine Wall."

Will wrote slowly, trying to maintain his composure. Even if John hadn't killed Kristen Gruber, witnesses now placed him on the boat, and the hair and shoe-print were probably his, too. That must have been why John refused to let the others call the police. He would be in deep shit and there was nothing that Will could do to protect him. He had done too much already. But at least John had an alibi for the time when Gruber was murdered.

He faced Heather, wishing he were interrogating them separately. "Is that how it happened?"

She nodded. "Yes." She immediately looked down and to the left.

Will didn't trust the story. Zack didn't seem like the kind of boater or human being that would check the welfare of anybody who couldn't do him a favor. But he also knew he had to fight against his bias to believe John was innocent.

"So let me get this straight. You go upriver, see the boat, and there's no activity on it. You party a few miles upstream. Then when you come back, you stop. Why?"

"There was blood on the portholes. It hadn't been there the first time."

Will asked him how he knew.

"I know boats. It was a Rinker Fiesta, in pretty good shape. The first time I was surprised that somebody would tie it up and leave it. But there were other boats and canoes on the river. When we came back toward downtown, it was the only boat left. This time I saw the blood, and it wasn't there before, when we were going upriver." The more he talked, the greater the confidence in his voice.

"So while you guys are partying, did you notice anything odd on the river?"

The smirk returned. "I was kind of occupied, but no."

"Only five young people on your boat?"

He lifted one shoulder. "Yep. Unless somebody used the Zodiac while I was busy or sacked out."

A muscle spasm kicked Will in his side, forcing him to fight to keep his expression neutral.

"What Zodiac?"

Chapter Twenty-two

Will handled a call as PIO and talked on camera. The idea was to have him out there in public as much as possible, to try to lure the killer. After dark, he drove back to Hyde Park, his car in the fast flow of traffic gliding along above the river on Columbia Parkway, his mind forced into a trench of unthinking, if only for now. He didn't look south, where the big river met its lethal tributary. He didn't look up the bluff to the north, where Kristen Gruber's condo perched.

In fifteen minutes, he was on the big-trees street in front of the sprawling Tudor, its blond bricks preening in the ornamental lighting. Every room inside was lit. It would have been a good account for Cincinnati Gas & Electric, if the company still existed, and hadn't been lost in the endless takeovers that had shaken the city in recent years. Dodds was following him, but it would have to be. Will could make excuses later. He was still running an errand for his ex, more than she knew.

The phone inside rang six times before a man's voice answered. Will watched him standing in the dining room, with a proprietary hand on his ex-wife's shoulder.

"Brad, it's your predecessor, Will Borders. Would you please put Cindy on the phone?"

"Will." He hesitated. "We sat down to supper a moment ago and Cynthia has had a long day. Maybe I could ask her to call you later."

"That won't do. I'll only take a minute."

After some muffles and distant, indiscernible voices, she came on the line, her voice brittle with anger.

"You're very rude."

She said it after she walked out of the brightly lit dining room and disappeared into some other chamber of the huge manse.

"Is John there?"

"Yes, he's going to join us for dinner."

"I want to talk to him now."

"You listen to…"

"Now, Cindy. I'm in the car right in front. This is police business. Send him out here."

It took a long time. Then the big front door opened and John walked reluctantly to the curb and climbed in. He was neatly dressed and his hair was freshly cut, but he was everything that Zack Miller was not: a little pudgy, a dusting of acne, no athletic grace in his movements. Will felt sorry for the kid, and reminded himself that John wasn't a kid anymore. But he also knew how much the surface, how much appearances mattered at John's age.

He started the car and drove down the street lined with fine houses, turning left on Edwards, crossing Observatory and gliding into Hyde Park Square, where Erie Avenue split around a narrow park that held a statue, fountain, flower gardens, and trees. Each side was lined with expensive shops, galleries and cafés, although it looked slightly ragged from the recession. The night was pleasant and couples strolled under period lampposts. Will had thought about taking a longer drive, maybe all over the city. But he was too tired. And he needed to get back into "bait" mode. He was running out of time. He slid the car into one of the angled parking places a few doors down from the landmark two-story fire station.

"What's up?"

Will stared straight ahead. He didn't want to look at John, didn't want to notice tells that he might be lying. He said, "Where were you on Saturday night?"

"I dunno. I'd have to think about it. Chillin', I guess."

He was lying already. Why was he lying? Will was afraid to speculate.

"I enjoyed having a beer with you the other night," Will said, fighting to change the tone in his voice from accusation.

"Yeah, me, too." John's voice was wary.

"I got the sense you wanted to tell me something," Will said. A young family went by on the sidewalk, two little children squealing in delight. What would they grow up to be? "John, if there's something you want to tell me, it's really important that you do it. Understand? It will really matter if you tell me on your own, if you make the decision to come to me and tell me what you wanted to say three nights ago."

He wanted to say something like, *you can trust me, I won't judge you.* And he wanted those things to be true, but he also had the badge and, had, as the young cop said to him, powers of arrest. The inside of the car was starting to warm up but he didn't crack a window. A noiseless expanse of time did nothing to stop the spasms in his legs. The next sound he heard was John crying. It was an ugly suppressed sobbing. The more he tried to hold it in, the worse it burst out after a few seconds. Will held back the instinct to put a hand on the boy's shoulder.

"She was...dead in there," he finally managed. "There was blood everywhere. He'd cut her up between her legs and spread them wide open. And...she was staring at me with those dead eyes..."

"Dead in where?"

"The boat. I went over to check. She was dead..."

"Was anyone else aboard?"

"I don't think so."

"Try to remember!" Will knew he shouldn't have shouted, but his ass was on the line now, too. "You said, 'he'd cut her...' Who cut her?"

"I don't know. It was only a figure of expression." John sniffled loudly. Neither of them had a Kleenex. Will usually kept a pack in the car for moments like this with the family or friends of a victim. "Nobody was on deck. I ran the flashlight into the cabin and I couldn't see anything at first. Then I saw her, and got out. I was really scared."

"How did you know she was dead?"

He hesitated, as if he hadn't even considered it. "There was so much blood," he said. "It was all over the walls, a big pool of it on the floor, and she was so white."

"You didn't check her pulse?"

"I was afraid to step into the blood."

Will didn't understand the contradiction: how John could go aboard to see if anything was wrong, but then see a bloody woman and not check to see if she were still alive. He'd been in Boy Scouts awhile and knew some first aid. This was the kind of thing that a skilled interrogator could start to break down, take apart, and drive a truck through. Will realized that he was desensitized to seeing the dead and being up to his elbows in blood. But John's story still didn't fit, unless you believed he first really did want to impress Heather Bridges and then, after he was aboard, became frightened and fled. It was all what a jury would believe—Will was that far down the line in his reasoning.

"What else can you remember about the boat? Anything on deck or in the cabin that seemed odd to you?"

"It smelled funny in the cabin," John said. "I couldn't place it at first, but now I think it smelled like bleach."

Will stared at the steering wheel, losing his last grain of hope that John's presence on that boat was all a big misunderstanding. He had been there. "Did you know who the woman was?"

"Yes." His voice was quiet. "Kristen."

Will rolled down a window and the sweet Cincinnati spring breeze unseemly intruded.

"Why were you even on the river that night?" Will demanded.

"I was on a boat with some friends from school."

He ran John through the same line of questions as he used on his supposed friends from school: What time did they leave the Serpentine Wall, who was aboard, when did they see Kristen's boat, how far up the Licking River they went, how long they were partying, and when they saw the boat on the return trip.

It all jibed. In fact, John had a more precise time for the second encounter with the death boat: a few minutes before four a.m.

"What were you doing upriver for so long?" Will asked.

"We had some drinks. Then Zack handed out E. Ecstasy."

"I know what E means. What else?"

John rolled down his window and stuck an elbow out. "People started hooking up. I was with Heather."

"Really?" Will didn't say it in a scandalized parent's voice, the way Cindy would, but with a sharp snap of skepticism. John looked at him with hate.

"I guess Zack fucked all three girls," John said darkly. "Maybe the girls played with each other, too. I don't know. I passed out."

Will made him answer it again. He sounded credible.

"I watched Zack and Heather bumping nasties, if you really want to know the truth," John said. "I didn't want to see any of it, but they woke me up."

"Why would you get on the boat with these kids, John?"

"I didn't want to! Heather and I were going to have a picnic at Sawyer Point. Only us. I asked her out. Thought she liked me. Then that douche nozzle pulls up in his fancy boat and she wanted to go. She invited me. Zack would have been happy to leave me at the wall."

Will took it in and said nothing.

"Are you carrying your knife?"

The boy stiffened in his seat and nodded.

"Let me see it, please."

John reluctantly reached in his pants pocket and handed it to Will, who switched on the dome light and unfolded the knife, which locked in place. It was heavy and all black, with a web-textured steel handle and spear point. "Blackhawk!" was emblazoned on the surface of the blade. It was very sharp. Although the blade looked a legal length, the whole unfolded knife appeared almost eight inches long. He examined it for dried blood; found none. John could have cleaned it. The Gruber autopsy showed such brutal knife wounds that it was difficult to determine the shape or edge characteristics of the blade, but it probably wasn't serrated. This blade wasn't serrated.

Will asked John if he had bought the knife. He said he had ordered it online for eighty dollars.

"And tell me again why you would carry a knife?"

"So I'd feel safe."

"Ever been in a knife fight?"

"No," John said softly.

"Ever use this knife for anything?"

He shook his head.

The motion made Will's own headache worse. He should have popped some Advils. It was probably only stress. Or a brain tumor.

"John, let me give you a scenario. While your friends were partying and high, or sleeping, or whatever, you unlashed the Zodiac from Zack Miller's boat and went downriver. You climbed on Kristen's boat. You threatened her with the knife and made her handcuff herself. Then you stabbed her over and over again…"

"No…No…" He was sobbing again.

"Then you got back to Zack's boat, tied up, and you have an alibi for when you all discover her later."

"It's not true!" he shouted, the streetlights shining on his tears. Some mannerly East Siders walked by a little faster, but didn't look at them.

Will let out a long breath. "I don't want it to be true, John. But the police found a shoe-print on the boat, and some hairs. The odds are they'll be yours."

John was completely silent.

"Where were you on Sunday night?"

"What is it with you?" John exploded. "I have to account for every second like a ten-year-old?"

Will wanted to say, then stop acting like a ten-year-old. But, calmly, "Two nursing students were killed up at Oxford, John. They were killed with a knife, like Kristen Gruber was."

A gasp came from the shadow in the other seat. It relieved Will.

"You don't think…? It wasn't me. I didn't do anything!"

"But you told me you partied up there. Did you see some pretty nursing students? Maybe they gave you the brush-off in a bar and you decided to get even."

"I was home with mom. You can ask her. We rented a movie."

Will finally let out a breath.

"You have to go to the police. I'm going to give you the name and number of a detective in Covington. I want you to call her in the morning. All you have to do is tell her what happened. Tell her the truth. You were scared. But you want to come forward and do the right thing. Now, did anyone see you with this knife that night?"

"No."

"Think, John. Did they?"

He almost cringed in the seat. "No! Nobody saw it."

"Then I'm going to borrow it. I've borrowed it for a month, okay? So you haven't had it."

"I thought you said tell the truth."

"Yeah," Will said, both temples throbbing. "Leave the knife out of it. If you're telling me the truth, then the knife has no part of your story, right?"

He nodded. "Are you going to tell mom?"

"You can do that. You're an adult now."

Will slid the knife into his pocket. He hated knives. The Mount Adams Slasher had used a knife, including on Theresa. He started the car and backed out. As he cruised slowly around the park to return the way they came, he asked, "John, why didn't you call the police when you found her body?"

"I wanted to. Zack wouldn't let me. He drove out of there as fast as he could, telling me he didn't want to get caught with drunk underage girls and E on his dad's expensive boat."

"Zack said you're the one who wouldn't let *him* call."

"You talked to Zack? He's lying!"

Of course he was, Will thought. Zack had control of the boat and could have chosen to stay. But there was a problem of corroboration, and it wouldn't help John.

"Ask Heather," he said. "She'll tell you."

"I did. Heather backed up Zack's version."

Will watched his stepson's face in the mirror as they drove back in silence. It held a rage that stole all his youth.

Afterward, Will stopped at a United Dairy Farmers store, bought Advil and a bottle of water, and swallowed four of the dark red pills at once.

Chapter Twenty-three

When all the lights had been turned off downstairs, Cheryl Beth walked through the darkness with a glass of Chardonnay. Upstairs, she ran a warm tub of water, lit some candles, turned off the lights, and undressed. The wine and the yellow-orange flickering light relaxed her as she stretched out in the tub. She dunked her head, pushed back her wet hair, and took stock.

She didn't want to hate Hank Brooks for being obsessed with Noah when the real killer was still out there, or for releasing Noah to his fate. Brooks didn't call her until late in the day. Then he didn't sound the least bit contrite. Instead, he said how he had doubted that Noah was the murderer, even in the hours after he had been arrested in the Formal Gardens. It was all about Brooks covering his ass. She barely got through the conversation without saying many unladylike things.

She couldn't imagine the horror Noah had felt there in the old graveyard. Was there something she could have done for him, when he found her in the bookstore? She couldn't think what is would have been, but she felt guilty nonetheless. Three of her students now dead. She took a deep drink of wine and felt warm water trickle down her back.

She thought of Will and looked at her body illuminated in the candlelight. She no longer had the bloom of seventeen, when she had been a reluctant cheerleader in Corbin, a national merit scholar finalist, too. She had scholarship offers from very good universities, but her mother said they didn't have the money to make up the difference. Nobody was on her side, the side of a young woman who dreamed of a world outside Corbin, who had the bus schedules out of town memorized.

So she went as far as she could, to the biggest city she knew, studying nursing at the University of Cincinnati. Her mother made her be practical in that choice. She had really wanted to study philosophy or theater. And she took her only boyfriend in tow, a nice but unambitious young man who really didn't want to leave town. They married too young. Now, past forty, she looked at a body whose changes she was only too aware of, and they were all changes for the worse. It didn't matter how many compliments she got or how many men hit on her. The years went by and they took and took and took. *What a silly, vain thought, when three of your students are dead.* Well, she still had nice legs.

As the candles painted shadows on the walls, she wished Will would call. But he was working. She had turned on the news before coming upstairs, and he was on camera twice as the police spokesman: a two-hundred-pound python found in a trash can in Sedamsville, below Mount Echo Park, and a shooting in Corryville, not far from the hospitals on Pill Hill, a few rough blocks from the now-closed hospital where she had almost lost her life. The television reporter said a man shot at a police officer but missed. Will made a statement, the man was now in custody, and then the chief of police talked. So much craziness and violence were a part of his life, and yet he seemed so steady and gentle. Could it be an act? She had been taken in before. Still, she liked the way he opened doors for her, old school, the way he was interested in her, how he kissed, and how he was tall. She liked the way her head tucked under his.

She wished she had brought the wine bottle upstairs.

When the phone rang, she was glad she had it by the tub. She dried off a hand and answered. It was Will, asking if he was calling too late.

"I'm a night owl," she said. "Too many years spent checking on patients around midnight when the pain got bad. I saw you on television. A two-hundred-pound snake?"

"He was the most pleasant creature I dealt with today. Anyway, lots of face time for Detective Will Borders. Now the question is whether the killer is watching." He told her about the minimal press release they had put out regarding Noah. "This guy has delusions of grandeur. He addressed the note directly to me. So the hope is if he doesn't get the publicity he's seeking, he might come after me." He sighed. "Or, he'll stop and we'll never find him, and in a few years he'll start again somewhere else."

"What kind of a person would do these things, Will?"

"There's a type," he said. "The scary thing is that sometimes they can fit right into society. They're not out in the country living alone in a doublewide. Or, like a lot of white folks in this town think, a scary black man asking for change on the sidewalk."

"Do you think you know who did it? Or shouldn't I ask that?"

"I met a man who I think is very capable of it," Will said. "He was one of Kristen's lovers. But he's very connected, and we'll need major probable cause to take it further. I'm not even sure the other detectives would agree with me. This guy's got an alibi, or he say he does. I'd love to poke a few holes in it and know where he was Saturday night."

"I hope you're being careful."

"Door's locked, and I'm upstairs with my Smith & Wesson and shotgun."

"You're getting me hot." She smiled.

"And, I have detectives watching from a car out on the street. It could be worse. They wanted me to wear a wire 24/7, so they could even listen in on our conversation. Dodds would especially like that."

"He's such a character." She looked at herself in the tub and thought, *Ask me what I'm wearing...*

"He is that." Will paused. "I'm wondering if we should go to the symphony tomorrow night."

"Are you kicking me to the curb, Borders?"

"No! I'm worried. I have skin in this game. You don't. I already nearly got you killed when I was in the hospital. I'm afraid of putting you at risk, at even greater risk, because we can't be sure the killer doesn't already know about you."

"As I recall, Detective, I nearly got *you* killed. The murderer was after me, and your buddies at CPD thought I was a murderer."

"You know what I mean…"

"And I have skin in the game, too, as you put it. My students are dead."

Another pause. "Fair enough. But I don't have the best history this way."

"Will, why does Dodds call you Mister President?"

He seemed grateful to laugh. "That bastard. Okay, if we're going to bare our souls, it's because my full name is William Howard Taft Borders. Named after Cincinnati's only president, and a failed one at that. My mom was a local history buff. He calls me that it to get under my skin."

Cheryl Beth smiled and finished the wine. "I like it. Look, Will, I know you feel guilty about what happened with Theresa Chambers. But that wasn't your fault. It's in the past and you can't live your life in fear. Unless…" Her smile faded. "Unless you don't like me, and if that's the case, all you have to do is tell me, before I get skin in that game, too."

"No, Cheryl Beth. I like you a lot. I have ever since I met you. No game."

"You're mighty forward." She exaggerated her accent.

"I didn't mean…"

"Relax, Will. I'm kidding you."

"Right." His voice relaxed.

"Maybe you don't even like the symphony. You probably use that line to get girls because you know we usually have to drag men to concerts."

"Yep, that's me. Be ready tomorrow night and you'll find out." His cadence changed. "Tomorrow's going to be hell day,

I'm afraid. I don't think I told you that my ex-wife has remarried and finally has her big house in Hyde Park. I went over there tonight to talk to my stepson. He's in trouble. He was on the river Saturday night with some other kids and they found Kristen Gruber's boat. He went aboard and saw her body. Lord, I wish he would have called the police then."

"Oh, no."

"I told him he's got to go tomorrow and tell what he knows." The phone line made a lonely buzz, then, "Even though he's not my biological son and things the past few years have put more distance between us, I feel for him like he's really my son."

She managed, "I know you must."

"Money's not a problem in his life. Far from it. So different from when I was growing up. But somehow the money is making things worse for him. So I'm not so much worried about the blowback on me tomorrow, and there will be. I'm worried about him. He's so isolated and...I don't know. You try your best to raise a child, but you finally realize that you can't live their life for them, that they aren't you. They can't be saved from all the mistakes you had to make. Inside, there's this individual soul that's going its own way, for better or worse. I'm rambling, sorry."

"Don't be sorry," she said. "Try to be good to you. I worry about you."

"I'll try. When do I get to learn some of your secrets, Cheryl Beth Wilson?"

She forced herself to speak. "Maybe I don't have any. Maybe I'm only a simple, small-town girl from Corbin, Kentucky."

"I doubt that."

"Then stick around. Sleep tight."

"You, too."

After he hung up, she sank into the water and smiled and sobbed.

Friday

Chapter Twenty-four

Will looked very debonair—yes, that was exactly the right word—sitting across from her. His charcoal pinstripe suit looked new, and his crisp white shirt was set off with a purple tie that had a subtle pattern. She was feeling the shortness of the black dress she was wearing, her legs encased in sheer black stockings, but he definitely noticed and complimented her twice about how good she looked. "Smashing," was one tribute; rather like "debonair."

It was wonderful to be out with him, and especially in one of her favorite places, the Palm Court at the Netherland Plaza Hotel downtown. She gloried in its long, spacious, art deco expanse. She always expected to see Fred Astaire and Ginger Rogers at another table. The rich, dark wood of the walls alternated with elaborate golden sconces and frescoes running up into the roof. The first time she ever saw the place, it looked like a combination of an ancient pagan temple and a glamorous setting from an old movie. The bar in the center of the room was right out of the 1930s and a pianist was playing jazz on a grand piano. They both appropriately ordered gin martinis.

It seemed like the right nightcap to the classical evening. Cheryl Beth also adored Music Hall, even though she hadn't been to the symphony in two years. To live in Cincinnati was to be immersed in music, from the symphony and chamber orchestra, to the Pops and the May Festival's choral extravaganza, which was coming right up. And Will had not disappointed. He had great seats in the orchestra section with as perfect sound quality as she had heard there.

As always, the stately old building seemed to levitate with an exciting glitter on a concert night. She didn't really know much about classical music. She knew what she liked, what transported her. But from the day she had arrived in Cincinnati, the symphony had been part of her self-improvement program, to lift herself out of the small-town South.

Will, surprisingly, did know classical music. Now he talked in that calm, sexy voice about the night's program, about the history of Beethoven's *King Stephen Overture* and the *Second Piano Concerto*. But he wore his knowledge easily. His face was relaxed and happy.

"Beethoven turned the piano into the monarch of romantic instruments," he said.

"You play, don't you?"

He gave a dismissive shrug. "I wouldn't call it that, now. It's hard to sit properly at the keyboard after my surgery and impossible to use the pedals… And I'm lazy and now I'm a little afraid of the thing. But I would much rather have been a pianist than a cop."

"Really?" This surprised her.

He smiled. "Who knows?"

"You wouldn't have to carry that." She indicated the small walkie-talkie radio sitting on the table next to his drink. "Maybe you'll play for me sometime. I'll sit next to you and stabilize you."

"Maybe I will."

"I thought the tribute to the cellist was very moving," Cheryl Beth said. "So much has happened this week that I had forgotten about that." She shivered slightly, and not only from the cool air on her legs. So much violence had been visited in a few days.

Tonight's program had been modified to include a piece dedicated to the murdered musician, with the cello solo played by a tall, willowy blonde. Although the program's listing of her accomplishments made it clear she was at least fifty, she looked much younger, with Nordic features and flawless fair skin.

"That was Stephanie Foust," Will said. "She was Jeremy Snowden's teacher and mentor."

"She said he could have gone to Julliard, but chose to stay in Cincinnati and study at CCM. If he hadn't stayed, he might not be dead. It's so sad. She seemed really on the edge of losing it. But she did a beautiful job."

Will nodded. "Rachmaninoff's *Vocalise* arranged for cello and orchestra. It's such a hauntingly beautiful melody. She chose well."

"It almost made me cry," Cheryl Beth said.

"I think it did the same to her. Remember the final statement of the theme, which actually occurs in the orchestra. Stephanie was playing a counter-melody. It closes the work in the upper stratosphere."

"I remember. It was magical."

"But if you listened closely, she was so spent, so devastated, that she missed her entrance to the final repetition of the melody."

Cheryl Beth hadn't noticed.

He said, "She recovered in time… Most people wouldn't even hear it. Sorry, I sound pompous."

"You don't!" Cheryl Beth said. She was rapt listening to him. "I love to learn about this from you."

"I've heard the piece many times. It's one of my favorites."

"Well, thank goodness the police got the guy."

Will's face was thoughtful. "They think they did."

"What?"

"I don't know." Will gave a smile short of sly. "Only a feeling I have."

She reached over and took his hand. The abrasions from his fall were healing, but she wasn't examining him, only wanting the closeness.

"There's so much to you, Will Borders."

He gave a self-deprecating shrug.

"The symphony president thought so. She specifically came up to you at intermission to thank you for your help. All those important people were watching her and wondering who we were. A cop and a nurse."

Will chuckled. "Notice how she avoided Dodds, even though he was no more than twenty feet away? He wasn't deferential enough to the symphony, which is a high crime in Cincinnati, so I had to go over and smooth ruffled feathers." His eyes brightened. "Here's a secret." He leaned in closer, still holding her hand.

"Her husband was one of Kristen Gruber's lovers."

Cheryl Beth felt her eyes widen.

"Yep. He berths his boat right next to hers at the marina. And he's a middle-aged bald man."

"Oh, my god…" She felt the big room closing in to envelope the two of them.

"He's a very high-powered lawyer. I met with him. He was belligerent. Of course, he doesn't want his wife to know he was with Kristen. He said he had an alibi, that he was with his wife last Saturday night."

"Too bad," she said.

Will leaned in closer. "It may be too bad for him. Remember when Mrs. Buchanan spoke to the audience before the Rachmaninoff tribute to Jeremy Snowden? How she said that it was only last Saturday night when she had heard him play there, and then she had gone to a party with him and other musicians after the concert. Her husband said they were alone at home Saturday night."

"The bald man who stalked Lauren…"

"If only I can sell it to the bosses."

Afterward, they walked across the street to Fountain Square. Will walked best when he could swing his left arm, but he took Cheryl Beth's hand and moved even slower. She didn't seem to mind. The most famous public space in the city was deserted except for the lights on the Tyler Davidson Fountain, illuminating the water falling out of the hands of the bronze woman who kept watch from her granite perch. Even many natives didn't know the fountain was actually called the Genius of Water. They sat on the lip and felt the spray in the cool night.

He couldn't keep his eyes off Cheryl Beth: she had never looked more beautiful.

"Are your friends watching us?" she asked.

He nodded. "See that Ford that's illegally parked?"

"So I guess we can't get naked in the fountain. Why are you doing this, Will? Making yourself a target."

Things had happened so quickly he didn't have an easy answer. It seemed to come naturally with the job. And with Dodds taking over as lead, he felt more insecure about even keeping the PIO position.

"Don't try to be macho," she said. "That's not you."

"No. I don't want this guy to get away, and this way is our best shot at luring him back. I'm careful. If you're worried about the cane and all…"

She touched his face. "I'm not worried about that. I want you to be safe. So I'm glad they're watching."

She asked him about his day and he told her. It started with a call from Diane Henderson in Covington; she wanted to meet across the bridge. There she told him that his stepson had come to her and said he had boarded Kristen Gruber's boat early Sunday morning. He acted surprised but told Cheryl Beth about forcing John to go to the police. Then he received a mega-ass-chewing from Fassbinder over the news, full of threats and menace. Fassbinder was a political commander and had forced better officers than Will out of the unit, even off the force. John hadn't been taken into custody—that was good. But Henderson said she considered him a person of interest—that was bad. Of course there was the mandatory call from Cindy, in hysterics over the developments with John, which were somehow his fault.

"He's fortunate to have you," Cheryl Beth said.

"I'm not sure he sees it that way."

"Why didn't you and Cindy ever have children of your own?"

He sighed. It was a question he had asked himself many times, and the straightforward answer was that Cindy didn't want more children. She became more and more invested in her career. He wanted to be supportive of that. And they had John, who for so many years seemed like his own son.

"Now I'm afraid for him." He watched the sparse traffic on Fifth Street and Vine.

"Of course, you would be," she said. After a pause, "Are you afraid of him?"

"Maybe." He paused. "Whoever wrote the note pinned to Noah Smith knew I was investigating the death of Kristen Gruber. Hardly anyone knew that, and almost nobody in the public. But I remember now that John stopped by my place a few days ago and I told him."

"Oh…"

For a long time they listened to the mesmerizing voice of the intricate Victorian fountain. Around them were flavorless modern box skyscrapers, except for the 1930 masterpiece of the Carew Tower, with its setbacks and soaring tawny walls, Cincinnati's own miniature Rockefeller Center. Will remembered Pogue's Department Store had anchored the arcade that was part of the tower and the Netherland Plaza. It was long gone, as was the big Shillito-Rikes over on Seventh. They had been so full of magic and big-city bustle, especially at Christmas. Now all that was left was the little Macy's west of the square, a concession to Macy's headquarters city and plenty of city subsidies. South of the Carew Tower, he could make out the lit whiteness of the 1913 PNC Tower, still the Central Trust Tower to natives, with its Greek temple at the top.

"Will, I've lied to you."

She took her hand away from his and faced toward the glassy front of the Westin across Fifth.

"You're married?" He tried to make light, but the change in her voice made him uneasy.

"Just hold me."

That was easy. He wrapped his arms around her and she leaned into him. He could barely hear her when she started talking.

"When I said I didn't have children, that was a lie. I've been telling that lie for so long that it comes naturally..."

She clutched him back tightly.

"I had a daughter. She died. She was born with a bad heart, and when she was three...I couldn't stop it. Her name was Carla Beth and today is her birthday and she would have been eighteen years old..."

All this came tumbling out at a speed to match the cascade of the fountain. He held on and kissed the top of her head. Her hair was very soft.

"I can't explain to you why I told this lie," she said. "There's no good reason. I loved that little girl so much. She was mine. And the grief was mine. Now I realize she didn't belong to me. She belonged to God, and if she had lived she would have made her own decisions. But for so many years I couldn't let go. I didn't want to try to have another baby because I couldn't stand another loss...couldn't face it again...and I never found the right man. But I had my grief... It was easier to wear this disguise. I don't want that with you."

For the first time in so long, his mind wasn't regretting the past or fearing the future. He was there in that space and moment, under the golden light of the fountain, feeling her heart beat wildly inside her chest.

She raised her head and looked at him straight on. Her eyes were wet but fierce. "Don't make me regret that decision, Will Borders."

He pulled her in and held her close, whispering, "Never... never going to hurt you...never going to let you down..." again and again. The splash and murmur of water, the song of this river city, under the statue's outstretched arms, consecrated their moment.

Chapter Twenty-five

They walked back to his car in silence, still holding hands. Cheryl Beth felt strangely free and light after telling him. She felt safe with him knowing. It was as if a new world had opened at her feet. He started slowly up Vine Street, past Piatt Park where the murdered President James Garfield looked out on the city from his statue, past the public library and Scotti's Italian restaurant with its red-and-green neon sign and red door. After Central Parkway and the monotonous Kroger tower, Vine would enter Over-the-Rhine and then climb into Clifton, back home.

"Let's go to your place." Her voice sounded normal again.

"Do you think that's a good idea?"

She put her hand on his knee. "Yes. It's a wonderful idea."

"Me, too."

She had never even seen the little street that held Will's townhouse. It was a block from the mishmash of wide Liberty Street, but it was quiet and secluded. The townhouse itself must have been more than a hundred years old and yet it looked to be in good shape. The interior was completely restored and modernized, even if the granite kitchen countertops weren't quite to her taste.

"Is this your son?" She held up a photo of a tall, dark-haired young man. He smiled awkwardly at the camera.

"Stepson," Will said. "His biological father showed back up, rich in Boston, and now my ex has remarried. The kid doesn't want for fathers."

She liked it that he had an old Baldwin upright piano, a bookshelf with titles that looked as if they had actually been read, and on the wall was a framed movie poster from *The Violators*. Will explained how he had bought the townhouse from a P&G guy who had done the rehab as he showed her though the downstairs.

"Play something for me."

"I can't really," he said, embarrassment clouding him. "I tilt now."

"I'll sit next to you."

So they did. His fingers tentatively began *The Blue Danube*, gathering confidence as he went. It was all wrong: he couldn't use the pedals. "I played this by ear when I was six. It made my mother think I was some kind of musical genius. Hardly."

"I love it," Cheryl Beth said.

Then he tried "Isn't It Romantic" from memory. She leaned into him. It felt like magic.

He left on a low lamp as they walked back into the living room. She mock-pushed him onto the sofa and straddled him. Now the dress was much shorter and she didn't mind. She felt his hands on each side of her face as he pulled her in close for a kiss. It was easy to respond to his lips and she kissed back, using her tongue, too. He was a good kisser. Then his hands were on her hips, pulling her closer. But his eyes held a wariness.

"Don't be afraid," she whispered and kissed him deeply.

"I worry..."

"I have worries," she said. This confession didn't keep him from nibbling on her neck, which set many nodes of her nerves into a delighted alert status.

He whispered, "What?" His mouth again met hers again and their tongues danced around together.

"I worry you won't be a legs-and-butt man and you'll want a 44-D woman."

His face gave up a broad smile. "I am a legs-and-butt man, all the way, lifelong. You couldn't be more attractive to me, Cheryl Beth." His hands were moving up her legs inside her skirt. It had been a very long time since she had felt this, and he had a light, teasing touch.

She leaned back and touched his nose. "Then don't worry. Remember what I told you after your surgery when you were still in the hospital?"

"You told me to stick out my tongue and wiggle it. I did. And you said, 'You have all that any man needs to satisfy a woman.' "

He lightly licked her wrist, ran circles around it with his tongue, and kissed the inside of her forearm. She sighed happily. "Oh, you do remember that. I had said that to so many patients, but with you I was very…"

"You turned red."

"Yes, I did, because I was attracted to you, Detective."

"And I was to you, pain nurse." Will pulled her in for more kissing. It had been so long since he had been with a woman. And this woman had been on his mind for so long. Part of him could barely believe it was happening, that he could be doing this after his surgery and with the day-to-day of his disability. But all of him was enjoying it, with every kiss, touch, and pressure of body on body sweeping away his apprehensions.

As she rocked against his pelvis, she let out a moan.

Still, he felt an obligation, almost like the need to give her a Miranda warning. "What if I get another tumor and end up in a motorized wheelchair or dead?"

She felt heat spreading down to her feet. "What if I get hit by a bus tomorrow?" she whispered.

Then she was taking off his tie, unbuttoning his shirt. "So stop worrying. Anyway…" Her hand was playing with the fly of his slacks. "Something's happening down here."

"Mmmmm?"

"Now relax, sir, I'm a nurse."

They lay together in his bed upstairs, the room dark except for pale blue light filtering in from the street. Cheryl Beth looked forward to taking in the view Will's balcony displayed, but they had other things to do when they first came up to the room.

His suit and her black pantyhose were downstairs. She felt spent and completely content. His face looked almost boyish, his hair curled up on the pillow, and his sleepy eyes barely open.

He stuck out his tongue.

She smiled. "You're a very good bad boy, Will Borders."

Slipping on his dress shirt, his only piece of clothing that made it upstairs, she stepped out on the narrow balcony.

"This is beautiful," she called back inside. To her left, she could see the back of Christ Hospital.

"Down below is Jackson Hill Park," he said. "It's where the old Mount Auburn incline ran. Most people don't even know that park exists. I wish they wouldn't have torn out all the old inclines."

She stepped back inside, closed the door, and lay beside him again.

"By the way," he said. "You have perfect breasts."

She ran a hand down his chest. "I'm glad you like." She had always thought they were too small.

"And legs and mind and face and…"

"What was that clicking on your radio after we turned off the light downstairs?" she asked. "It was like, click-click, then a pause and it happened again."

"Oh, those jerks. They were only messing with me."

"I hope they couldn't hear us." She giggled, not really concerned.

Will explained how a double-click of a mic button could signify "okay" or "affirmative." After the second double-click, a dispatcher had come on to tell the units to keep the channel clear.

"You guys are as bad as nurses," she said, nestling her head into his shoulder. The sheets smelled like Will, and now like both of them, and that made her happy. His heart was beating normal sinus rhythm. That made her happy, too.

His right leg suddenly thrust up in a crooked position.

"Did you do that deliberately?"

"No, it's the spasticity. It usually kicks in an hour or so after I lie down. Then I have to sit up and shake my leg until it calms down, or I fall asleep in the chair and have bad dreams. Whine, whine, whine."

"Poor baby." She kissed his right thigh. It was remarkably muscled up compared with the left. "Here." She pushed it down and it immediately pulled back up. "Going to be stubborn, eh?" She rose up from beside him and swung across his leg, sitting on the quads. The muscles fought her but gradually eased up.

"Better?"

"It feels great."

Cheryl Beth felt a little sizzle from pressure of his quads between her legs, and managed, "Uh-huh."

She was about to come again when the phone rang.

Late-night phone calls were never good. As a pain nurse, Cheryl Beth knew they meant something was wrong with a patient, that she would have to throw on clothes and rush back to the hospital. She felt Will's body tense beside her but he made no attempt to answer. In a few seconds, a voice came on his machine. The voice sounded distorted, like a robot out of an old sci-fi movie.

"Detective Borders, are you fucking with me? 'Cause of death unknown…may be suicide.' Are you not taking me seriously? If your situation didn't interest me, I would immediately release the truth about my deathscapes to the public. Let the police be shown for fools. Let the city live in fear. I know you're there, detective. I know you can hear me. Don't assume you or the pretty nurse are safe…"

Will grabbed for the handset, nearly sending Cheryl Beth tumbling off the bed.

"Gone," he said and cursed. He spoke into his hand-held radio. "He called a minute ago. Did you get it on the land-line tap?"

"Affirmative, 7140. Too short for a trace. Sounded like the voice distortion machine you can buy in any spy shop."

"He's watching my house."

"It's all clear out here. He may have seen you at Fountain Square or the symphony."

Will set the radio back on the bedside table and pulled her close to him. She laid her head on his big chest and listened to his heart slowly stop its race. She could feel her own, whacking away under her sternum.

"He knows I'm a nurse," she whispered.

"Oh, baby, I'm so sorry I got you into this."

"You didn't." She liked it that he called her "baby." She said, "He killed three of my students. For all I know, I was in this before you were."

He stroked her hair and thought about that. Then: "Do you know how to handle a pistol?"

"My daddy taught me."

"Good. I won't let anyone hurt you."

"I know."

He started to speak again, but she held her hand against his cheek, "Now, hush," gently, and they held each other, skin on skin from face to toes, the best feeling in the world, no matter what waited tomorrow, what waited outside the bricks of the wall. She felt a brave peace.

Saturday

Chapter Twenty-six

Lieutenant Fassbinder called an all-hands meeting for ten. Everyone was fueling up on coffee and in a bad mood for being brought in on the weekend. Once again, Will was back on the fifth floor of 800 Broadway, sitting at his old desk. He was the only one not in a bad mood, and the reason, Cheryl Beth, was sitting in the waiting room.

"Ideas, people," Fassbinder was saying, pacing a trench in the floor. His voice was businesslike, but his hands kept clenching and unclenching. "I need ideas. The brass are on me like white on rice and that means I'm going to be kicking every little turd from them right down on you. Ideas!"

"We need somebody with Cheryl Beth," Dodds said.

Fassbinder stopped and gave Will a stare so filled with anger that no one would have been surprised if he had started foaming at the mouth. "I think Borders has that covered. Don't you, Detective Borders."

Dodds persisted. "Starting Monday, she's going to be back on the job. She's a target. Do you want me to replay…"

"No, I don't want you to replay the goddamned recording. We've heard it five times." Fassbinder stalked to Dodds' desk and rapped his fist on it. "Do you know how much overtime this is costing?"

"The chief said we could have unlimited overtime," Will said.

Fassbinder fixed him with the suppressed homicidal look again. "Well, your friend the chief doesn't cut me that kind of slack, Borders. My old man wasn't killed in the line of duty. I don't limp with a fucking cane. It's a week since Gruber's death and we don't have shit. That's the world I live in. The only thing Covington has is your goddamned son as a person of interest. *Your son!*"

"John only stepped on the boat," Will said. "After the murder took place. He voluntarily came forward as a witness."

The lieutenant ignored him. "Do you know we have eleven open homicides this year besides Gruber and this kid in the graveyard with his cock cut off? Last year, we had seventy-two and half of them are unresolved." He wheeled back around and continued pacing. "Skeen. You play nurse, starting Monday."

"I hope it's as much fun as playing doctor," she said, but no one laughed.

That gave Will some piece of mind. So did arming Cheryl Beth. He had given her his old backup weapon, a snub-nose .38 Chief's Special. It was small, lightweight, and lethal. When he handed it to her, butt-first, she immediately opened the cylinder to make sure it wasn't loaded. Then she hefted it and did some dry-firing. Will had kept it clean and oiled for years, and the mechanism worked like new. She had been taught well by her father. He loaded the revolver and she gently slid it into her purse.

Fassbinder kept talking, "I'm bringing in narcotics and Central Vice to help tail Borders." Everyone groaned and cursed. There was a long-standing feud between narcotics and homicide. Several years ago, a narc had tossed a firecracker into the homicide office. One of the old homicide detectives, now retired, had fashioned a bomb from a printer cartridge filled with shredded paper and set it off in narcotics as retaliation. It took them years to get the burned paper off the walls and desks. Unfortunately, Fassbinder had come over from narcotics four years before. So no one took it further than assorted "fucks" and "shits," spoken in the tone of members of the police department's most elite and seasoned unit.

"What do you want me to do?" Fassbinder said. "I need homicide detectives working this homicide case, not tailing Borders."

"What if the killer is on the force?" Dodds said. "Whoever wrote that note knew Will was working the case. We need to keep this in-house, inside homicide."

"No." Fassbinder said. "What are you still doing on Gruber, Borders?"

"I'm going though her old arrests and I have a disk off her hard drive with twenty-one-hundred photos, give or take."

"Hand off the arrest records to Kovach," Fassbinder said. "He's the new liaison with Covington, too. You've got a conflict of interest. Dodds, make sure you have the Gruber casebook from Borders. He can go through the pics while he's sitting at home." He wagged a finger at Will. "And that's what you will do when you're not on a PIO call. Now, people, listen up: I don't want to get distracted with this Oxford homicide. Focus on Gruber. What do we know?"

Will said, "Lieutenant, Gruber is connected to the Oxford murders, and sooner or later somebody is going to put this together and it's going to be public. We have four murders in four days committed by the same guy. Jack the Ripper only killed five in two months, and then he disappeared forever. What if this guy does the same? Covering our asses will be the least of our worries."

"Oxford P.D. and Butler County have agreed to sit on our story for now," Fassbinder said. "Nobody's mourning Noah Smith and calling the media about him."

"These killings are all connected," Will said. "We need to go public."

A long, furious silence sat in the room. Finally Will went through Kristen Gruber's last twenty-four hours. She had worked day shift out of Central Vice a week ago Friday, made eight routine arrests, nobody resisting or making threats. She went off duty and spent Friday night with her sergeant friend at her condo. They had breakfast at First Watch at Rookwood Pavilion on Saturday morning a week ago. At 2:38 p.m., she withdrew a hundred dollars from an ATM. Sometime after that, she took her boat out from the marina. Nobody saw her leave. Not one tip had a witness placing her on the water; therefore, they didn't know who was on the boat with her.

Fassbinder said, "I want something real, and I goddamned want it before Sunday night." He called out names and assignments, and Will knew springtime weekend plans with families were being demolished.

Will tried to stay in the zone of the previous night, with Cheryl Beth sitting astride him on the sofa and lying beside him in bed. He could still feel her sweet breath on his eyelashes. He said quietly, "I want to bring in Kenneth Buchanan for an interview."

The room was silent for a good minute. Even the radio monitoring eight police frequencies didn't make a sound.

Will made his case: the attorney gave a false story about his whereabouts a week ago Saturday night; he was Kristen's estranged lover who said he was jealous of her other men, jealous enough to fight with her about it. He moored his boat next to hers at the marina, he phoned her on Saturday afternoon, and a middle-aged bald man had stalked one of the Oxford victims. Kenneth Buchanan was a middle-aged bald man.

"Are you out of your mind?" Fassbinder said. "He'd call every city councilman, the mayor, the chief, and have a harassment lawsuit filed first thing Monday."

"He said he was with his wife Saturday night. He wasn't. She told a thousand people last night that she was at the symphony last Saturday night, listening to Jeremy Snowden play for the last time, and then she went to a party with the musicians. So either he was with her, and he lied to me about going to the symphony, and why the hell would he do that? Or he lied because he wasn't with her. He was on the river. Let's bring him in."

Fassbinder shook his head. "You call that probable cause? You're crazy, Borders. We can't do that."

"Why not?" Dodds said. "Because he's white? Because he's rich and lives in Indian Hill? If we had the same P.C. against some black kid in Avondale, he'd be in jail."

"Don't." Fassbinder aimed a finger. His face was nearly crimson.

"Just sayin'. You didn't complain when I brought in the guy who did the cello player. Right color, I guess…" Dodds knew how to push everybody's buttons. It was one of his useful characteristics, as long as you weren't on the receiving end.

Will persisted. "Let's put a tail on Buchanan. See where he goes. Let's interview people at the marina about him. Maybe somebody saw him leave on Saturday evening in his own boat."

"No." Fassbinder's eyes were bloodshot with anger. "I mean it, Borders. You're hanging by a thread here. I'll take your pension. I'll make sure you end up on Social Security disability eating dog food. Do not go off the reservation. The only reason I don't bring you up right now is the chance our guy might try to kill you."

Dodds caught up with Will and Cheryl Beth at the elevators.

"Fassbinder was way out of line," he said, "bringing up your father like that. The whole unit thinks so."

"Thanks," Will said, feeling raw and tired from the meeting.

"I'll have your back," Dodds said. "You ask for it, I'll do it. I think I can speak for everybody."

"Then you be the one who tails me today. Keep the others away for a few hours."

Dodds didn't ask why. He merely nodded.

Chapter Twenty-seven

Cheryl Beth arrived well before the service was scheduled to begin. She hadn't been to Dayton in years. It was still a pretty city, laid out in a valley where the Great Miami River makes a wide bend. But she was stunned by the sense of collapse: the shuttered factories, empty buildings, and dead downtown. Even NCR's headquarters was gone. It was the story of the Midwest now.

She diligently checked her rearview mirror, but was sure she wasn't being followed. She felt Will's absence and thought about the previous night. She had held her love for a long time and now she could see herself falling for this man. He was smart and gentle. She was not a girl now, and yet she felt emotions that made her feel seventeen. All her life, she had wanted to be kissed in Fountain Square underneath the statue with its falling waters. Will Borders was the man who had done that for her. It was thrilling and frightening. She had never let a man this close, this fast. Yet it felt right.

Through the thin partition at the homicide bureau, she had heard the raised voice directed at Will. She didn't want to hate his lieutenant but it was hard. His father had been killed when Will was only twenty-two, a rookie patrolman. It was one of their bonds: she had lost her father when she was ten. She had felt like an orphan girl after that day. She was now older than her father was when he died.

Woodland Cemetery was a lovely garden of graves southeast of downtown Dayton. Everything was blooming and budding.

She parked behind the long procession of cars and made her way across the grass to a group of three dozen people. Her students all came, and for a long time they stood in a tight circle, hugging and talking.

Then she introduced herself to Lauren Benish's parents. They were only a little older than her, but had the shattered, numb look of the grieving. She had seen it so many times in the hospital. It contained a special dark quality when it was a parent facing the death of a child. To outlive your child: she knew it so well and struggled not to let her own tears turn into sobs.

April Benish looked nothing like her sister. She was short, trim, and blond. Her work as an R.N. at Miami Valley Hospital had inspired Lauren to go into the nursing program. She and Cheryl Beth had a long, deliberately light conversation while everyone waited for the minister. Lauren's casket sat in a silver frame, a spray of lilies on the top, the hole in the ground in which it would descend kept well concealed.

Then April struggled through a eulogy, even mentioning Cheryl Beth as Lauren's favorite instructor. It embarrassed and moved her. Lauren's brother played a guitar and sang *Amazing Grace* in a scratchy tenor voice. She closed her eyes and listened to the minister. She was very conscious of the revolver in her purse as the reverend started his talk.

"Friends, we have gathered here to praise God and to witness to our faith as we celebrate the life of Lauren Benish. We are here together in grief, recognizing our human loss. But beyond these tears, we celebrate Lauren's life. We pray that God grants us grace, that in pain we may find comfort, in sadness hope, in death resurrection..."

Cheryl Beth tried to pay attention. Lauren's death was so senseless, the act so evil. The man who did it was still out there, and maybe even here. She looked around the cemetery with fresh, suspicious eyes. Will was aware she was coming up here to the memorial service, but she knew he didn't want her to play amateur sleuth. Still, her gaze patrolled the crowd.

She joined in by rote: "Our Father, who art in heaven, hallowed be thy name..." hearing an echo with the other voices among her.

Someone had sought out Lauren, Holly, and Noah. Was it even someone in her classes? Could it have been one of the janitors who cleaned the classrooms in Hamilton? Patients: what creepy or odd people had Lauren cared for as a student nurse? She would have to go back through the records. No one immediately came to mind.

None of this would explain the murder of Kristen Gruber. She was a cop. But a monster that saw murder as an art chose each of the victims. She looked for a bald man, found none, looked for a serial killer out of a movie, a creepy unshaven fat man or a sleek sinister-looking figure. All she saw were people fighting unbearable sorrow. She thought about Will and took comfort.

"...Keep true in us the love with which we hold one another..."

It had been years since Cheryl Beth had been to church. She considered herself a believer, and certainly spiritual. But something about leaving a small town where church attendance was mandatory, whatever was in your heart, had driven her away from organized religion. Or maybe she was lazy. She would have to think about that.

"...In all our ways we trust you. O Lord, all that you have given us is yours. You gave Lauren to us and she enriched all our lives. Now we give Lauren back to you..."

And suddenly it was over and people were walking away in twos and threes, the car engines starting amid the silence in a cruel benediction that life would go on. When Cheryl Beth felt the brush against her sleeve, she jumped.

"I'm sorry!"

The young woman beside her had short brown hair parted in the middle, a pleasant heartland face, and permanently sleepy eyes. She apologized again and introduced herself as Melissa.

"April said I should talk to you."

"What about?"

She hesitated. "Lauren. I was with her that night at Brick Street."

"The bar in Oxford?"

The woman nodded. "Lauren and I were best friends since high school. We both went to Miami. But I saw less of her after she started spending more time in Hamilton for the nursing classes. So we decided to catch up that day. We went riding, and then we changed and came into Oxford to have a few drinks."

"When was this?"

"It was two weeks before..." She looked away at the casket, where only Lauren's parents now stood wordlessly.

"Two Saturdays before she was killed?" Cheryl Beth asked.

"Exactly."

Melissa said the bar was crowded and they were standing, drinking beers, when a man approached Lauren and started a conversation.

"He was very funny. He obviously knew how to talk to girls."

"What did he look like?"

"I didn't get a great look at him. At first, I was pretty much ignoring him. Then I got separated from Lauren and was talking with some friends at a table. He had a great body. It wasn't that warm outside, but he wore tight jeans and a T-shirt. He was very well built. He had no hair. He was bald or shaved his head, and didn't have a beard or anything."

"Middle-aged?" Cheryl Beth said. "April told me that Lauren said it was a middle-aged man."

"Lauren couldn't tell age. This guy might have been a little older, but not like my father, you know? He was obviously more interested in Lauren than me. I was used to that. She was always the pretty one." She stifled a sob. "She told me he said he was an artist and wanted her to model for him."

The skin on the back of Cheryl Beth's neck tingled. It was enough to make her look around to confirm that they were alone.

"And Lauren said no..."

"That was when he got mean. By that time I was watching them. He called her names, really nasty stuff. I swear to God he went from Mister Charisma to Mister Creep in a heartbeat. She wasn't mean to him. But she had a boyfriend and wasn't interested in whatever this guy wanted. The bartender told him to leave and I went back over to Lauren to make sure she was all right."

"Was he a student, Melissa?"

"I'd never seen him before around campus, but there are fourteen thousand students. Something about him didn't fit in…" She dug in her purse and produced a cigarette. "Do you mind?"

"No." In the presence of so much else that could kill a person, Cheryl Beth wasn't going to give a healthy living lecture. Melissa lit up and took a long, deep drag.

"This reminds me," she said. "Sense memory. I'm a theater major. Lauren and I ducked outside a few minutes later to have a smoke. And he was there, maybe half a block away, watching us. He was under a streetlight. His look was really unnerving. We got a couple of guys to walk us to our cars that night."

"Lauren told April she thought this man was stalking her."

"She told me the same thing. We talked on the phone and texted, I didn't see her again. But I know she saw him once at Hamilton and again on campus at Oxford. Both times, he started following her."

"Oh, my god. Why didn't she go to the police? That would have been the first thing I did."

"She thought she was being paranoid. She thought if she ignored him he'd go away." The reality set into her tear-reddened eyes. "Do you think he was the one who…?"

"Have you talked to the police?"

"I got back to town this morning," Melissa said. "I've been in Chicago for a week. When I heard about Lauren, I went to pieces. I thought they had the killer in custody."

"They had the wrong man."

Cheryl Beth dug into her purse and handed her Will's card. "I want you to call this man. He's investigating this case. You need to tell him everything you told me." She thought about it. "What are you doing this afternoon?"

"Well, I…"

"I want you to come back to Cincinnati with me, Melissa. This is life or death."

She wore her tough nurse expression and the young woman didn't argue. They walked toward their cars.

Cheryl Beth ran the new information through her head. Then, "So this guy picked Lauren out of a crowded bar?"

"I guess so," Melissa said, blowing a plume of blue smoke away from them. "No. No, that's not true. He said he'd seen us that day on the bike trail."

"What bike trail?"

"On the Loveland bike trail."

Chapter Twenty-eight

The bad thing about stakeouts in Indian Hill was that the wealthy enclave was built for privacy, with winding streets, cul-de-sacs and plenty of trees. The good thing about Kenneth Buchanan's manse was its proximity to Indian Hill Middle School. Nobody could come or go from the dead-end street without passing the school. Will pulled into the parking lot and shut down the car, preparing himself for the dullest part of the job. In any event, he wasn't going to sit and wait for the killer. He was going after him. Only Dodds knew he was here. Now, if only Buchanan was home, and if only nothing major happened that required the PIO. So far, the radio was quiet.

It was difficult to think of much beyond Cheryl Beth. He was worried about her going to Dayton for the dead girl's funeral. Mostly, he kept reprising their night together. He had gotten and maintained an erection, no small accomplishment. That he had even kissed, much less made love with this woman seemed like an impossible fantasy. Yet it was real, and he had slept last night without dreaming. Now, he missed her intensely.

The dark Mercedes hurried past, going south, Buchanan's distinctive head clearly visible.

"That didn't take long." He started the Crown Vic and sped out of the parking lot.

Buchanan turned onto Shawnee Run Road and Will gave him a quarter-mile distance as they passed more expensive real estate and made the green light at Miami Road. A car from St. Gertrude's Church pulled between them. That was good, especially when the driver matched Buchanan's speed. The three vehicles continued west to Camargo Road. Buchanan barely stopped and turned south again. Will did the same. Camargo cut through hills and thick trees. Traffic was light and Will gave him plenty of distance. A right on Madison and they were headed toward the city. Big cotton-ball clouds were floating in the sky.

"7140, check in."

If it would have been anyone's voice but Dodds', his gut would have tightened.

"7140, all secure."

Two clicks of the mic responded. Anybody listening thought Will was still at home.

By this time, they were crossing Red Bank Expressway and almost to the point where Madison juked southwest. Buchanan could have taken Red Bank north to hit the interstate. He didn't. He was definitely headed into the city. Traffic was getting thicker and Will worked to close the gap, letting two cars stay between him and the Mercedes, but sticking close enough that he wouldn't get caught at a light. As it was, they moved at a unit, making and stopping at the same intersections. As they passed through Oakley, Will thought of ice cream with Cheryl Beth. That hadn't even been a week ago.

They stayed on Madison past the Rookwood shopping center, which was packed, past the edge of Hyde Park and the Cincinnati Country Club and the old mansions of Annwood Park and Scarborough Woods. The street changed as they approached the imposing St. Francis de Sales Catholic Church and touched East Walnut Hills. The traffic became thicker still, and Will had to gun it to make the light at Woodburn. Madison became Dr. Martin Luther King Drive and Buchanan turned south again on Gilbert, for the long dip into downtown past old factories that had been turned into offices. Buchanan was driving into his own downtown office on a Saturday. Oh, how Will wished he were going to the marina to get on his boat.

But he did neither. He crossed over Interstate 71, got on Reading Road, and then turned again on Liberty Street. The steeples, spires and towers of the old city spread out ahead. It was as if he were driving to Will's house. Will was about to alert Dodds when Buchanan sped past the familiar turnoff and kept going. They were in the heart of the city now. People were on the sidewalks. It occurred to Will that all this time he had been following Buchanan, he had never checked to see if someone was following him. The rearview mirror looked benign, but would he really know?

They drove straight through Over-the-Rhine doing fifty, making every light. Buchanan slowed at Linn Street and turned left, barely missing a pedestrian. Will was right behind him. It couldn't be helped if he was going to make the light. Now he backed off and gave the Mercedes plenty of room. Only an unmarked police car in the West End, where the old housing projects once stood—nothing suspicious, Mr. Buchanan, drive on. Enjoy the majestic half rotunda of Union Terminal off to your right. They were not far from the Laurel Homes, now demolished, where Will's father had been gunned down on a domestic abuse call. It was a reality never far from his mind.

After several blocks more, Linn lifted up over the massive gash of Interstate 75. Buchanan turned west again on Eighth Street and they plunged into the warehouse district and under the railroad tracks. The main police channels remained on routine business.

Now Will was growing curious. Despite what many east-siders thought, there were some lovely neighborhoods west of I-75, the Sauerkraut Curtain—although old-timers applied that term to Vine Street—but Buchanan was not driving into one. When the sunlight found them again on the other side of the railroad underpass, they were in Lower Price Hill. He could keep going and follow Glenway's rightward arch around the tree-covered bluff ahead of them and keep going uphill. But he was slowing down.

They weren't on a hill. The real Price Hill was directly ahead, and it, too, had once been connected with an incline railway, but Will couldn't say exactly where. Lower Price Hill was in the basin above a broad swoop of the Ohio River, and although the city had designated it a historic district that couldn't make up for the blight and crime. He had been on a shooting call here a week ago Wednesday, on Neave Street. Many of the rowhouses held the classic Italianate features found in Over-the-Rhine, but few people were trying to gentrify the properties. Vacant lots and junk cars proliferated. It was slowly falling apart.

If Kenneth Buchanan "spoke Cincinnati," he would know that he was among the briars, the local term for poor Appalachian whites. This had long been a closed, clannish part of town. Once the briars had migrated down the river, then on the railroads, finding decent jobs in the factories around the rail yards of Mill Creek. It was their way out of the coalmines. Now most of those manufacturing jobs were gone. The factories were being gutted, their scrap sold to China. Some of the junkyards were in this neighborhood. Poverty was high. The place was also growing more African-American, and that made for racially charged confrontations. Like most of the older, poorer parts of the city, it was losing population.

And here was Kenneth Buchanan, white-shoe downtown lawyer.

He turned down two-lane State Avenue, going twenty-five. Will waited for the red light and sat, watching him slow. Then a truck passed, obscuring the view, and when it was gone so was Buchanan's Mercedes.

Will turned left and cruised slowly down the street. Some large old multi-story brick apartments were on the left, and a few forlorn rowhouses stood on the right.

"Hello," he said to himself.

Buchanan had parked in an empty lot next to a two-story brick rowhouse that had lost both its siblings. The front windows were boarded up with old wood and the paintless door looked barely on its hinges. Buchanan's car was empty. Will picked up speed, went to the next intersection, turned around, and found a place behind a rusty pickup truck. He called Dodds.

"Guess where I am?"

"Hope it's more interesting than my life, sitting outside a cop's house."

"Lower Price Hill. Buchanan drove over here. He parked and went inside a house."

"No shit?" Dodds thought about it. "Maybe he's a secret meth head."

"Maybe." Will watched a young man with mussed light-brown hair, hard-muscled in a wife-beater shirt, walk past giving him the eye. He ignored him. "It's about the last place I'd expect him. You see anything around my place?"

"Nope," Dodds said. "I'm encouraging my hemorrhoids."

Will made a note of the address and waited. It took nearly half an hour before Buchanan stepped down on the crumbling sidewalk and walked purposefully to his car. He was wearing a light-blue shirt, tan slacks, and expensive tasseled shoes. His face was set in a hard look, and he didn't even turn his head in Will's direction. Then the expensive car's backup lights flared and it was on the street. Will decided to stay.

It was another half hour before Will saw movement at the door. First a bicycle tire, then the whole bike being pushed by a woman. She wore blue jeans and a Bengals T-shirt, but what you first noticed was her hair, vivid red and flowing down over her shoulders. She swung a leg over the bicycle seat and pedaled north. Will let her go for a moment, then started the car and followed slowly. Her hair caught the sun and wind, making a lovely orange sail.

"7140, 7140."

He muttered a profanity and picked up the mic.

The dispatcher came back: "Meet the officers, signal nine, Queensgate Playfield. We have a sixteen at large. Respond Code three."

"7140 responding."

It was a shooting with a suspect at large. He gripped the steering wheel tighter but stayed on the girl.

She stopped at Meisner's market and went inside, bike and all. Will parked in front.

No more than two minutes later, she came back out, stuffing a red-and-white carton of Marlboroughs in her purse. She started to swing over the bike, when he tapped the horn. She looked him over and ignored him. He hit the emergency lights and she paid attention.

He flashed his badge when she came to the driver's side. "Climb in."

"What about my bike?"

"Lean it against the front of the car where we can watch it." For all he knew, it was one of the few things she owned in the world. As she did so, he tossed his cane in the back seat.

Once she was in the car, he could see her more clearly. She was younger than he had first assumed, and her fiery hair framed a lovely face, the home to startlingly blue eyes. Her features were uniformly delicate and her skin was as flawless as Kristen Gruber's. Put her in different circumstances on the east side and she would have worlds offered to her.

"I didn't do anything."

"I didn't say you did," Will said. Time was running against him, even if the call location was close. If Fassbinder knew what he was really doing, all his dreams of revenge could be quickly visited on Will's head. He kept the agitation out of his voice. "You had a visitor a few minutes ago, well-dressed man, middle-aged."

"So?"

"So, are you a pro?"

"No! I don't turn tricks, don't do drugs." She pointed out the window at a passing man. "Why don't you people do something about the niggers overrunning our neighborhood, instead of hassling me?"

East side, west side, race was never far below the surface in Cincinnati.

"What's your name?"

"Jill."

He asked her to show him her driver's license and wrote down the information: Jill Evangeline Bailey and the addressed matched the shabby place she had come from. She was nineteen.

"You ever been in trouble, Jill?"

"No."

"Not even a DUI?"

She shook her head.

"You have a job?"

"I'm a waitress at Tucker's. I ride the bus."

"So how do you know Kenneth Buchanan?"

She hesitated and ran her hands though her hair.

"Is that his name?"

"That's his name and you didn't answer my question. This is a homicide investigation."

Her small frame went rigid. "I don't know anything about any homicide." Her voice became small and trailed off into silence. Finally, "He gave me some money."

Will waited a few beats. "Why would he do that?"

"I didn't do anything!" The blue eyes filled with tears. "I was raped last fall by one of these niggers and you people didn't do anything about it. He dragged me right behind that church one night and raped me three damned times. Right there behind a house of God. This used to be a safe neighborhood. Now the white people can't even go out at night. You people never caught him. You never even tried…"

"I'm sorry."

"Don't think I wouldn't be gone from this shithole in a heartbeat, but after my momma died that house is all I have. I don't even have a car."

"Now you have some money from Mister Buchanan."

She stared out the window.

"He wants me to get an abortion."

"How many months along are you?" She wasn't showing.

"Six weeks."

"And it's his baby?"

Again, her silence, and the clock tormenting him. He had to be an asshole cop. "Jill! Talk to me, right here, right now, or downtown and as long as it takes. I don't care. You'll only mean more overtime pay for me. Maybe your bike will be here when we get back, probably not. I guarantee you one thing: we'll take as much time as we need to find out why you were screwing a big-time lawyer."

"It's his son, okay? His son and I had sex. One time. I got pregnant. How insane is that? One time and I'm pregnant. Now he wants me to go away."

If it was the same son, Will thought of the foul-mouthed young man in the ball cap he had encountered at Music Hall.

"You didn't ask for money?"

"No! I want to have this baby!" she yelled. "I won't kill it."

"Sounds like a case of blackmail to me. That's against the law. You won't look so pretty after ten years in prison, Jill."

"His dad gave the money to me! I didn't ask for anything! I didn't want anything. I'm sorry I ever told Mike I was pregnant. After he found out, he never took my calls again. Then I started getting calls from his father. He threatened to sue me and take my house. He said I'd taken advantage of his son. As if! I was afraid."

Yes, he was an asshole cop. He had never seen a human being look more helpless. And here was Kenneth Buchanan cleaning up his son's casual disaster. He thought about John and his own cleaning up, the knife that he had stashed in his dresser drawer.

"How much did he pay you?"

She stared into her small lap. "Ten thousand dollars."

He let her get the bike and ride off, then lit up his unmarked cruiser, turned east on Eighth, and accelerated to sixty, the big twin-turbocharged Interceptor engine sounding like a fighter jet closing in on its target.

Chapter Twenty-nine

Melissa spent three hours with Dodds and a police artist. More overtime for Fassbinder to bitch about. She kept protesting that she hadn't gotten a great look at the suspect, that the bar had been too dim, but a sketch was produced. At five p.m., Will called all the television and radio stations, as well as the city desk at the *Enquirer*: a press conference would be held in an hour regarding the Gruber murder. That would be enough to draw a crowd. It was agreed that Will would conduct the briefing, the chief overruling Fassbinder's objections. Will was the one the killer knew, the one he had threatened.

Once again, the room at police headquarters was flooded with television lights. Will wore a dark suit and French blue shirt with a blue-and-burgundy rep tie. He was flanked by the brass and tried not to tilt or hold on too tightly to the podium.

"Thank you for coming," he began. Cheryl Beth sat in the front row and gave him a secret smile. "Tonight we want to tell you about a new development in the investigation of the murder of Officer Kristen Gruber. What's being passed around is a sketch of a person of interest in the case. You can also see it on the screen to my right. He's a white male, twenty-five to thirty years of age, at least six-feet-three inches tall, muscular build, and bald."

The room rustled with paper and whispers. He waited for it to die down. "Based on our investigation, witness interviews, and a profile of the murderer, I can tell you a few things. He's a loner and has an anger-management problem that would be noticeable to his friends and family. He might have threatened them. This person might have been seen around the Seven Hills Marina last weekend. He might also have been on the Loveland Bicycle Trail." He slowed down the next part: "This suspect is impotent and was probably sexually abused as a child." Maybe those words would smoke him out. He heard a still camera clicking. "It is entirely possible that the person of interest shown in this sketch is our murderer. He is extremely dangerous. If you see this man, you should call nine-one-one immediately. We won't be taking any questions tonight. Thank you for coming."

It was eight before they had dinner at Joe's Diner on Sycamore. The old standby with its chrome walls and a neon sign had been revived from the riots. It was only a few blocks from home. The night was gentled by light rain, and the streets shone. Inside, they got a table without a wait and talked about the day over burgers, fries, and onion rings. "I'll eat onion rings if you will," she said, and it was decided. He praised her again for finding the witness and convincing her to come down immediately. She asked about his shadowing of Kenneth Buchanan, and he told the story.

"Do you still think Buchanan did it?"

Will took in a deep breath, took stock. "I don't know. Sometimes in this job you have to avoid the hammer and nail thing…" She smiled widely, a beautiful thing. "When you're the hammer, everything looks like a nail."

"I feel for that girl," Cheryl Beth said. "But ten thousand dollars is a lot of money."

"Not in Buchanan's world. And, he wants her to go away. I wonder how many other times he's had to bail out his son's stupid mistakes."

He talked about John and the parallels.

"You love him," she said. The words made him uncomfortable in that context. He couldn't say exactly why. It was something to do with the many separations and alienations of recent years: Cindy drawing apart, then a complete rupture, John's sullen and difficult adolescence, and then the reappearance of his biological father.

"I think my old man would have let me spend a night in jail to get my mind right," he said. Comfortable in her presence, he talked about his dad. He wasn't cruel or abusive, a typical father of his era. He didn't want to be your buddy and you damned sure weren't his equal. "We didn't have a bunch of stuff. We didn't go shopping for recreation. I don't know. I see kids like John, or this Buchanan son, or the one who was piloting the boat on Saturday night. They're ruined by money."

"I never got that chance," she said.

"I hear you."

He went on. "My dad really disapproved of me becoming a police officer. He wanted me to be a lawyer. 'Something respectable,' he'd say. I never understood why he devalued himself that way." He felt safe enough with her to go on. "I was working the night he was shot. I was on patrol, District Five, up around Winton Hills. He was a patrol sergeant in District One. Could have been a captain, a fine detective. But he couldn't stand the politics, he disliked the detectives, and he liked the street. So, that night was busy in his district. He was the first on the scene. A couple was mixing it up in the projects, dad went in and separated them, and the man came back with a gun in his hand and shot him. Once right in the heart." He had to slow down. "And that was that."

She reached across and took his hand, holding it tight.

The food arrived and Will let her take the first onion ring; she preferred the small ones. "A perfect match," he said. "I like the big ones."

He lowered his voice. "If Buchanan's not our guy, I don't even know where to begin. Her two other boyfriends have solid alibis. They've found another guy she had an affair with a year ago. He moved to Denver last August, swears it was an amiable separation, he hadn't heard from her since. He has an alibi, too." He bit into the ring and soon the whole thing was gone. "Except for your witness, nothing's going our way. If he doesn't make a move against me, we're screwed." He sighed. "And here I am putting you at risk, too"

"We've been through that," she said. "I hope you don't have that many girlfriends going." She put a straw in her mouth and sipped Diet Coke.

"Only one, but she's really hot."

"So tell me how you tailed this guy, got an emergency call, and didn't get caught."

He laughed loudly and any weight of the day or the past flew off.

They were still laughing as they left an hour later. The rain had stopped so they did not get soaked as Will did his slow-walk with the cane to the car, which was parked in a lot across Grear Alley. One big building, once the School for Creative and Performing Arts, filled the view to the north. Sirens were yowling off to the west. He opened the door for Cheryl Beth and closed it. Then he walked around the car, making an inventory of their surroundings, touching the raindrops on the trunk and fenders. His right hand was hurting from holding the cane. A couple was fighting fifty feet away. A man yelled, "You think because you're beautiful and men want to fuck you…"

As he started to open the door, he felt something hard and cold right behind his left ear.

"Hello Detective Borders." The voice was low, barely audible. "Your friends aren't tailing you tonight." A small laugh. "I guess they went for donuts. You've been searching for Kristen's gun. I thought I'd bring it to you." The barrel tapped hard against his skull. The fighting couple got in their car and drove away. They were alone in the lot now.

"Now don't think about doing anything cute," the voice said. "You're going to do exactly what I say."

If Will were not crippled, he would teach this man cute. If Will didn't yearn for a future with Cheryl Beth, and couldn't take chances with her so near, he would give this a lesson. When somebody was holding a gun that close, it was possible to quickly step inside the reach of his arm, inside his firing radius, and disarm him. It was easier when done from the front, but he could do it. He once could have done it.

The hoarse whisper continued: "The first thing you're going to do is pull out your gun, left hand, please. Then toss it in front of you."

"That's not going to happen." Will decided not to attempt to turn his head and look at the man.

"You're going to do it, or I'll shoot you now. Is that your friend, Cherry Beth, sitting there? She's going to find out if I'm impotent like you said. I'll fuck the little cunt in every orifice and then watch her die slowly. There's nothing you can do about it. How does that make you feel, detective?"

He almost looked back, stopped himself. Will was very conscious of each breath, how it barely seemed to fill his lungs. He could see Cheryl Beth's legs and lap, but couldn't tell if she could make out his predicament. He asked, "Why did you pick me to send your messages?"

"Later. I may answer your questions, or not. But right now, quit stalling and pull out your gun with your left hand, toss it on the pavement in front of you."

Breath in, breath out. His right wrist was aching, his hand gripping the cane tightly. His gun was an impossible six inches away.

"Agh!"

Will heard this half-grunt, half expression of pain as the gun that had been behind his ear went airborne and landed a few feet in front of the bumper. Somehow it didn't go off. A black-clad figure fell to his side and rolled.

Another man yelled, "Motherfucka', what you think you doin'?" Then he kicked Will's assailant in the side. "This here's an officer of the law. Don't you be disrespecting the po-lice!"

Will said, "Junior?"

"I made bail. Glad to see me?"

Indeed, it was the gang thug he had stopped from stomping the man beside Central Parkway on Monday. The shadow on the asphalt vaulted up and ran. Oh, to see a face, but there was none. And he had hair.

"Yes," Will said, drawing his service weapon, "glad to see you. Get down."

But big Junior was chasing the other man and blocking Will's aim.

"I'm gonna nail you, sucka'. Citizen's arrest! "

"Get down, Junior!"

Junior's three-hundred-pounds made the chase last, at best, a third of the way across the parking lot. Then he was bent over, struggling to catch his breath. The time elapsed for the clumsy pursuit, with Junior's huge body in the way of Will's aim, consumed no more then ten seconds. But it was enough. The man in black was gone.

Chapter Thirty

Two hours later, the twenty marked and unmarked units that responded to Will's broadcast had scattered. The suspect was gone. The unmarked unit shadowing Will and Cheryl Beth had been drawn off by a report of a shooting three blocks away. It wasn't a shooting. Someone had rigged a fuse with a cigarette to a string of M-80s which did a good job of impersonating gunshots. By the time the unmarked car from Central Vice got back to the parking lot, Will had already taken off, searching for the man who had held Kristen Gruber's gun to his head. And it was Gruber's—the serial number matched.

Now they cruised slowly through Over-the-Rhine. Cheryl Beth sat in the passenger front seat, Dodds in back. Nobody talked at first. She was certain that if she were hooked up to an EKG her heart would still show tachycardia. She blamed herself for those moments when Will was in mortal danger. The car had cloaked her from the threat he was facing. She couldn't see what was happening until the gun flew in front of the car and the big black man was chasing someone. Will had given her gloves and told her to retrieve the gun, then, when she returned, he had revved the car across the parking lot, its spotlight sending a dazzling white cone against buildings and into alleys. After that, it seemed as if the entire police force had descended upon them.

"Here we are again," Dodds said. "The three musketeers."

"Let's hope it's a little easier this time," Cheryl Beth said. "Last time, we were trapped in the basement of the hospital, nobody knew where we were, the killer had knocked you out, he was beating the crap out of me, and Will, who was stuck in a wheelchair, had to save us."

"Details, details," Dodds said.

Cheryl Beth prided herself on a professional steely calm, hard won in the five years she had spent working in the emergency department. But that was a controlled environment compared with this, even when a gang member would try to barge in and finish off the guy he shot an hour before. She hated to admit it: she was over her head. She stuffed her shaking hands into her lap. Her emotions roiled in a wild bundle of fear and adrenaline, some anger was down in there, too. The son of a bitch had nearly killed Will and he got away, almost as if he were a ghost. The city seemed bathed in an invisible evil.

Will stopped at Central Parkway and Vine, where he pointed to the grand mural on the building on the southwest corner. It looked like a statue standing inside a temple.

"Cincinnatus," he said. "The entire face of the building is blank, and everything you see is a trompe l'oeil painting. 'Trick of the eye.' Done by Richard Haas to mark Kroger's centennial."

"I like the statue of him down at Sawyer's Point better," Dodds said. "Looks like a real bad-ass. He saved Rome, refused to be dictator for life, and went back to his plow. If it hadn't been for Cincinnatus, we'd be called Losantiville."

"Well, technically, we were named after the Society of the Cincinnati, the Revolutionary War veterans," Will said.

"Okay, know it all," Dodds said. "What was that building called?"

Will shrugged.

"The Brotherhood Building," Dodds said. "Which is appropriate as the gateway to Over-the-Rhine, where all the brothers are hoods."

Cheryl Beth felt her face smile. That was a start, at least, to feeling human again.

Will turned north onto Vine and began an impromptu tour of Over-the-Rhine. A turn of the wheel, and they entered a different world. He pointed out this building in the Italianate style, that one in federal, a hidden garden behind another, and the commercial buildings with their cast-iron fronts. Renaissance revival, Romanesque, Queen Anne. Some had been restored, most had not. She thought the neighborhood was stunning, despite its problems. It held an intimacy and living history that appealed to her. Its streets were meant to be walked to be really appreciated, but the slow drive with Will's narration was the next best thing. He wore his knowledge lightly and it was coated in the sweetness of his joy of the place.

A man who liked something other than sports and cars: that was a find.

She also realized he was doing this to calm down, and it was helping to calm her, too.

He jigged over to Walnut and lingered in front of the Germania Building with its statue, a woman in a robe, holding a shield. She stood on a setback in the second story of the ornate building.

"This was the German Mutual Insurance Company," he said. "In World War I, the anti-German feeling was so hysterical, the company became Hamilton Mutual and they draped the statue. They renamed a bunch of the streets, too. English Street used to be German Street. Bremen Street became Republic…"

"You see what it's like to ride with Mister President," Dodds said.

"Cheryl Beth, do you know what J.C.'s nickname was when he played football at UC?"

"Now don't start that!" Dodds grumbled.

"It was 'Sweet Dreams' Dodds."

"Sweet Dreams." Cheryl Beth suppressed a laugh. "I assume that's because you hit the other guys so hard it sent them to nap time, along with a potential concussion."

"Damn straight." Dodds adjusted his posture. "See, she gets it."

"Then why are you aggravated when I bring it up?"

Dodds faked a punch at the back of Will's head. "Man, Borders knows every building, every cobblestone here. He's a frustrated architect."

"Maybe an architectural historian," Will said. "I hate most modern architecture. Except for the Contemporary Arts Center and the P&G headquarters."

"Which looks like Dolly Parton's..." Dodds stopped himself.

"Oh, please," Cheryl Beth said. "Everybody calls them the Dolly Parton Towers. Nurses can match cops any day in inappropriate language. We're as weird as you guys."

Dodds chuckled.

"If we're going to have to do this," he said, "Why don't you drive over to the Samuel Adams Brewery. While you regale Cheryl Beth with Over-the-Rhine's beer history, I'll break in and get us a six pack."

"This is the heart and soul of the city," Will said.

"It's the heart and soul of scumbaggery," Dodds said.

"Jeez, Dodds, some guy killed five people in a little town in southeast Indiana last month. Crime happens anywhere. The city has to warehouse so many of the poor and uneducated because they're zoned out of suburbia..."

"Complex socio-economic-cultural drivers behind this." Dodds face dropped into mock seriousness. Then his teeth gave an 880-key smile. "My travel tour would be to point out every building where we had a dead body. I could put up about a hundred red targets as a tourist attraction. See that intersection? Three homicides in one week a couple of years ago. That building: stinker on the fourth floor, middle of July..."

Cheryl Beth laughed, glad for the release. "If you do that, I'll tell you really nasty E.R. stories..."

Will drove on slowly. The streets were deserted, a steady rain now coming down. Not even a wino was sleeping inside a doorway.

"He told me he had 'Kristen's' gun," Will said. "Not the woman I murdered, or the lady cop, or even Kristen Gruber. But 'Kristen.' He said it familiarly. He called me 'Detective Borders,' like the letter-writer and the voice on the phone. Then he called you 'Cherry Beth.' Has anyone called you that?"

"Not since I was teased in fifth grade. It sounds like a soft drink."

He went on, "You know what else he said to me? He has the gun to the back of my head, he's making threats, demanding that I give up my weapon, and he says, 'How does that make you feel, detective?' Those are the exact words Kenneth Buchanan used the first time I met him and he wanted me to know he'd already leaned on the chief."

Dodds took it in and said nothing. Cheryl Beth was interested in the dynamic between the two of them, imagined how effective they had been as partners, but she also checked again to see that her door was locked.

"What else did he say about me?" she asked.

Will hesitated. "It wasn't good. I would never let anything bad happen to you."

"I know that." At that moment, she felt strangely unafraid for herself. She was more concerned for Will. "Did he mention your father?"

"No. No, he didn't."

"So he doesn't know you that well," she said. "Otherwise, he would have used that to get at you."

"Good point," Dodds said. "That might mean he's not law enforcement. I still don't know why he chose Borders. So how do we get probable cause that will let us really go after Buchanan?"

They passed a marked unit. Two officers were standing on the sidewalk, talking to three young black men. All were soaking wet.

"I'm not sure," Will said.

"So let's find something. Screw Fassbinder."

"I mean, I'm not sure a man Buchanan's age could have absorbed that punishment from Junior and still outrun him and gotten away. Also, nothing from ViCAP about homicides in the Atlanta area that match the M.O. here."

Cheryl Beth asked about ViCAP, and Will told her of the FBI database. Buchanan came to Cincinnati from Atlanta when his wife took the job with the symphony.

"Our guy has killed before," Will said. "He knows the right moves. He's disciplined. But Buchanan was in Atlanta for thirteen years and nothing. He only decides to start killing now because he's in Cincinnati? I don't know..."

"So you're doubting yourself now?" Dodds sounded annoyed.

Will shook his head. "I'm missing something..."

"Don't go soft on me, Borders. It's becoming a bad habit. You don't believe I caught the cello player's killer, either."

"No," Will said. "I don't. Your golden gut is lying to you."

"Oh, fuck you."

"Calm down, boys," Cheryl Beth said. A dark shape caught her eye: some kind of bundle or bag. "What's that?"

They were at Fourteenth and Sycamore, back near the diner. Will swung the spotlight toward some bushes at the edge of the Cutter Playground. He pulled across the street and put the car in park. Dodds got out, snapping on gloves.

The intersection was completely empty. A pair of headlights lingered several blocks south, and then turned.

He came back toting a black gym bag and something else.

It was a wig.

He tossed them in the back seat and climbed back in.

"More ammo against Buchanan," Dodds said, holding out a wig of long, dark-brown hair. "The cure for baldness. Got any large evidence bags?"

Will shook his head.

Cheryl Beth heard a long zipper.

"What have we here," Dodds said. "Two pairs of handcuffs, his and hers. Two ball gags. Gloves and footies to put over his shoes. He's very methodical. A folding combat knife that I bet will match the wounds on the four vics. And a bottle of lye." He carefully placed the items and the wig back in the bag and re-zipped it.

"There won't be any prints," Will said.

"You never know," Dodds said. "I will say you owe Clarence Junior your good word to the D.A. He saved your lives."

Will was quiet for a long time. The rain was now coming down hard enough that it sounded like small pellets hitting the roof.

Finally, he spoke quietly, all the exuberance of the tour drained from his voice. "We're not going to get another chance. This was it and we blew it. He won't be careless enough to come back again."

"Unless," Dodds said, "he really has a thing for you."

Will stared into the wet windshield. Cheryl Beth took his hand and squeezed it. He returned the pressure, but she could tell his mind was elsewhere.

Sunday

Chapter Thirty-one

Cheryl Beth could feel Will's left leg start to twitch. It was only forty-five minutes after they had gone to bed. He was still asleep despite the movement. The spasticity must have kept him in a state of REM sleep much of the time. She hoped he had nice dreams, at least. With that thought, she gently snuggled against him, pushed aside all that had happened that night, and fell into a deep slumber.

"Oh, hell!"

His words woke her. He was sitting by the bed, shaking his right leg, his face illuminated by the screen of the computer perched on the arm of the chair. She rolled over and checked the clock: five fifteen.

"Are you okay, babe?"

"I'm sorry I woke you." His voice sounded miles beyond weary.

"Is it your legs?"

"I wish. I had to sit up to calm down my left leg, so I thought I'd go through the photos from Kristen Gruber's computer, and I found…"

She waited but he didn't finish the sentence.

She climbed out of bed naked, surprised how comfortable she was with him. Coming behind the chair, she wrapped her arms around him and leaned forward. He rested his head against hers.

"What?" She asked. Then she saw the photo on the screen.

"Oh, Will…"

"There are more."

"What are you going to do?"

He sighed. "I'm not going to do what Kenneth Buchanan does. I'm through with that. At six, I'm going to call Dodds and the lead detective in Covington."

Chapter Thirty-two

The interrogation room at Covington was nicer than Will was used to: clean, new, with unmarred furniture, pristine fluorescent lights in the ceiling, and walls that might have graced a modern conference room. The seats hadn't yet been beaten down by thousands of felonious butts sitting in them. Will sat in the adjacent room, looking through the one-way glass. With him were Dodds, Cheryl Beth, and an assistant prosecutor from the Kenton County Attorney's Office. He got Cheryl Beth in on the pretext that she was a witness under protection, which was true.

Only one person was sitting in the interrogation room: John.

Already it was a busy day. A fifty-six-year-old man had been decapitated and dismembered in his apartment and the Covington cops held three suspects in custody. It had been a struggle to get a free room.

Will watched John sit uncomfortably. He was still handcuffed. His expressions moved through anxiety, anger, and dreaminess. This was the sweet boy with the fine singing voice, now an adult under arrest. Will shook his head.

The interrogation room door opened and Diane Henderson stepped inside. She was dressed in jeans and a peach-striped shirt, carrying a tan portfolio. She pulled up a chair across from John and sat. They could only see her back. Will imagined that Cindy was frantically trying to get a good criminal lawyer. They didn't have much time.

Henderson started a tape recorder, gave the date, location of the interview, suspect's name, and her name and badge number. She Mirandized John again as he stared down. He mumbled that he understood his rights. Then she slowly laid out sheets of paper like playing cards. Soon they covered the table.

"Do you recognize the photographs, John?" Her voice was calm and almost motherly. It was obvious from his face that he was surprised by the images.

He managed, "Do you know who my dad is?"

Will wanted to melt into the floor.

"I do," she said. "How about answering my question."

"I know what they are. Can you take off these handcuffs? They're really uncomfortable."

She ignored his request. "So tell me what they are?"

"They're me and Kristen."

"Kristen Gruber."

He nodded.

"Is that a yes?"

"Yes." He stared angrily at her in a face that looked alien to Will.

"Who took them?"

"She did."

"When?"

He hesitated, then told her: last fall.

"So you knew her?"

"We were friends."

"Some of these show you naked in her bed," Henderson said. "Looks like you were more than friends. Why didn't you tell me this the last time we talked?"

He stared down. She prompted him with his name.

"I was scared," he said. "She and I had a fling."

"Last fall?"

"Yeah, last fall."

Will felt acid boring a hole in his stomach.

"So you picked her up? What? She was a good deal older than you, and a celebrity to boot. Why would she want a kid like you?"

He didn't answer.

"I'm about her age," Henderson said, her tone changing from sympathetic to mocking. "I can't imagine a bigger turn-off than some baby barely out of his acne stage…"

"She picked me up, okay!" He wiggled in the chair, trying to find a comfortable position without success.

"I find that hard to believe."

"That's because you're not Kristen, lady."

"You can call me Detective Henderson, or detective, or officer."

"Whatever," he said. All his sobbing from the night at Hyde Park Square was gone. In its place sat a fuming defiance.

"So why'd she pick you up? You look pretty ordinary to me. Are you some hot lover on the prowl for cougars?"

"As if." He gave a mordant laugh. "She wanted to deflower me. It excited her."

Will resisted the involuntary urge to shake his head. He listened to the intonations of John's voice; could it have been the one he heard behind him the previous night? Then there was John's pale, short hair: someone might mistake him for bald, especially if she didn't get a good look. He forced his jaw to unclench.

Henderson sat still for a few beats. "It must have been exciting for you."

"I wanted somebody my own age. But the girls my age don't like me. Kristen did. She thought I was mature. She said I had good judgment, that I acted very mature."

"You're not showing it so far," Henderson said. "She's dead. We have your admission that you were on her boat the night she was murdered and the evidence to back it up. Now we know you were her lover. It's not looking good. I'd say when you were on the Licking River with your friends and saw her boat. It put you in a rage. While they were passed out, you unlashed the Zodiac, went back, and murdered her."

"I didn't kill her!" His face contorted.

"You're slick," she said. "You got off the Zodiac, forced her back into the cabin, handcuffed her, and then you got out your knife…"

"No!" he screamed.

"Then you went back to your friends, and you were with them when they went back downriver and saw her boat. You could claim you found her for the first time. You could have called the police, but you didn't."

"I already told you, I wanted to!"

"That's not what your friend, Zack Miller, said."

"He's not my friend," John said.

That was true enough, Will thought. He also knew that Henderson had interviewed the three girls on the boat individually and they all admitted that John had wanted to call the police after he found Gruber's body. But Henderson kept that to herself, kept the pressure on John.

Leaning forward, she said quietly, You must have really hated her to do such a horrible thing…"

"I cared about her! I was grateful to her!"

The room stayed silent for a long time. The prosecutor was getting antsy. Henderson turned motherly again. "I can understand. So you started out a little reluctant with her, you wanted a girl your age. And then you fell for her. She was attractive. Did she know you cared about her? How did she react?"

"She laughed at me afterwards and never took my call again."

"Did that make you angry?"

"It hurt."

"And made you angry."

"Yes." His mouth turned down violently.

Will saw a stranger's face. It chilled him. His right quads starting jumping. It had come to this: what if he was wrong? What if John were about to confess?

Henderson said, "You wanted to get back at her."

"No." The stranger's face went away.

"These photos: you on the bed, you and her. Where were they taken?"

"In her condo." But Will already recognized the surroundings. At least that wasn't a lie.

"It must have really pissed you off when she dismissed you."

"It hurt," he said. "I didn't understand."

"Did you know she saw other men?"

"No." He sounded surprised.

"You sure? She broke up with you, she was two-timing you. That would make any man really angry. Mad enough to take revenge."

"No! Never!"

"Mad enough to kill her."

"I didn't kill her!" Now the tears were coming down and his hands were helpless to wipe them away.

She let him stew for several minutes. Will had a sudden sense of disorientation. For a moment, from the back with her fair hair, Henderson looked like the avenging ghost of Kristen Gruber. The ghost pointed and spoke: "How about these pictures here?"

"We went bike riding."

"Where?"

"The trail out in Loveland, that used to be train tracks."

Will whispered, "Goddamn."

"It's a nice place," Henderson said. "Do you go there often?"

"A few times."

"Have you been there this spring?"

He nodded.

"Speak up, John."

"Yes," he said. "I was out there a few weeks ago."

"With some friends?"

"Alone."

Henderson flipped through her portfolio and put a photo of Lauren Benish in front of him.

"Did you see her?"

"No."

"You sure?"

"I'm sure. She's pretty. I would have noticed."

"I bet you would have. I bet you did. She was also murdered last weekend."

John's face lost all its color.

"Now wait a minute…"

"John, we know you went to bars at Oxford. She was a nursing student at Miami. What if I have a witness who said you were on the trail with her and then started stalking her?"

"That's crazy! I never…"

Henderson said, "Let's go through this again."

Dodds turned down the speaker and said, "What do you think?"

"We don't have enough to hold him once his mother gets here with a lawyer," the prosecutor said.

Will shook his head, looked back at Cheryl Beth for some reassurance. She telegraphed it. He said, "I don't know what the hell to think, J.C. He's lied and lied. But he's not bald."

"You can buy a bald cap from the Internet. It'd be a good disguise, because that's the first thing any witness would remember."

Will said, "You don't really think…"

"No," Dodds said. "He's tall but looks out of shape. I don't see him overpowering Noah Smith. He doesn't have a knife."

Now the hole in Will's stomach was big enough to drop a baseball through.

"But," Dodds continued, "It's all what a jury believes."

He turned the speaker back up.

"So she liked it rough," Henderson was saying. "Liked to be tied up."

"Not by me," John said. "I didn't like that. It scared me."

"You never tied her up?"

"I wouldn't. She wanted me to. She wanted me to call her names and slap her, force myself on her. She said it helped her get off."

Henderson shook her head and pushed back the chair. "Now you're lying to me again, John. Why would any woman enjoy that?"

He tried to answer but couldn't form the words through his sobs.

When he was able to speak, they could barely hear him. "I tried to understand why she was that way. Finally, she told me she'd been raped when she was twenty-five. She'd been on duty when it happened. I don't know if that had anything to do with how she was, but that was all she'd tell me."

A tap came at their door and a uniformed officer stuck his head inside.

"His mother and lawyer are here, raising hell."

Chapter Thirty-three

They made it out to the parking lot and into the car before Will's phone rang. Cheryl Beth could only hear his side of the conversation.

"Yes, chief…I told Detective Dodds this morning and Covington brought him down for interrogation…No, sir, he lives with his mother, my ex-wife…No, sir…" She watched his face lose its color. "I haven't read it yet…I don't know how they could have put together the information about Noah Smith…"

She felt her body tense at the mention of Noah's name.

Will kept talking, "So the Oxford cops said nothing?" The voice on the other end talked a long time. Will silently gripped his leg. "Sir, with all due respect to Lieutenant Fassbinder, he's misremembering. I urged him to go public with the connection between Oxford and Gruber. I think it might help bring forward some new witnesses, throw the suspect off balance. Lieutenant Fassbinder declined my advice…Yes, sir…I'd really like to be there. If for no other reason because I think the suspect still might try to make contact with me…"

The police jargon both amused and horrified her. "Contact me." Sure as hell.

"I don't believe John is the suspect, sir," Will said. "He's stupid and was in the wrong time and wrong place. Based on that, he might end up like Noah Smith, who was a suspect once himself…"

Cheryl Beth hadn't even considered that. She watched Covington cops coming and going.

Will gave a final "yes, sir" and put the phone down, a defeated look on his face.

"The *Dayton Daily News* had a story this morning saying the suspect in the Miami killings had committed suicide in Cincinnati last week. The chief wants to know how they put that together. How the hell do I know? We never released Noah's name. The newspaper didn't even call me for a comment. Hank Brooks was helpful, giving a 'no comment,' which makes a good reporter think something's being hidden. Goddamn it to hell…"

She put a hand on his arm. He slumped into the seat.

"Now I have to explain this disaster with John. And Fassbinder told the chief that I was the one who said we shouldn't go public with the connection between Gruber and your students. Damn him. If you don't mind, would you pull the knife out of my back?"

She smiled. He didn't.

"They're going to give a media briefing this afternoon and bring in the Oxford murders and their connection to Gruber. I'm not to be there. The chief wants me to take a leave."

He suddenly slammed his fist on the steering wheel.

"I'm useless! I'm done! All they see is this fucking cane and they judge me. They keep it to themselves in their nice Cincinnati way, but they judge me and stab me in the back. I've cleared more homicide cases than anyone in the unit except for Dodds, but does that mean anything? No. I didn't even want this case, but the chief assigned me. Now I'm a liability. I'm a cripple who can't cut it anymore…"

"Stop that!" The words were out of her mouth before she realized it, and all the tension and anger that she had held inside blew out like a high-pressure oil well. "You are not useless, or done, or a liability! The only one who sees that cane is you. The only one who doesn't see a tall, handsome, impressive man is you. Do you know how lucky you are, Will Borders? Do you remember all those people in neuro-rehab, the quads who couldn't move the arms and legs? I see people every day who are sick and dying. You're alive and strong! You got a second chance that so many people never get!"

She was fighting tears now. She tended to cry when she got mad. But her anger quickly dissipated.

In the silence, he took her hand and held it to his face. She could feel his tears, too. His kissed her palm, whispered, "I'm sorry. Forgive me."

The car's layout, with radios and a computer between the seats, made it difficult, but she scrunched over and gave him a long hug. She didn't care who was watching.

"No displays of affection in an official police vehicle!"

It was Dodds, standing by Will's door.

"Check this out." He handed an official-looking piece of paper to Will. The upper part showed a mug shot of a hard face staring at the camera and above it no hair.

"Charles Wayne Whitaker," Will said. "Registered sex offender. Convicted of raping a woman in Columbus ten years ago."

"Yep," Dodds said. "It gets better. Remember Kristen's fan mail? We took it back from Covington. They didn't have the manpower. So I had police recruits go through two-hundred letters yesterday. Mister Whitaker wrote to Kristen, telling her all the things he's like to do to her."

"No shit? Does Henderson know?"

"I'm going to tell her. Why do all your white psychos have Wayne as a middle name?"

"Yours have De-Wayne," Will shot back, but she could see his body relax.

Dodds put a hand on Will's shoulder. "We're going to get him. All this is going to work out."

"Chief wants me to take a leave."

"Oh, bullshit."

"Yes, sir, Chief Dodds."

They rode back through Covington's old streets in silence. From the bridge, she could see the river filled with pleasure craft, as if Kristen Gruber's murder had never happened.

"Turn here," she said quietly once they reached the other side.

She gave a couple more directions and he knew where she wanted to go. In five minutes, they slipped out of downtown, around Mount Adams, and into Eden Park. It was the grandest of Cincinnati's hilltop parks, with its abundance of trees, grass, gardens, and a view into the distant blue-green hills that instantly relaxed her. The flowers were in full bloom, in more colors than she could count or name. He illegally parked where they could look across the shallow reflecting pond of Mirror Lake at the gazebo. Its jet-stream fountain shot six stories in the air. For a long time, they sat and took in the views, the sweet spring air, and the people walking and sitting in a happy normality, where babies didn't die, men weren't struck down in their prime, and killers didn't roam the darkness.

"I've been thinking," she said. "I should call the university and get them to send my students home. I should have done this before, but first I thought..." Noah Smith's face hovered before her and she stopped herself. "First I didn't know if Noah was the killer. Then, I thought my students wouldn't be in danger because the killer was after you, after us. There's no excuse. They've worked so hard for this clinical time and it's almost the end of the semester. They want to get this over with. That's the way I felt when I was a student nurse. But they can make it up in the summer. They're all potential targets of this Charles Whitaker."

"I think you're right," he said.

"Do I have your permission to tell them there's a killer at large?"

"Yes."

"I don't want to get you in trouble."

He smiled. "I'm already in trouble. It's my middle name. William Howard Taft Trouble Borders."

"Then, I'll be at loose ends," she said. "They probably won't even pay me for the rest of the semester."

She watched him carefully. His eyes looked so tired.

"Maybe if you're not sick of my company," he said, "we could..."

She smiled. "I'm not sick of your company, Will."

"If you want to leave, I understand," he said quietly. "Now would be a good time because…"

"I don't!"

She spoke over him, regretted it, because he might have thought she didn't hear the rest of his sentence.

"I'm falling in love with you, too," she said. "You're the bravest, truest man I've ever known. I lost my temper back there because I can't stand to hear you talk about yourself that way. Maybe a year after my daughter died, a friend of mine was talking about something in her family, and she said, 'I guess everything happens for a reason.' I asked her if she really believed that, because at that moment I thought the whole universe was so fucked up that nobody knew why anything happened. That's how angry I was for years, and I still don't know why these things happen, why life is so unfair. I know how much discomfort and pain you're in. I know how hard it is to stand and walk and make it look easy. You carry it off with such grace. I'm not sure I could. But you do it every day. You can tell me stories that make me fall in love with this city all over again. You're a wonderful lover. You're kind. But more than any of that, Will Borders, you stand for something good. You're willing to fight for it. In this fucked-up, unfair universe, the only hope and protection we have are people like you. And if your bosses are acting like assholes, it's not because of your physical condition. It's because they're assholes."

He ran his hand across her hair, touched the curve of her cheek, and brought his lips to hers. The kiss lasted until they heard a tap on a horn. A marked police car behind them was saying, *move along, get a room*. When the cop swung alongside, she waved and Will saluted back.

She laughed. "No displays of affection in an official police vehicle."

Will's phone rang. He answered it and listened, then put it away.

"Well, that was short but pleasurable. I hope it was good for you, too." His voice had a cutting tone. "That was Dodds. Turns out Charles Wayne Whitaker has been in jail in Indianapolis for the past month. Hell."

Cheryl Beth sighed. "So back to square one?"

He dropped the shift into drive.

"Maybe not," he said, "Let's go catch a killer."

Chapter Thirty-four

The Seven Hills Marina sat on the other side of Lunken Airport, where Kellogg Avenue crossed the Little Miami River. It was separated from the river by a tree-lined sandbar. Hills covered with more thick trees rose up in every direction. Through the marina's mouth, a boater would steer into the brown Little Miami, turn south, go around a bend, and the big Ohio River awaited: running fast nearly a thousand miles from Pittsburgh all the way to the Mississippi near Cairo, Illinois. There, the Ohio was actually the larger river.

The marina seemed in the country and a little down-market for Kenneth Buchanan, although it was fairly close to his house. Aside from parking lots, outbuildings, storage sheds, and boats for sale, it had room for five sets of floating berths, each one having several slips. They had wide walkways in the center and then narrow walks out to the boats. You learned many things working homicide and from a case several years ago, Will knew the narrow walkways were called fingerfloats.

He also knew from the reports of the detectives that had already been out here where Kristen's boat had been moored. It was gone now, evidence. Buchanan's big boat was tied up and looked deserted. About half the slips were empty. In others, groups of people were aboard their boats, either coming back or preparing to go out. It was a warm afternoon and everyone looked happy. Will parked where he had a view and turned off the engine.

"What are you looking for?" Cheryl Beth asked.

"I don't know. I keep thinking about the river…"

"Mind if I make phone calls?"

He didn't mind. While she called her bosses and explained the situation, Will watched.

When his phone rang, he stepped outside to take the call.

"Detective Borders?" It was a man with a heavy Southern accent, a harsh sound with none of the lilt and music in Cheryl Beth's voice.

"This is Special Agent Ricky Northcutt with the FBI," the man said. "I've been out on vacation and only got back to Atlanta yesterday. I saw your ViCAP request."

Will leaned on the hood and his pulse picked up. "That's right. It came back with no matches."

"That might not be quite true," the fed drawled. "There was nothing for metro Atlanta. But we had a case in Athens two-and-a-half years ago. A coed at the University of Georgia was kidnapped and her body turned up the next day. It had the same genital mutilation you describe. And the scene was clean as a whistle. Not a damned bit of DNA or much other evidence."

"Much other?"

"She was restrained," he said. "Her wrists seemed to have been tied with duct tape. There were marks on her wrists and some duct-tape fiber. Works for everything, right?"

"How far is Athens from Atlanta?" Will had never been to Georgia.

Northcutt said about sixty miles. "I'm not sure if that's any help to you. I would have called sooner, but our resources are stretched so thin now on criminal cases. Anti-terrorism is the priority…"

"Any suspects?"

"Not a one. The other thing that caught my eye about your report was the word 'deathscape.' There was an index card pinned on this girl's forehead that said, 'Deathscape Number One.' It was written in block letters with a felt-tipped pen."

Will stood and nervously walked around the car, taking the information in.

"Was she a nursing student?"

"No," Northcutt said. "I think she was computer science. But she was out on a secluded trail near campus, riding alone on her bicycle."

Will heard the women's laughter before he saw the boat, a sleek new model with several young women wearing bikinis and acting as if everything they heard or saw was the funniest thing they had ever experienced. The boat slowed and came to a halt three slips down from where Kristen's craft would have been docked.

Then he saw the man.

He was standing at the water's edge and looked to be somewhere north of sixty with the mien of a Civil War general: bushy beard and moustache and long, white hair combed back from his forehead. The image was broken by his clothes: an old T-shirt and shorts. He was filming the girls on the boat with a video camera.

Will left Cheryl Beth to her calls and walked in his direction, which, as usual, took quite a bit of time. But the man was so distracted that he didn't notice until Will was right behind him.

"Hi."

"Oh, howdy." The man put down the camera and faced him. He had skin the color of Spam.

"Nice view."

"You better believe it, and I'm not talking about the boats." He chuckled.

Will used his left hand to show his badge and identification. "I'm Detective Borders, Cincinnati Police."

"Whoa." The scraggly face tensed. "I don't want you to get the wrong idea here, officer."

"Relax," Will said. "Do you come out here to take pictures often?"

The general hesitated, then nodded. "It's only harmless fun," he said sheepishly. "My boat's over there on that trailer. It's not like I'm trespassing. There's so many pretty girls, and, hell, it's not like I'm going to get any now, but at least a man can dream, can't he?"

"I said relax," Will said, sounding a little less relaxed now. He felt time working against him. The detectives Fassbinder had sent out earlier last week interviewed everyone who was at the marina, a small group during a weekday, and then called each slip owner at home. This man might have fallen through the cracks.

Will asked him if he had been here the previous Saturday afternoon.

He had.

"Did you see a young woman who owned the boat that would have been tied up over there?" He pointed fifty feet to the empty slip where Gruber's craft would have been.

"The lady cop." He nodded slowly. "Kristen. That was a damned shame, a tragedy." Then he stepped back and held out a hand. "God, man, you don't think I killed her, do you?"

Will stepped in closer. "No, I don't. But did you see her? Did you film her?"

He stared at the ground and kicked it, the camcorder held limp at his side.

"I taped her several times. I knew who she was. I liked her show. She was real friendly, spoke to me and all, knew my name. So, yeah, last Saturday, I saw her. She was such a beautiful girl."

"Do you have that footage on your memory?" Will pointed to the device in the man's hand. "It would really help us."

"Well, let me see. Walk over to my truck where there's a little shade." The older man moved quickly ahead, Will following as fast as he could, watching every curve and break in the pavement that could bring him down.

The general leaned inside the cab of an old Ford pickup and ran through his files. It took at least fifteen minutes. Will leaned on the wall of the truck bed.

"This is it," he said, standing up again. "You can see the date and the time displayed digitally." He showed Will how to work the camcorder.

In the shade of the cab, Will looked into the little screen. Kristen Gruber was alive and smiling, walking down the fingerfloat, and hopping aboard her boat. Buchanan's boat was clearly visible nearby. She wore shorts and a white shirt tied to expose her waist. She waved at the cameraman and disappeared below. In a moment, she came back up and her head turned, as if someone had called her name. A man appeared on the fingerfloat beside her boat. He was tall, muscular, and wearing a ball cap. He looked familiar, even though his back was to the camera. At first she seemed to be only listening while he talked. It was too far away and the quality of the recording was too grainy to make out her expression. Then she shook her head.

The man gesticulated—oh, for some sound. His gestures were adamant, and her body language returned the favor. Again, she shook her head and spoke. This went on for a minute.

The man pointed at her. His face was turned enough that he seemed to be shouting. Then he pulled off his cap and walked away. Kristen shrugged and waved again at the general.

"Did you hear that exchange?" Will said. "Between Officer Gruber and the guy in the cap?"

"I couldn't hear the words, but he sounded mad as hell."

Will rewound the segment, replayed it. He replayed it a third time, slowing and freezing the screen.

And he knew.

He said, "What happened next?"

"Oh, she shoved off in a few minutes."

"Alone?"

"Yeah," he said. "She did that sometimes. Other times, she had male company, if you know what I mean. But she told me she liked to go out on the river by herself to relax. I'm really sorry about what happened to her."

"What about this man? What did he do after he talked to Officer Gruber?"

"He stomped away, real mad. After that, I don't know. My fishing buddies showed up and I launched my boat."

Will took a deep breath. "Have you seen that man around here before?

The old general squinted into the sun. "I don't pay much attention to the guys. But, yeah, I've seen him."

Chapter Thirty-five

Will climbed back into the car, a curious expression on his face. Cheryl Beth had completed the calls to her bosses.

"Now I'm about to start calling students and ruin their semesters," she said glumly.

"Hold off," Will said. He pulled over the computer that was mounted on his dashboard and started typing rapidly. "Now, if only the computer-aided dispatch system is working." Lines appeared and he scrolled through. He typed in keywords and a blank screen appeared.

"What?" she said.

He laid it out for her. Then he went through it a second time, more slowly. She felt a coldness creeping up her legs, no matter the warm air coming in the windows. Will had his cell at his ear.

"I want you to meet me somewhere." He gave the address. He mouthed to her: Dodds. "I don't care if you're going to the ballgame, they'll probably lose anyway." She heard Dodds' deep and angry voice floating out of the phone. "Well, get there when you can."

He put the phone down and turned to her. "What if I let you off?"

"No way," she said. "I'm a witness under your protection. I'm coming with you."

"Good."

He sped out of the marina parking lot and regained Kellogg Avenue, turning west. At the first intersection, he flipped on the siren and the emergency lights. They drove that way across town. Sometimes the speedometer hit eighty.

The forlorn brick building in Lower Price Hill looked abandoned. Its front windows were covered in old plywood and the second story curtains looked ancient. But Will parked in front and got out. She picked her purse off the floor and followed him.

After several minutes of banging on the door, it opened and a wisp of a girl with red hair stood there. She wore shorts and a NASCAR T-shirt.

Will said, "Can we come in, Jill?"

"Why?"

"Because we need to talk."

She reluctantly stepped aside and they walked in. The interior smelled of mold and cabbage. It was dark, which was to be expected from the boards over the front windows. A couple of old lamps provided illumination. The living room was painted a faded burgundy and filled with too much furniture, all of it shabby. Family photos were scattered atop the mantle above a fireplace that probably hadn't been used in decades.

Still, Cheryl Beth was struck by the young woman's beauty: the flame-colored hair falling to her shoulders pin-straight, a face with perfect features, and flawless fair skin. She seemed out of place here.

Will sat in a wooden rocking chair, while Cheryl Beth sank down to the boards of an old sofa, fearful of what the fabric might transmit to her clothes. Her Coach purse was wildly out of place. The girl settled next to her, clutching small hands in her lap.

Will waited a long time before he spoke. Then: "Jill, you told me that you were raped near the church down the street. Do you remember that?"

She gave a slight nod. "Yes." Her voice was faint.

"You said the suspect was black."

"Yes."

"And that we never caught him."

She stared into her lap and repeatedly fluffed out her hair.

"Isn't that right, Jill?"

"Yes, sir."

Cheryl Beth heard the soft Appalachian twang in Jill's voice, looked around at the raggedy surroundings, and thought, *There but for the Grace of God…* The only thing missing was a second-hand crib and crying baby. She thought of all the girls in her high school that had gotten pregnant and never gotten out of Corbin.

Will was plainly uncomfortable in the rocker. He rearranged himself and leaned forward.

"But that never happened, did it?"

"These niggers yell at me all the time, 'hey, baby,' they yell. They follow me. They try to break in here…"

Cheryl Beth winced at the slur but sat there watching.

"But a black man didn't rape you, did he?" Will's voice was soft and soothing, inviting confession.

She sighed. "No, sir."

He asked why she told him that.

She faced him and flushed. "Because I was afraid." Her voice sounded grown up and battle-scarred.

After another long pause, Will said, "You don't have to be afraid, Jill. Why don't you tell me what really happened?"

The silence lasted minutes, with the girl staring at a large mirror on the far wall. Cheryl Beth could hear the old building breathing and settling, as if every brick and piece of wainscoting wanted to tell a story, every one tragic or worse. When Jill began to speak, her voice breaking the quiet startled Cheryl Beth.

"It was last fall. October. I like to ride my bike, and when I can do the hill, I like to go to Mount Echo Park. It's got the best views of the river and the city, even if all the loaded people over in Hyde Park have never been there. I like it that way. It's peaceful. I always thought of it as my park…"

She looked at Cheryl Beth, who gave her best reassuring smile.

"It was Saturday afternoon and starting to get dark. The days were getting shorter, and I was in the park later than I thought. Nobody else was around. I'd stopped for one last look at the skyline, when somebody tackled me. Knocked me off my bike, knocked the air out of me. I was mostly surprised at first, and then scared. He started dragging me by my hair. I screamed but no one was around. He picked me up and held me by the throat, and he had a knife in his other hand. I'd never been so scared in my life.

"He said he'd kill me if I made another sound. He was going to rape me, he said, and if I went along, I'd live…"

The room was warm, but she wrapped her arms around herself.

"So I went along. He pulled me into the trees and made me take off my clothes. He was really picky. Wanted me to fold them. Then he made me turn away from him, and he pulled my hands back behind…" Her voice faltered.

"Take your time," Will said.

"He handcuffed me. And I started to panic, but he held the knife to my throat and said if I wanted to live, I'd better settle down. He said the handcuffs turned him on, and he wouldn't hurt me."

"What happened next?"

"He raped me. He pushed my face into the dirt, pulled my legs apart, and did it from behind. It went on a long time…God, forever. He was calling me every awful name: cunt, whore, little bitch. Said that I was asking for it, riding out there by myself. When he stopped, he made me stay that way, bent over, on my knees. I couldn't hold out my hands. It hurt. It all hurt. Then he was back for more. 'You got lube?' he asked. I didn't even know what he meant at first. Of course, I didn't have any. 'Too bad for you,' he said and laughed."

She shuddered. "Then he raped me that way."

Cheryl Beth resisted the urge to gather the young woman in her arms. She stopped herself from clawing at the worn fabric of the sofa arm. She rearranged her purse to the middle of her lap, anything for something to occupy her hands.

"When he was done," Jill said, "he made me get dressed. My knees were scraped. The side of my face was bruised from being shoved down on the ground, and I felt blood from my behind.

Then he handcuffed me again. He said he was going to drop me off, away from the park."

She took deep breaths, her complexion ghostlike. "So he pushes and pulls me to his truck. It's a brand new black Dodge Ram. He opens the driver's door and shoves me in ahead of him. I'm really hurting and scared shitless, and then he tells me that he's changed his mind. That he's going to kill me. He starts talking crazy. I remember he said the word 'deathscape.' That I was going to model for him. I don't understand..."

Her voice trailed off into exhaustion. Cheryl Beth put a hand on her arm and Jill didn't push it away. Her face looked as if tears were coming out of her capillaries.

Will said, "But he didn't kill you."

"No."

"And you're not pregnant, are you, Jill?"

"No, sir. I lied to you about that. I can't have babies. I had cysts on my ovaries."

"What about the ten thousand dollars from Kenneth Buchanan? Was that a lie, too?"

"No." The word was said neither adamantly nor softly; one dead syllable. "He promised to pay me ten thousand a month cash for a year if I didn't go to the police. He was real nice at first, but then he started that lawyer shit and said if I claimed rape nobody would believe me, that he'd make me out as a whore in court and take everything I owned. At that moment, I was so glad to be alive and so scattered in my head. I really needed money, too. They sent my job to China and I was getting by waiting tables. I went along with it. He's a rich, powerful man and I'm nobody in Lower Price Hill. I know how this city works."

Waves of horror and rage washed over Cheryl Beth. She had heard many dreadful stories, but she was usually going Mach Five in the hospital, doing something to make it better. Here she could do nothing.

Jill continued "He found out where I lived, said he had a private detective watching me. And every month he'd drive over and give me an envelope of cash and ask how I was doing. What

I was doing was saving every cent so I could get away from this! Honestly, I didn't even know his real name until you said it to me the first time, detective."

"How did you know his son's real name?" Will asked.

"He called it out when he ran over and pulled me out of that pickup truck. He saved my life."

Will took a long pause, idly turning the shaft of his cane. "Why would he do that?"

The girl bit her lip. "He said Mike was mentally ill and off his meds that day. They had a terrible fight at home and Mike said he was going to find someone to kill. So Mister Buchanan followed him. Not close enough I guess. Thank God he found me when he did."

"And you never thought about going to the police?"

"I thought about it, but you heard what I said. I wouldn't have stood a chance with those fancy lawyers downtown. Mister Buchanan said Mike was his only son, and he promised to get him treatment, get him in a hospital so he wouldn't hurt anyone ever again. He told me his wife was very sick, and if she knew this had happened, it might kill her. Anyway, Mister Buchanan was real good with words, real good. But there was always something behind them that didn't take a college degree to understand."

"And what was that?" Will asked.

"That if I didn't do things his way, he'd tell Mike where I lived and he'd come finish me off."

Chapter Thirty-six

Jill jumped when she had heard the knock. Then she walked hesitantly to the door.

Will assumed it was Dodds, but something inside tightened. "Wait!"

But it was too late. She flew back into the room so violently it was as if an explosion had happened. It was the sound Will had heard many times when a door was kicked down. A man came right behind her. He kicked her in the stomach and turned toward Will and Cheryl Beth.

He was tall, bald, and had a face that almost looked like a mask. But it was no mask: it was a younger man with an older face, one sculpted and creased by God-knew-what. Except for the dark eyebrows, he looked like Mister Clean. His clothes were Indian Hill preppy: expensive chinos and a light-blue shirt with a Polo logo.

Mister Clean was carrying a sawed-off shotgun and pointing it their way.

"Ah-ah-ah," he said.

But it was too late. Will had his Smith & Wesson out and leveled at the man's chest.

"Get the fuck in there, little whore." He grabbed Jill by the hair and shoved her to the sofa, all the while keeping the shotgun pointed in Will's direction.

"You weren't easy to follow, Detective Borders, using your siren and all, but I did it, all the way from the marina. I sat outside waiting for you, and when I realized you didn't have any of your cop buddies nearby, I decided to come on in. And what do I find: my little red-haired sex slave."

Jill was crying and shivering, bent over with pain, her face hidden by her hair.

"And this must be the famous Cherry Beth I've heard so much about." He stepped closer. For the first time, Will noticed the black backpack he was wearing. "This is going to be even better than I fantasized, and I fantasize a lot."

Will kept the gun steady. It wasn't the first time he had been on the wrong end of a shotgun. Thanks to years of training and experience, his insides were calm. Suddenly the dread of the next MRI, the possibility of another spinal-cord tumor, didn't matter. The notion that he would join his father on the wall of police officers killed in the line of duty was over in a second. He had civilians to protect. Not only that, he had Cheryl Beth.

"Put down the gun, Mike. You're under arrest."

The man laughed, high-pitched and raw. "No, Detective Borders, you are going to hand me your gun, stock-first, please. That, or I'm going to blow off redhead's head."

"You might want to reflect on that, genius," Will said. "You shoot her, I shoot you, multiple times, end of story." He studied the man's weapon: It appeared to be an Ithaca Auto & Burglar Gun, 20 gauge, with no stock and no more than a foot in length. It was rare but still lethal.

"You like my gun? It's a collector's item, very expensive. I stole it from my dad's cabinet. An armed society is a polite society, right? Now…hand…over…your…fucking…gun!"

Will said quietly, "That's not going to happen."

Mike's rubbery face held the exact same expression as the day when Will had first encountered him in Music Hall, on the way to meet the mother. Will realized that he had been talking to the wren in the miniskirt that day about her friend in pain and he had mentioned Cheryl Beth's name. That's where Mike must have misheard it.

"One way or the other." Mike smiled. It was an ugly sight. "I have some things with me to make this fun. Had to bring duct tape. I was all out of handcuffs. But I'm going to make you watch, Detective Borders, make you watch your friend get raped, watch red get raped. As many times as I want. 'Impotent'? You'll find out. Then, I'm going to kill you as slowly and painfully as I can figure out. When all that's done, I'm going to burn down this hole and disappear. Part of the art is knowing when to stop."

Will would have shot him as he talked, but the shotgun was no more than two feet away. He wouldn't survive the blast. He had to play for time, hope that Dodds would be there soon.

"Tell me why?" He felt his right quads getting tighter.

"Why?" Mike shrugged. "Killing each other is the only thing humans do really well. But to kill with style, that's an art. To watch and listen as they beg and bargain and then scream. It makes me feel like God."

"Every psycho says shit like that," Will said, watching the man's gun hand. He was half an hour past his Baclofen dose. All he needed was for one leg to start jumping. "Why Kristen Gruber? Why the nursing students? Why Jill?"

"Is that your name, sweetie? I hope you have some lube in the house, because you're going to need it. So is Cherry Beth."

Will wanted to look at Cheryl Beth, intuit what she was thinking, but he kept his focus on the man with the gun.

Mike cocked his head. "There's never one single reason. I went after Kristen to get back at my dad, but she let me down. It could have been perfect, but it was spoiled. With Jill—what a cute name—I saw her and wanted her. Same with the brunette on the bike trail, only I didn't realize I'd get three for the price of one. That was close to perfection. I have a thing for girls on bicycles, what can I say? Those pumping legs. But that wouldn't make great art, would it? I want models that look vulnerable on the outside and yet are strong inside. What's the expression? Strong at the broken places? The man I took to the graveyard? It was perfection. That's why I chose you, Detective Borders. You and your cane." He paused. "That, and you got in my way."

Will looked at him unimpressed. Then it was as if someone had inserted a key into his quads and they unlocked. His leg relaxed.

"Did the girl in Athens, Georgia, get in your way?"

"Very good, detective. She was my first. I made mistakes. But I learned. No, she didn't get in my way. She was in one of my classes and I kept having a vision of killing her. One day I did. All the shrinks and medication my parents spent money on never changed me. Death is my art. I won't be stopped."

"But you've got to know when to stop." Will started to wonder whose arm would tire faster. Mike looked very steady, those muscled arms doing well by him. Will was conscious of the instability of the rocking chair.

"You said it yourself, Mike," he went on. "You've got to know when to stop. If you would have stopped with Gruber, we might never have caught you. Now it's too late. How does that make you feel, Mike?"

Mike's face tensed at the phrase he had probably been hearing from his father since he was three.

"Hand me the shotgun. Stock first."

Mike's face was growing redder with rage when Cheryl Beth said, "Mike!"

He swung his torso toward her, dropped the barrel of the shotgun forty-five degrees, and almost got out a reply. Then the room exploded and he lurched back, a red stain on the shirt where the polo logo once sat. Jill screamed. Mike screamed and struggled to regain control of the gun. It went off, an even louder blast, the load of shot hitting the floor. Cheryl Beth held out the .38, ready to fire again.

Two seconds had expired as Will shot him three times, nearly point blank, in the torso.

The shotgun dropped harmlessly from his hand as his body swayed backward and collapsed by the door. Will kept the gun trained.

His ears were still ringing even though the only sound in the room was Jill's screaming. Cheryl Beth stood and started to the door. "I should help him."

"No," Will said. "Stand back. He might have other weapons."

He was up, his legs miraculously working without the cane, walking slowly to the sprawl of a human being on the floor. Mike Buchanan lay face up, very pale. One leg was twisted beneath the other. His arms were clutching at his chest, which stuck out unnaturally because of the backpack he was still carrying.

Will bent down and got on his knees. He tried to ignore the sharp pain that immediately struck, patting down Mike's shirt, pockets, pants legs, and shoes. He was clean. He nodded and Cheryl Beth was instantly on the other side. She checked his pulse and opened up his shirt. A blood pool was emerging from underneath him.

She said, "Stop screaming, Jill." The young woman stopped. "Are you hurt?"

She said she wasn't.

"We're losing him," she said. "If I had a surgical team here right this second…"

"Detective…"

Will looked at Mike's face. It was turning alabaster and the premature wrinkles were fading. He struggled to breathe, the sound coming from his throat like the grinding gears of an old truck. Will had shot him close to the heart, into one lung, and probably near the aorta.

"What, Mike?"

He whispered. Will bent closer.

"Kristen…"

"What about her?"

"She…" He gasped, his speech slurred. "She was all ready…"

"All ready?"

"No…" And he repeated the word so softly that Will could barely hear it.

All ready for what?"

Will heard one last quick intake of air, and then the man's eyes went black.

Chapter Thirty-seven

A month later, Will was back in the Homicide offices, and not as a visitor. Along with a medal of valor, he had gotten his old job back. Along with the medal, the chief had given him a dispensation for his physical condition in honor of solving the murder of Kristen Gruber. Fassbinder had retired suddenly and Skeen was taking the lieutenant's exam. For now, she was the acting Homicide Commander. He sat across from Dodds, who was idly tossing a football in the air. The names of Gruber and Smith had been shifted to black on the white board. But plenty of other names were still written in unsolved red.

A folding knife had been found in Mike Buchanan's backpack, along with duct tape, a gallon of gasoline, and matches. The knife had been sterilized, so it contained no blood or DNA evidence from the victims. After a search warrant had been executed on the house in Indian Hill, they found four pairs of women's underwear, one pair of men's underwear, and Gruber's badge, keys, and wallet in a hidey-hole of the garage. The DNA matched the young woman in Georgia, Holly Metzger, Lauren Benish, and Noah Smith. There was more: photos of Lauren taken on the bike trail.

Kenneth Buchanan had been arrested and was being tried as an accomplice to rape and murder. They were working with detectives from Georgia to find out whether Buchanan had known about the Athens killing and had concealed Mike's role in that, too. Buchanan's former colleagues who went to Elder and Moeller quickly deserted him. Kathryn Buchanan resigned from the symphony.

Will passed his MRI with no new tumors. He had gained another year of bonus time. But, then, the one thing he had learned on this job was that we were all living on bonus time, only most people didn't realize it.

The *LadyCops* producers moved their location to Florida.

"Pretty kinky about Kristen, huh?" Dodds tossed the ball hard at Will, who caught it. "Handcuffs, ball gags, sex toys. And such a wholesome face. No disrespect to a fallen comrade."

"You have a dirty mind." Will spun the football at his chest.

"Only thing that keeps me going."

"I'm not a Cincinnati moralist," Will said.

"Apparently not." He fired a shot that hurt to catch.

"So are you going to Jimmy Buffett at Riverbend this weekend?"

"No," Will said. "Cheryl Beth and I will probably take in a movie at the Esquire. And Grammers has reopened in Over-the-Rhine, so we'll have dinner there. She's going back to the hospital, you know."

"Good. Give me back that ball."

Will tossed it. "You're the only black parrothead in Cincinnati."

"That's an unforgivable racial stereotype." Dodds faked a pass, kept the ball. "There are at least four of us. You can't really be a Cincinnatian unless you love Jimmy Buffett."

"Why is that? We're about as far from the tropics as you can get."

The ball came his way, another expert pass. "Partner," Dodds said, "That's one of life's mysteries."

Skeen intercepted the next pass. She stood between their desks. "Don't rest on your laurels, gentlemen." She tapped the casebooks and files that rose several inches high. "They may not be exciting, but they need to be cleared."

"Yes, ma'am," Dodds said. "Send my poor bones back out into the fields…"

She bopped him on the head with the football.

"I like it when homicide's boring," Will said. "Anyway, he's on call tonight and I'm out of here until Monday."

Summer had settled its hot towel over the city, so Will took off his suit coat on the elevator ride down. When the doors opened, he noticed the woman talking to the guard. She saw him and immediately walked toward him.

She was tall, blond, and attractive, with a face you'd never forget. But it was one of those out-of-place moments, as if you saw the president serving slop at a chili parlor. It only lasted few seconds. Before he had never seen her so close. He had only seen her onstage, dressed in black, with the mournful cello between her legs.

"Detective Borders," she said. "My name is Stephanie Foust."

"I know," he said. "I've admired your music for years. I'm so sorry about Jeremy's death."

When she heard the name, her composure melted, second-by-second, and she seemed to age in sudden bursts. Her eyes flooded with tears.

"I can't…" She started to hyperventilate. He told her to slow down her breathing.

"When he told me he was going to marry that little bitch, I couldn't believe it."

"Ms. Foust…"

"We had been together for so many years! That he would do that. Marry that girl! She didn't understand his gifts. She barely listened to real music. She saw him as a ticket to wear Prada. I tried to talk him out of it. We argued over and over."

"Ms. Foust…"

"Then when I saw that man had been arrested, I couldn't let him go to jail." She pulled on his sleeve. "I didn't mean to…"

"I know," he said. "Now I want you to stop talking. You have the right to remain silent."

"I know that!" For a second, the imperiousness of matchless talent handed out by God surfaced, then she started crying. He Mirandized her.

"Take the elevator upstairs," he said. "Ask for Detective Dodds."

He watched the elevator doors make her disappear and then walked out to the street, his cane steady, his right quads arguing with his brain. He thought about Cheryl Beth, a short drive and a bottle of wine away, and allowed himself a smile.

John ran down Observatory Avenue past the fine houses. The lights were on and the drapes open. The people inside seemed so happy in the cheerful light and the company of others. Even in a T-shirt and shorts, he was dripping sweat and sucking in the humid air in search of oxygen. Maybe if he lost weight running, he might be welcome in one of those rooms someday, and not because of his mom's money and connections.

He thought about his stepdad. Will seemed happier than he had ever seen him. It was the girlfriend, of course. John had told him a week ago that he had decided to stay in Ohio and enroll in Miami, like Will. His grades from prep school were certainly good enough. Will was supportive. He seemed cooler when John said he wanted to be a Cincinnati police officer, like Will. But John knew if he got in shape and got a degree, the service of his grandfather and, yes, his *father*, would help him onto the force.

Will was the closest thing he had to a real father. He would come around.

John never got back his knife. He bought a new one and it seemed to weigh ten pounds as he jogged through the muggy night. He always had it with him. You couldn't be too careful.

Paying My Debts

I'm grateful once again to Ellie Strang, R.N., who was generous with her time and indulgent of my questions about Cheryl Beth's professional world. In my professional world, the best luck was getting to work with Barbara Peters, the finest editor a writer could imagine. The crew at the Poisoned Pen Press, especially Robert Rosenwald, Jessica Tribble, Annette Rogers and Nan Beams, continue to impress me by their commitment to excellence. I made use of some rightly beloved Cincinnati institutions in this book. It is, of course, a work of fiction. I also fiddled a bit with the city's recent timeline. Blame me for any errors, deliberate changes, or inconsistencies. Winston Churchill said Cincinnati was America's most beautiful inland city. It's still true, so visit if you haven't. Bring your heart and soul. It's certainly a gift to a writer.

To receive a free catalog of Poisoned Pen Press titles, please contact us in one of the following ways:

Phone: 1-800-421-3976
Facsimile: 1-480-949-1707
Email: info@poisonedpenpress.com
Website: www.poisonedpenpress.com

Poisoned Pen Press
6962 E. First Ave. Ste 103
Scottsdale, AZ 85251

ML   5/12